Hark! The Herald Angel Screamed

ALSO BY

Mignon F. Ballard

AUGUSTA GOODNIGHT MYSTERIES

The Angel and the Jabberwocky Murders

Too Late for Angels

The Angel Whispered Danger

Shadow of an Angel

An Angel to Die For

Angel at Troublesome Creek

The Christmas Cottage

The War in Sallie's Station

Minerva Cries Murder

Final Curtain

The Widow's Woods

Deadly Promise

Cry at Dusk

Raven Rock

Aunt Matilda's Ghost

Hark! The Herald Angel Screamed

An Augusta Goodnight Mystery
(with Heavenly Recipes)

MIGNON F. BALLARD

ST. MARTIN'S MINOTAUR
NEW YORK

This is a work of fiction. All of the characters, organizations, and events portrayed in this novel are either products of the author's imagination or are used fictitiously.

www.minotaurbooks.com

Library of Congress Cataloging-in-Publication Data

Ballard, Mignon Franklin.
Hark! the herald angel screamed : an Augusta Goodnight mystery (with heavenly recipes) / Migon Ballard.—1st ed.
p. cm.
ISBN-13: 978-0-312-37667-3
ISBN-10: 0-312-37667-7
1. Goodnight, Augusta (Fictitious character)—Fiction. 2. Guardian angels—Fiction. 3. Women detectives—South Carolina—Fiction. 4. South Carolina—Fiction. I. Title.

PS3552.A466H3 2008
813'.54—dc22

2008026430

First Edition: November 2008

10 9 8 7 6 5 4 3 2 1

For my readers, with thanks and appreciation

Hark! The Herald Angel Screamed

Chapter One

"Lucy Nan, are you sure we're on the right road?" my cousin Jo Nell asked. "Seems like we've been driving an awfully long time."

"Mama said the church was outside of Winnsboro," I told her, "and this *is* outside of Winnsboro, isn't it?"

"I'm sure she didn't mean this far outside. We must be halfway to Columbia by now and I haven't seen one sign of a small white church with a stone wall around it."

My cousin sat ramrod straight beside me in the same black wool suit she's been wearing for at least twenty years. Jo Nell never gains an ounce—the rat! On one bony knee she balanced a box holding her "Joyed-It" jam cake made from our grandmother's special recipe and so named because when anyone ate it they always said they "joyed-it." In her other hand my cousin clutched the black leather purse she carries every day from September through March. Sighing, she shifted the cake on her lap. "We should've turned left back there like I told you. Funeral's going to be over before we get there."

"You didn't tell me to turn *left*, you said turn *right*. This is Old Grange Road, isn't it? Here's an intersection coming up. Hurry, look and see what the sign says."

At the request of my mother, Jo Nell and I were on our way to the funeral of a relative, Mercer Vance, who was our second cousin or first cousin once removed. I never can get that straight.

My parents live in a condominium a couple of hundred miles away in Mount Pleasant, South Carolina, and pleasant it is, but it isn't a mountain at all but an island off the coast of Charleston.

"Mercer was my favorite cousin when we were growing up and I hate it that I can't be there," Mama told me, "but it's hard for your daddy to get around after his knee surgery and I don't feel right about leaving him." She gave me a chance for that to sink in. "You really don't mind going, do you, sugar—as a favor for your poor decrepit mother who suffered through twenty-seven hours of labor to bring you into the world?"

Although she's nearly eighty, my mother swims almost every day and plays golf at least once a week. I laughed. "Do spare me, please! Of course I'll go, but it's been years since I've seen some of those relatives and I can never remember who's who."

My family never let go of a name. Most of the men all the way back to Genesis were named Grayson, Mercer, or Vance while the women passed around Julia, Virginia, Lucinda, and Nellie. I'm named for my grandmother, who was named for her great-great-grandmother Lucinda Vance, who in 1835 with her husband, Mercer, built the columned home they named Willowbrook on the outskirts of my hometown of Stone's Throw, South Carolina. My grandmother was born there and lived there most of her life, but Mimmer's been gone for twenty years and except for some off and on tenants, the house has been empty since. Jo Nell claims it's haunted.

Now my cousin leaned forward shading her eyes to read the road sign as the pale November sun glinted off her bifocals. "I told you we were on the right road, Lucy Nan! Old Grange Road—plain as day—right there on that sign we just passed."

"Jo Nell Touchstone, you never told me any—"

"And there it is—white church with a stone wall. That's got to be it right up ahead . . . see it? *Slow down*, Lucy Nan! You're about to pass it." Jo Nell unbuckled her seat belt before we came to a complete stop. "Lord, I hope they haven't already said the benediction."

I parked and looked around as we wove through the rows of cars to the front of the church where two somber men waited. "Did you see a sign anywhere?" I asked. "I hope we're in the right place. Are you sure this is Capers Methodist Chapel?"

Jo Nell tramped ahead, pocketbook swinging from her arm. "What else can it be? Hurry, they're already singing a hymn."

I hurried. We were just in time for the last stanza of "In the Sweet By and By" when we took our seats in the next to the last pew.

I nodded politely to the people on either side of me, neither of whom I knew. They nodded back. It was close in the small sanctuary and heat blasted from a vent nearby. Jo Nell loosened the scarf around her neck and fanned herself with the memorial program. "Can you see Cudin' Grayson and them up front?" she whispered. "I don't see anybody I know."

"It's been so long I'm not sure I would recognize Cudin' Grayson if I saw him," I said, "but I'm pretty sure that's Mercer under all those flowers down there."

"*Lucy Nan!*" Jo Nell's eyes widened. "For goodness' sake—"

"Shh!" I said primly. "I think they're getting ready to start."

The minister mopped his face and stood. He wore a black robe and a stole as red as his glistening face and took a long drink of water before he opened the Bible to read the Twenty-third Psalm. His voice was low and soothing and I tried to picture myself in a shady green pasture where not-so-still waters rippled over mossy stones. Pausing at the end, he closed the Good Book softly, gave it a loving pat, and set it aside.

"Our good friend Lizzie Frye has left us for a better place," he began.

Lizzie Frye? What does she have to do with the price of eggs in China? I thought.

A lot, I soon discovered when I looked at the program. It was Lizzie Frye, not our cousin Mercer, under all those flowers down front.

Too late I glanced at the words on the hymnal in the rack in front of me: *Presbyterian Hymns*. We were in the wrong church!

Beside me Jo Nell leaned forward in the pew as if she couldn't believe her ears while the minister extolled the many virtues of the late Lizzie Frye. A faithful wife, loving mother, and dedicated church worker, she was especially noted for her generosity with homemade pepper jelly and watermelon rind pickles.

"We've gotta get out of here!" Jo Nell whispered to me from behind her program.

I made a face and shook my head. It was too late now. We couldn't just get up and walk out in the middle of a funeral service. Besides, someone else was stepping up to the pulpit to eulogize the departed. It turned out to be her daughter who was followed by another. Fortunately she had only two. Lizzie seemed like such a likable, down-to-earth sort of person, I was sorry I hadn't known her. Apparently so was Jo Nell as she sniffed a couple of times during the recessional hymn and blotted her eyes with a lace-trimmed hankie.

"I'm so sorry," I said to the family gathered outside as we filed from the church. And I *was* sorry, but I was also in a hurry. If we could just get away in time maybe Jo Nell and I could still get to poor Cousin Mercer's funeral before they put him in the ground.

Jo Nell, however, felt it her duty to extend her sympathy to each and every one, and when one of the family members responded with a hug, my cousin broke into tears. "Gone but not forgotten," she sobbed as I led her away. "She's going to be missed."

"And so are we if we don't make it to the right funeral," I told her. "Save some of those tears for Mercer, will you?"

As it turned out, we *were* on the right road but had been going in the wrong direction—which was entirely my cousin's fault, but I wasn't going there.

Capers Chapel, we were told, was about five miles down the road in the direction we had come and we got there just as the mourners lined up to follow the hearse to the cemetery. Jo Nell and I fell in behind them.

"No need to say anything about the extra memorial rites," I said later as we gathered around the grave site. "Maybe they'll think we've been here all along."

Nodding, Jo Nell agreed. "I guess what they don't know won't hurt them," she said. "I just hope we can get home before dark. I don't want to get lost out here again."

Of course Cousin Grayson and his wife Angela insisted that we come to the house after the service and I was glad for a chance to visit with my relatives inside where it was warm. It was the last week in November and sunlight was fading fast as we walked back to our cars from the cemetery. I hadn't seen Grayson and Angela ("my sweet angel," he calls her) since they were in Stone's Throw for my husband's funeral over four years earlier, but I was in such a zombie state at the time I barely remember their being there. Charlie was killed in a traffic accident while on a business trip and the shock of it turned my heart and my life inside out and upside down for a long time after that.

Augusta has helped me come to terms with losing Charlie as well as with several other of life's major bumps—such as murder—in what was once our peaceful little town. I must admit I had my doubts when she first showed up on my doorstep in her voluminous emerald cape, but there was something so right about her, something so good, I soon invited her into my life. I haven't regretted it. Augusta Goodnight is a guardian angel—*my* guardian angel she tells me, but sometimes she seems to end up watching out for most of my friends as well. It was a pity she wasn't around that day, I thought, to steer us to the right funeral.

"Come and sit with me and tell me all about that grandson of yours. How old is he now?" Grayson's daughter, Nellie Virginia, said as we helped ourselves to the buffet on the dining room table. It seemed as if their friends and neighbors had brought enough food for the whole town and I was having trouble deciding between baked ham and fried chicken. I took some of both. Jo Nell's "Joyed-It" cake, I noticed, was going fast.

Nellie Virginia will be forty-seven in March—ten years younger than I am, and I always thought of her as a little sister following me like a shadow at family reunions. With little encouragement it didn't take me long to light into my favorite subject, my six-year-old grandson, Teddy. But when Nellie Virginia's eyes began to glaze over, I knew it was time to change the subject or shut up.

"Sorry," I said. "I should give people a buzzer or something so they can let me know my time's up."

My cousin laughed. "One of these days I'll probably be the same." She glanced at her young son Vance Tate, who was in deep conversation with Grayson, his grandfather, at the far end of the room. "And from the way things look, I might not have too long to wait."

I had been introduced earlier to Vance's girlfriend, Jamie, a willowy blonde, who now stood sipping wine with Angela and several of her friends in the living room.

"Oh? Is a wedding imminent? Vance was hardly more than a child when he came with you to Roger's wedding. Has it really been that long?" It was hard to believe our son and his wife Jessica would soon be celebrating their tenth anniversary.

"Believe it or not he'll be graduating from law school in June." She glanced at her son with a secret smile. "And it wouldn't surprise me one bit if he gave Jamie a ring for Christmas."

Jo Nell joined us with her plate piled high and began buttering a couple of what had to be homemade yeast rolls. "I know I shouldn't have rice casserole and candied sweet potatoes, too, but I just couldn't resist," she said, digging into the latter.

"I hate you, Jo Nell," I mumbled under my breath.

"That was such a lovely service," Nellie Virginia said later over dessert. "I think Uncle Mercer would have approved, don't you?"

Jo Nell, who had just taken a bite of pecan pie, suddenly went into a coughing fit and had to leave the table.

Nellie Virginia rose to follow her. "Is she all right?"

"I think she'll be fine," I assured her. "Emotional, you know." Thank goodness she didn't bring up the subject of Cousin Mercer's service again.

After about an hour Jo Nell began looking at her watch every few minutes so I knew it was time to go. My cousin hates to be on the road long after dark.

"I suppose things are all right out at Willowbrook," Grayson said as we prepared to leave. "I know I should get out there more than I do, but Preacher Dave does a pretty good job looking after things."

My great-grandfather left Willowbrook to Mimmer's brother Sonny, who didn't want to live there and was glad to have her stay and look after the place. My mother and Jo Nell's were both born there. When Sonny died a few years after Mimmer, Willowbrook went to his sons, Mercer and Grayson. Mercer never seemed interested in the property, but a couple of years ago our cousin Grayson decided he'd try his hand at long-distance farming. He bought a small herd of Hereford cattle, had several acres planted in pines, and hired Dave Tansey, a jackleg preacher, to keep an eye on things.

Preacher Dave and his wife Louella live in a cottage on the place with their grown son, Jeremiah. I'd never met his wife and son, but Preacher Dave had recently taken a job filling in for the sexton at our church, Stone's Throw Presbyterian, after Luther, our longtime maintenance man, fell and broke his hip replacing a lightbulb. He seems to be doing a pretty good job because Pete Whittaker, our minister, says Dave even polished the brass lamp in his study that Luther had ignored for years.

I was almost out the door before I remembered to ask about the tree. Our church has been cutting a large cedar tree from Willowbrook for about as long as I can remember. It goes up in the fellowship hall the first week in December, and "angel" gifts for needy families are collected underneath the tree to be distributed in time for Christmas.

"Of course you can cut a tree! Cut as many as you like. You don't have to ask me," Cousin Grayson said. "I wish my sweet angel here would let us have one," he whispered loud enough for his wife to hear. "Nothing smells like Christmas like a real live evergreen, but she insists on putting up that artificial thing she ordered from some catalog."

"He's not the one who has to sweep up after it," Angela said, giving her husband her long-suffering look. "But you know you're always welcome to cut what you want."

"Want to drive out to Willowbrook with me to pick one out next week?" I asked Jo Nell as we started home. "Preacher Dave said he'd cut it down and take it to the church if we'll show him what we want. And we can get some greenery for the Advent wreath while we're there so Opal won't have an excuse to use that tacky plastic thing."

Opal Henshaw has taken it upon herself to be the unofficial chairperson of the decorating committee at Stone's Throw Presbyterian and everybody, including me, is too chicken to suggest somebody else.

"I don't like going out to Willowbrook," Jo Nell said, holding her hands to the heater.

"Why not?"

"Makes me sad to see it empty and neglected like that. Mimmer loved that place so. I'm glad she can't see it now. Besides, you know it's haunted."

"We're just going to pick out a tree," I reminded her. "We won't be going inside. And you know very well all that talk about poor Celia is a lot of hooey."

Almost 150 years ago young Celia Vance was supposed to have thrown herself from the balcony at Willowbrook after her fiancé was killed in the battle at Manassas Gap. Mimmer claimed you always knew when Celia was around because you began to hear music and smell gardenias. They were Celia's favorite flowers, and according to our grandmother she was said to have been an accomplished violinist. Mimmer liked a good story.

"Hooey or not, you won't catch me out there," Jo Nell said. "Now, for heaven's sake, Lucy Nan, don't miss the turn up there and get us lost like you did coming over here."

Chapter Two

"That tree over there looks nice," Augusta said.

"Too skinny." Ellis Saxon frowned and shook her head. "You can see right through it."

I stopped to untangle my sleeve from a blackberry briar. "Here's a nice fat one—smells good, too."

Ellis inspected it closely. "No way. Double trunk. Keep looking."

The three of us were on a mission at Willowbrook to find the perfect Christmas tree for our church fellowship hall and so far nothing had met with Ellis's approval.

With a few exceptions, my friend Ellis is the only person besides me who can see and speak with Augusta. As the angel explained when she first appeared at my front door at 101 Heritage Avenue, Ellis could use a little looking after as well. And didn't *that* turn out to be true!

Augusta wrapped her voluminous green cape about her and shivered. She has never gotten over that treacherous winter with General Washington at Valley Forge. A host of heavenly help was on hand during those times, she tells me, but she has suffered from the cold ever since.

"Why don't you wait for us in the car?" I suggested. "We shouldn't be much longer." But Augusta had already disappeared behind a clump of cedars until all I could see was the gleam of her candle-bright hair as she moved among the branches.

The ground had been covered with frost when we first arrived, and now at mid-morning grass still crunched underfoot. Even in thick socks and my old clodhopper boots my feet were beginning to feel numb and I beat my gloved hands together to keep them warm.

"With it being this cold so early in December, maybe we'll have a white Christmas," I said.

"Remember that big snow when we were in the fourth grade?" Ellis said. "We slid down that hill behind the school on cafeteria trays, and I almost got hit by a car when mine ran into the street because I didn't know how to stop."

"How could I forget?" I said. "You scared me half to death."

"I was so terrified I couldn't think straight until you hollered at me to roll off—probably saved my life."

"Just remember that when Teddy comes around selling gift wrap for his class this year," I reminded her. "And for goodness' sake, will you please hurry and decide on a tree before my feet freeze to the ground!"

"I believe I see one over here!" Augusta called. "Come and look. What do you think?"

"I've already looked over there, Augusta. I didn't see a single one taller than I am." But Ellis plodded after her, holding aside limbs for me to follow.

"Now, where did *that* come from?" Ellis stopped so suddenly I almost stepped on her heels. "It's—it's perfect, but I'll swear it wasn't here earlier."

The lofty cedar lifted its feathery branches in majestic splendor over all the others around it. I pinched the tip of a frond to release a fragrance like Christmas perfume. "This one's just right," I said. "Hurry and tag it, Ellis, so we can collect the greenery we need and go home." I had already made note of a smaller cedar I'd seen that would be perfect for that spot in our living-room window, but we could come back for that later.

I looked around for Augusta, who stood quietly in the background. "Lucky you saw this one, Augusta. It should be a big hit at the church."

Ellis tied a strip of yellow ribbon to a branch of the tree so Preacher Dave could find it. "It's the strangest thing! I don't understand why I didn't see it before."

"I think I know why," I told her, noticing Augusta's secret little smile. "It's because it wasn't there."

With a stroke of her fingers, the angel gave the elegant tree a parting caress. "Of course it was," she said. "It just grew a bit." With graceful steps she hurried along beside us in dainty fur-trimmed boots, her radiant hair escaping from a purple-tasseled hat. "And I believe I will wait for you in the car if you don't mind."

"Of course," I said, concerned. "Augusta, are you feeling all right?"

She smiled. "Fit as a banjo. Take your time."

Ellis rolled her eyes and grinned over the angel's choice of words. Augusta sometimes gets her expressions a little bit jumbled. "Why didn't you give her the keys so she can warm up the car?" she asked as we watched Augusta walk away.

"She won't use them," I said. "Augusta's never been comfortable with the internal combustion engine—says she much prefers a horse."

Ellis laughed. "She seems quite at home with other modern conveniences like the refrigerator, for instance, and the washing machine, and I know better than to interrupt when she's watching those old movies on TV."

"But she still practically jumps through the ceiling when I turn on the garbage disposal," I said, smiling at the thought. Augusta had come to my house the year before when I advertised a room for rent in our local paper, and although she has served as a guardian angel "temp" from time to time throughout the ages, she's just now becoming accustomed to some of our more recent inventions.

I skirted a scattering of pine saplings as we made our way to the house. Willowbrook reminded me of a once proud lady who had met with unfortunate times and was in dire need of a visit to the beauty parlor, or better still, a good plastic surgeon. The old house looked bare and forlorn standing in scruffy undergrowth with sagging shutters and peeling paint. Jo Nell had a point. I was glad Mimmer couldn't see it now.

"There's a holly tree by the portico around front," I said, "and there should be plenty of hemlock and pine on the other side of the house."

"Maybe we'll see the ill-fated Celia," Ellis said. "Isn't that where she was supposed to have fallen?"

"Or jumped." I stopped to break off a few branches of pine, making certain to choose the ones with the prettiest cones. "Remember that poem we made up about her?"

Ellis laughed. "Poor Celia! Weren't we the callous lot—you, Joel, and me? I think your mother got kind of upset with us."

"But not Mimmer! In fact it was her idea," I said.

My great-grandmother Nellie had written a verse about Celia sometime in the early nineteen hundreds and it had even been published in *The Messenger,* our local weekly, which must have been having a light news week at the time. Mama kept a copy of it in her scrapbook, and much to her dismay my brother, Joel, came across it and delighted in quoting it on every occasion while I fluttered in the background in an old window curtain.

Now, striking a pose, I touched my palm to my chest and chanted:

"When there's music in the air
You'll see Celia standing there.
Quietly now she moves in grace,
Soft the smile upon her face.
Then, like a shadow, Celia's gone,
But the scent of flowers lingers on."

Ellis responded by climbing on a convenient tree stump to echo the parody the three of us had collaborated on years before:

"Did Celia jump or did she fall
When she landed in a sprawl?
Or maybe someone gave a push
To send her tumbling on her tush.
Poor Celia! What a sad demise!
It must have been a big surprise,
At least I think it would to most
To have to end up as a ghost."

I laughed. "Well, I hope she's not around today. It's cold enough out here without ectoplasm."

"We'd better hurry before Augusta turns into an icicle," Ellis said, adding more evergreens to her bag. "How much holly do you think we'll need?"

But I didn't answer because either somebody had dumped a scarecrow on the porch beneath the balcony or poor Celia had jumped again.

"Hurry! Get Augusta," I said—or tried to say, but the words came out in a squawk. And it wasn't necessary anyway because suddenly Augusta was standing there beside us.

Ellis dropped the greenery she had collected. "Is he still breathing? Do you know who it is?"

The man lay on his stomach with his legs bent beneath him in the center of the porch between two Doric columns, and from the peculiar angle of his head, it looked as if his neck had been broken. I knelt and felt for a pulse, finding none, while Augusta checked for breathing. She looked at me and shook her head. "Maybe you should give him artificial insemination," she said.

"In his case I don't think that would do any good," I told her, realizing what she meant. "I'm afraid he's beyond help now."

"My phone's in the car. I'll call nine-one-one!" Ellis took off running, but we both knew it was too late to help the man sprawled on the portico at Willowbrook.

"He's still warm. It must have just happened," I told Augusta. "Looks like he fell from the balcony up there. The railing's broken."

"Do you know who he is?" Augusta touched the man's face as if in a silent benediction, her eyes filled with compassion.

"Never saw him before," I said. The dead man, dressed in faded jeans and a tan jacket, was stocky and seemed to be of medium height. His dark curly hair was badly in need of a trim and he had the beginnings of a beard.

"Oh, dear God!" I stepped back as it occurred to me that this might be Preacher Dave's son.

"The man who looks after this place has a grown son who lives with them but I've never seen him. Do you suppose this might be Jeremiah Tansey?"

"Do you know his age? This fellow looks to be in his late twenties or perhaps his early thirties." Augusta stooped to examine him more closely.

I considered searching the man's pockets for some kind of identification but couldn't bring myself to do it. We would find out soon enough anyway, I thought, as Ellis returned to tell us the police and an ambulance were on the way.

Stepping back, Augusta looked up at the balcony. "Why don't you keep an eye on things here? I believe I'll step inside for a minute."

"Keep an eye on what? He isn't going anywhere." Ellis hugged herself for warmth. "And it isn't any warmer in there than it is out here."

"We can't get in anyway," I said. "The house is always kept locked to discourage vandals."

I knew of course that wouldn't deter Augusta but didn't take to the idea of being left here with the dead man while both of us grew colder by the minute.

And neither did Ellis. "Why do you want to go inside?" she asked, slowly backing away from the house and the body that lay beside it. "There's nothing in there to see."

"He must have gotten in somehow or else how did he manage to fall from the balcony?" Augusta said. "And, as you can see, the front door is slightly ajar. Perhaps whoever was with him is still in there."

"What makes you think someone was with him?" I asked, glancing up at the shadowy balcony. But Augusta had already slipped inside.

Through the glass panels on either side of the heavy door I glimpsed peeling wallpaper and layers of grime on the sturdy old heart-of-pine floors, which were in sharp contrast to the elegant gold acanthus leaves on the hallway arch as well as on the ceiling medallion in what was once the drawing room. Years ago Joel and I had played hide-and-seek under the graceful curving stairway. I was not going inside that house—angel or no angel!

"What if there *is* somebody in there?" I said, joining Ellis in the yard.

"If there is, Augusta will let us know, but what would anybody be doing in there?" She glanced briefly at the still form beneath the balcony. "What was *he* doing in there?"

"I don't know unless he turns out to be Jeremiah Tansey," I said.

Ellis frowned. "Is that Preacher Dave's son?"

"Right. Lives with his parents in the Green Cottage over there."

The Green Cottage where the caretaker lives was now painted more of a pale yellow and hadn't been green since I was a child, but old habits die hard here in Stone's Throw. I still refer to most of my high school classmates by their maiden names and some of them have been married for almost forty years.

But Ellis shook her head. "Nope. Dave's son is fair and kind of skinny—not nearly as large as this man. I saw him when he helped his dad hang those new curtains in the ladies' parlor at the church. This man isn't Jeremiah Tansey."

"Thank God for that!" I said, relieved that we wouldn't have to be the bearers of sad news to Preacher Dave and his wife, Louella. But then the dead man was somebody's son or husband or brother and I felt ashamed of myself for being so grateful. Must be Augusta's influence.

Ellis was still for a minute. "Lucy Nan, do you hear that music?"

"What music?"

She cocked her head. "For a second I thought I heard violin music—you know—like Celia was supposed to have played."

"No, and I don't smell gardenias, either," I told her. "What you probably hear is a siren. Here comes an ambulance now, and finally the police."

Although Willowbrook had been a country estate in my grandmother's day, and even in my mother's, the city limits of Stone's Throw had eventually crept out to include it.

Captain Alonzo Hardy of the Stone's Throw Police Department stopped in mid-stride when he saw me. "*You!*" he said, shoving back his cap to reveal his fiery red hair. He didn't look happy to see me, but I didn't take offense because I was certainly glad to see him.

"Captain," I said, going to meet him. I was relieved to see he was accompanied by my friend Kemper Mungo instead of that nincompoop Police Chief Elmer Harris. During the recent troubles at the local college I learned I would much rather have Sergeant Mungo on my side than against me.

"Any idea who this man might be or what he was doing out here?" the captain asked after a preliminary look at the dead man.

I shook my head. "None. Could be a vagrant looking for a place to get in out of the cold."

Kemper glanced up at the splintered balcony railing. "Looks like he might've had a little too much to drink last night."

Ellis approached with an armful of pine that filled the air with its clean fresh scent. "There's no way it could've happened last night," she told him. "He was still warm when we found him."

"And when was that?" Captain Hardy asked.

"About fifteen minutes ago," I said. "We were gathering greenery for the Advent wreath—"

"And were about to clip some holly from this tree right here when we saw him," Ellis pointed out as she shook one of the lower limbs of the evergreen.

"I don't suppose you saw or heard anyone else around here?" the captain asked as Kemper roped off the area.

Ellis, who had been busily adding holly to her collection, looked quickly at an upstairs window. "No, but . . ."

"But what?" he asked, squinting against the late morning sun.

Ellis avoided looking at me but I knew what she was thinking. *Augusta might have seen something when she went inside the house.*

"The Tanseys live over there in the Green—I mean the yellow house a little way down the road," I said. "Dave Tansey sort of looks after this place. Maybe they'll know something about him."

Kemper frowned. "Tansey. That Jeremiah's folks?"

"That's right," Ellis told him. "You know him?"

"I know him," Kemper said. It didn't sound as if the two were on a friendly basis.

The captain gave Kemper a look that clearly read, *Keep your mouth shut.* "I expect we'll be finding out more about this fellow here before too long," he said, giving Ellis and me a dismissive nod as the coroner and a couple of police cars pulled into the yard behind him. "I think you've told us about all we need to know for now," he told us. "No reason for all of us to freeze out here—that is if you think you have enough holly there."

This last was directed at Ellis, who crammed one more limb in her bulging bag. "We'll be in touch, and if anything comes to mind, you will let us know, won't you?"

Ellis looked over her shoulder the whole time as we walked back to where we had parked the car, bags of evergreens bumping along between us.

"If you're looking for Augusta you're wasting your time," I told her. "You know good and well she'll be waiting for us in the car."

And of course she was. We found her muffled from head to toe in a throw I keep for that purpose. "It's going to take about a pot of coffee to warm me up," Augusta said from the backseat. "Do you think you might get that heater going soon?"

Ellis and I didn't speak as we quickly crammed our fragrant gatherings into the trunk and drove away. Both of us were eager to put that dreadful scene behind us.

Ellis turned to Augusta as we entered the main road. "Well?" she said.

Augusta pulled her knitted hat closer about her ears. "Well, what?"

"Did you see or hear anybody when you went inside the house?" I could tell Ellis was trying to hide her exasperation.

But Augusta only shivered and drew her wrap more snugly about her.

"For heaven's sake, Augusta, tell us! You *did* see something, didn't you?" I caught her eye in the rearview mirror but she quickly looked away.

"I was so hoping it might snow," she said, scanning the sky. "Do you think it will?"

I glanced silently at Ellis, who shrugged. I could have told her that if Augusta Goodnight had anything to share she would tell us when she was good and ready, and not a second before.

Chapter Three

"I'm going to have to quit hanging around with you—in fact, it makes me a little uncomfortable having you right next door," my neighbor Nettie McGinnis said.

Bellawood, the restored plantation where I work several days a week, was planning its annual Christmas candlelight tour and Nettie had brought over her punch bowl for the occasion.

"I'm sorry to hear that," I said. "How come?"

She set the box on my kitchen table and plopped into a chair. "How many bodies have you found in the last year or so? Three? Four? I've come to the conclusion it might be in my best interest to stay out of your way."

"I wasn't even there when that man fell from the balcony yesterday—cross my heart." And I did. "The police think he probably spent the night in there to get in out of the cold. It wouldn't be the first time somebody found a way inside Willowbrook. Preacher Dave tries to keep the place secure but he says he had to run off a couple of teenagers making out in there a few weeks ago."

Nettie frowned. "Preacher Dave? Isn't he the man the deacons hired to fill in for Luther at the church?"

"Right. He and his family have been living out there for over a year since Cudin' Grayson decided to try his hand at farming. Kinda looks after the place."

Nettie helped herself to one of Augusta's apple spice muffins as I poured coffee for both of us. I had known our neighbor for as long as I could remember, but when Charlie and I moved into the house on Heritage Avenue over twenty years ago she became an integral part of our lives. "This man who fell—do they know who he is—or should I say, *was?*" she asked.

"Kemper said they didn't find any kind of identification on him," I said. "They don't seem to know a lot more than they did."

"Had he been drinking?" Nettie stirred another spoonful of sugar into her brew.

"I guess they'll know more about that after they get the autopsy report. According to Kemper they found several empty beer cans and an old whiskey bottle or two upstairs but he didn't know if any of them belonged to the dead man. Preacher Dave said he could've sworn he locked that front door up tight but it wasn't closed when we saw it. Looks like he just walked right in and made himself at home."

My neighbor clicked her false teeth, a sign which usually meant she was studying on something. "How do they know he fell from that balcony? Could've been pushed, you know."

I passed her another muffin. "Or jumped like poor Celia. But why come all the way out to Willowbrook to do away with himself? Nobody here seems to have even known the man."

She chewed on that for a minute. "What about the preacher's son—Joshua, isn't it?"

"Jeremiah. His mother says no," I told her.

"Or that's what he would want her to believe, but I wouldn't put too much faith in what that boy says. Kim—you know Kim, does my hair at the Total Perfection—well, she says she's seen him hanging out with that rough bunch over at the Red Horse Café."

"What was Kim doing at the Red Horse Café?" I asked, but Nettie didn't bother to answer. "I don't reckon you all had a chance to get enough evergreens for the Advent wreath," she said.

"Then you reckon wrong," I told her. Geraldine Overton is working on it as we speak. Says she'll keep it in that big refrigerator at the church until Sunday." Geraldine Overton used to work part time at a flower shop.

"You could do just as good a job as Geraldine," Nettie told me. "Back when you used to help out at Bud's Blooms I thought you made some lovely arrangements, Lucy Nan."

I laughed. "My children called them '*de*rangements,'" I said. "Besides, I don't want to risk the wrath of Opal Henshaw. She's already on the warpath about our using fresh greenery."

"Opal's always got her drawers in a wad about something," Nettie said, lifting the punch bowl from its box. "Do you think this is gonna be big enough?"

"If it was any bigger we could swim in it," I said. "But I'd hate it if anything happened to your pretty cut-glass bowl, Nettie. Are you sure you want to let us borrow this?"

"Cut glass, nothing! I got that old thing at the Five and Ten Cent Store for three ninety-eight back when I was first married. Tell 'em they can keep it if they want. I can't remember the last time I used it."

Nettie blew off my attempt at thanks. "What are they going to serve?"

"Just a few simple things: shortbread cookies, gingerbread, orange-cranberry punch, and peppermint sticks for the children."

My neighbor snorted. "What? No syllabub? I was always told that's what they used to serve for Christmas, weddings, and almost any festive occasion. Every house worth its salt had a syllabub churn."

"So does Bellawood," I said. "I've seen one in the kitchen, but that's kind of like eggnog, isn't it? Lord, Genevieve Ellison would have a cow if we brought alcohol onto the property!" Genevieve, a strict teetotaler, was on the board of directors at Bellawood and I wanted to keep my job. I had been hired to take care of publicity and public relations for the plantation over a year ago, and although the pay wasn't anything to brag about, I could take care of much of the work from home.

"They've asked The Thursdays to help greet visitors," I told her. "I think you and Jo Nell are supposed to be in the schoolhouse."

"Well, I hope they'll have a fire in that old stove out there. I just about froze my ass off that year they stuck me in the upstairs hall." She frowned. "Where are you going to be?"

"Entrance hall, I think. Of course I'll get a chill every time somebody opens the door. Lucky Ellis gets to help in the kitchen."

Two other members of our book club, The Thursday Morning Literary Society (which now meets on Monday afternoons), Idonia Mae Culpepper and Zee St. Clair, were scheduled to guide guests through the upstairs rooms. Our seventh and youngest member, Claudia Pharr, planned to attend a holiday program at her son's school and wouldn't be available to help out that night.

"Some of the schoolchildren plan to decorate a small tree with cranberries and popcorn for the parlor," I said. "I remember Mimmer helping us string those for our tree when I was a little girl."

"I'm glad your grandmamma can't see the sad condition her old home has fallen into," Nettie said with a sigh. "Grayson ought to be ashamed for not taking better care of that place—Mercer, too, God rest him. It's a wonder it hasn't burned to the ground."

"It was rented off and on for a while," I reminded her, "but the last tenants couldn't afford to heat those big rooms. You remember my cousin Nellie Virginia, don't you? Well, she told me her son Vance has shown an interest in Willowbrook, but of course he's young and has no idea how much it would cost to keep it up. His mother thinks he's crazy. Says he's got his head in the clouds because he's in love."

Nettie nodded. "Bless his heart, I hope his girlfriend has money."

My neighbor hadn't been gone five minutes when Ellis phoned. "Got something to tell you," she said.

"What?"

"Tell you when I get there. Just wait till you hear this! Need anything from the store? I have to stop by the market first."

"Why do you do this?" I asked. "You *always* do this, Ellis Saxon!"

"Do what?" Innocence dripped from her voice.

"You know very well what. You bait me with the promise of some tantalizing news, then leave me hanging while you go running—"

But I was talking to a dial tone. Ellis had hung up.

I was washing a handful of dishes a few minutes later when a gust of cold air ruffled the pages of a magazine on the kitchen table and Augusta, followed by our dog, Clementine, came in from their afternoon romp in the backyard. The magazine was one of those publications that featured an article on "How to Lose Ten Pounds in Ten Days" and a recipe for Christmas trifle with eggnog custard and whipped cream, both in the same issue. Augusta had seemed especially interested in the trifle.

"I do believe it's getting colder," she said, hurrying to warm her hands by the sitting room fire. "Must have dropped ten degrees since morning."

I followed her and curled at one end of the sofa where Clementine reached up to nuzzle me with her frosty nose. "Colder than yesterday?" I asked. "I think I was almost as cold as you were while we waited for the police to come. I wonder if they ever found out what that man was doing at Willowbrook."

"I don't imagine it was for any good purpose," she said, turning to warm her angelic behind. "I'm afraid we haven't seen the end of the difficulties out there."

"Does that mean you saw something when you were inside?"

She added a stick of firewood to the blaze. "Not at all."

"Augusta Goodnight! You're every bit as exasperating as Ellis! I do believe you're teasing me on purpose." I told her about Ellis's earlier telephone call.

"Lucy Nan, you must know by now that I dislike leaping to conclusions."

Augusta sat on the rug with the big dog's head in her lap and stroked the animal's ears. If Clementine had been a cat she would have purred. "If I had *seen* something I would have told you."

"Ah," I said. "But you *heard* something, didn't you?"

Augusta stared into the flames. Her long necklace of glittering stones reflected the blue and amber of the fire's blaze. "I'm not sure," she said finally.

"What do you mean you're not sure?"

"It could have been a mouse—and old houses do creak."

"What's this about a mouse? Should I jump up on a chair and scream?" Neither of us had heard Ellis enter by way of her usual route through the kitchen.

"It would take more than a mouse to make you scream," I told her. I had made up my mind I wasn't going to mention her earlier hint of news.

"We were referring to a noise I might have heard while I was inside the house at Willowbrook," Augusta explained. "It was rather like a . . . scuttling sound as if someone were trying to keep quiet."

"Could you tell where it was coming from?" I asked.

"I thought at first someone might be hiding in the room to the right of the stairway, but there was no one there," she said. "It was almost as if it came from inside the wall."

Ellis brightened. "Really? How exciting!"

I made room for Ellis on the sofa. "Mimmer used to say there was a secret stairway in there somewhere but she never would let us look for it. She pretended she didn't know where it was, but I'm sure she did. Said she was afraid the steps might be rotten and we would fall through."

"Well, whoever might have been there is probably gone now," Augusta said, "although I'm afraid we haven't heard the last of this. And I would hope your friends from the police will check to see if there really is a stairway there."

"Do you think they'll come back?" I asked.

"I suppose it all depends on what they were doing out there in the first place." Augusta gently dislodged Clementine from her lap and stood, shucking her serious tone. "At any rate, it's a bit early to worry about it just yet. Would anyone else like hot chocolate?"

Ellis waved her hand in the air. "I would! But doesn't anybody want to hear my news?"

I yawned. "What news?"

Ellis shrugged. "Well, if you really don't want to know . . ."

"Depends," I said. "Does it involve scandal, intrigue, or romance?"

Ellis grinned. "Romance."

"Whose? Yours?" I asked.

Ellis laughed. "Of course not! Bennett and I are *married*—not that we don't—oh, never mind! It's about Idonia," she said.

I think I gasped, but shame on me if I did. "Idonia? *Idonia Mae Culpepper?*"

Ellis nodded. "The very same."

Augusta stood in the middle of the room with her arms folded.

"I don't understand. Why shouldn't your friend have love in her life?"

"Well, she should . . . could . . . I guess," I stammered while Ellis readily agreed. "Of course, of course," she said. "It's just that . . . Idonia . . . well . . ."

Augusta twined her necklace through her fingers. "Well, what?"

"It's just that she's *Idonia*," I admitted finally. "Actually Idonia was married briefly when she was a lot younger but it didn't work out. He turned out to be a rotten apple."

"An *apple?*" Augusta shook her head.

"Ran around on her," Ellis explained. "Rotten to the core. She's been kind of sour on men ever since."

Augusta paused in the doorway. "A sour apple . . . I see," she said, although I wasn't sure she did. "So what were you going to tell us?" she asked Ellis.

Ellis paused to get the full benefit of our attention. "Idonia has a gentleman friend," she announced.

"Really? Who? Anybody we know?" I asked.

"Does the name Melrose DuBois ring a bell?" she said.

"Should it?" I laughed. "You're kidding, aren't you? You made that up. Nobody is named Melrose DuBois!"

Ellis stood to follow Augusta into the kitchen. "Idonia's fellow is. Works part time for Al Evans over at the funeral home. I think he and Al are cousins or something."

I trailed along after them. Clementine trailed after me. "How do you know all this?" I asked.

"Opal Henshaw told me. He's taken a room with her at the Spring Lamb."

"God help him," I said. The Spring Lamb is a bed-and-breakfast, so called because of the two cement lamb planters filled with plastic flowers on either side of the front door. I hoped Idonia's friend didn't have a big appetite because he wouldn't get much to eat under that roof. Opal Henshaw could squeeze a nickel till the buffalo bellowed.

"When did all this come about?" I asked, adding a dollop of whipped cream to my hot chocolate. For some reason since Augusta arrived I've had trouble zipping my pants.

"Opal tells me he's been with them about a month," Ellis said. "I think he and Idonia met at Harris Teeter over a bunch of grapes. He asked her to help him pick out some fruit."

Probably to supplement the breakfast menu, I thought. "Romance in the produce department . . . sounds like the title of a book. Has Idonia said anything to you about him?"

Ellis sipped her hot drink slowly. "Not yet, but The Thursdays are meeting at my house Monday. What do you bet we get a full report then?" She closed her eyes. "Mmm . . . tastes like cinnamon in here. Augusta, this hot chocolate is heavenly."

Augusta smiled. "Of course it is," she said.

Chapter Four

Zee St. Clair flung her crimson cloak over the back of Ellis's living room sofa and took a stance. The Thursdays had just finished reading *Zelda*, a biography of Zelda Sayre Fitzgerald, and Zee had been acting even more flamboyant than usual. "I think we should have a caroling party for Christmas this year," she announced, "instead of going out to dinner like we always do."

Jo Nell, who had just settled comfortably in the wing chair by the fireplace, sat up so suddenly she frightened Ellis's cat, Cookie, who had been sleeping underneath. "You mean walk around out in the cold and sing on neighbors' porches?"

"Why not?" Zee tossed her brightly tinted curls. "We used to do it all the time. Remember what fun we had? We could have a few glasses of wine before we start, then come back to Lucy Nan's for a covered dish."

"Fine with me," I said, since it was my time to host anyway.

Idonia looked thoughtful. "Would it be all right if I asked Mel—" she began.

"I think it's a great idea!" Claudia Pharr set her steaming cup of Russian tea on the marble-topped coffee table and took a calendar from her purse. "When?"

"Would next week be too soon?" I asked. "We can work it in between rehearsals for Lessons and Carols and the candlelight tour at Bellawood . . . and by the way, I'm counting on some of you to help us decorate out there."

Nettie said she'd be glad to help decorate and would even go along with the caroling if we would agree to carry her home in a pack saddle if her feet gave out.

I laughed. I had almost forgotten about the term we'd used as children for making a seat with four crossed arms.

"I think I'll be able to help, Lucy Nan, and I'd like to invite Melrose to join us for caroling if that's all right." Idonia spoke louder this time.

Zee nodded. "Of course—Melrose *who?*"

"Melrose DuBois—he's someone I've been seeing." Idonia sipped calmly from her cup but I noticed her hands shook slightly when she set it down.

And then the bombardment began:

"Where did you meet him?"

"When did you start seeing him?"

"Is he from around here?"

"How long were you going to keep this from us, you sly fox?" Zee asked, perching on the arm of Idonia's chair. "Tell us, is he handsome? What's he like?"

"All right! Enough!" Idonia shook her head, laughing, and told us how she had met Melrose in the produce department at Harris Teeter. He had taken her to dinner twice and they had seen several movies together, she said, and until he could find a more permanent place, he was staying with Opal Henshaw at the Spring Lamb.

Her face flushed almost as red as her hair. "He's merely a friend," she stressed, "but it's nice to have someone to go out with—something to look forward to . . . and well . . . I find Melrose pleasant company."

"I think that's wonderful," I said, "and of course you should invite Melrose to the party. I plan to ask Ben as well."

Benjamin Maxwell and I had been seeing one another for over a year and it hadn't taken me long to learn that he was not only an extraordinary spinner of yarns, but sang a pretty good baritone as well.

"There are a lot of older people here in Stone's Throw—especially in the neighborhoods right here in town—who might enjoy having carolers come by," Claudia said brightly.

Ellis passed around a tray of sandwiches. "In case you haven't noticed, we *are* the older people here in Stone's Throw," she informed her.

"I hope your friend won't have to stay at the Henshaw place long," Jo Nell said to Idonia. "That Opal Henshaw's queen of the skinflints—and fussy! Lord, everything has to be just so!"

Idonia smiled. "I think Melrose just tries to stay out of her way. He said once he accidentally brushed against a picture hanging on the wall and she about knocked him down to straighten it."

Ellis nodded. "Probably obsessive-compulsive."

"More like obsessive-*re*pulsive," Nettie said. "That woman gets on my last nerve."

"I think she's just plain bossy," I said. "Everything has to be Opal's way. I heard she practically had a fit and fell in it when she heard we were going to use fresh greenery in the Advent wreath this year."

Claudia shook her head. "I dread having to go with her on the fruitcake run," she said.

I laughed, picturing panicky people fleeing from giant fruitcakes with legs. "Fruitcake run? I suppose you're running *from* them."

But Claudia waved my comment aside. "Every year our Sunday school class takes fruitcake and homemade cookies to shut-ins and we've always included Luther and his family, as well. Since

Preacher Dave is filling in as sexton, we voted to take the Tanseys some, too."

"Lucky Tanseys," Ellis whispered under her breath.

"I always seem to get stuck on the committee with Opal," Claudia said with a groan. "I wish I could think of a good excuse not to go."

"Cheer up! Maybe you'll come down with smallpox or typhoid fever or something," Zee told her.

"Smallpox? My goodness, Zee. People don't get—" Claudia smiled as realization dawned. "Oh, you're pulling my leg again!" She shrugged. "Well, we're not going for another week so with luck I might catch a mild cold."

Nettie clicked her teeth in annoyance. "For heaven's sake, Claudia, just tell the woman you won't be able to help out that day."

Claudia paled. *"Tell Opal Henshaw that?"*

"Melrose is taking me to a choral concert at the college tonight," Idonia said, "and I'm having a terrible time deciding what to wear."

"Your black sheath always looks nice," Zee said. "Or what about that blue silk you bought last year?"

Ben and I had made plans to go to the concert, too, but I didn't want to steal Idonia's thunder by mentioning it. "You'd look great in either one," I told her, "but I kind of favor the blue."

"Will Julie be home for Christmas this year, Lucy Nan?" Jo Nell asked as we helped clear away teacups.

"For five whole days! She saved part of her vacation time and we're—I'm making new curtains to jazz up her room a little."

"*You're* making curtains?" Nettie didn't even bother to hide her amazement. She has never forgotten that clown costume I made for Teddy's third Halloween. I forgot to put an opening in the neck and he couldn't get his head through.

"Well, my goodness, it's not that big a deal!" I told her, not daring to look at Ellis, who knew who was *really* making the curtains.

"Or I could wear that turquoise pants suit I made last winter," Idonia mused aloud. "Melrose says that color shows off my hair."

Everyone agreed that the turquoise pants suit would be a good choice.

"Have you heard any more about what happened to that poor man you found out at your grandmother's old home?" Zee asked me as The Thursdays prepared to leave. She frowned. "You don't suppose somebody pushed him, do you?"

"If somebody did, the police aren't saying," I told her. "Kemper said they looked around inside but didn't see anything suspicious."

Idonia shrugged into her coat and tucked her purse and her book under an arm. "Well, I must be off if I'm to have my hair done this afternoon. Melrose doesn't like to be late."

"Did you tell Kemper about the secret stairway?" Ellis asked after the others had left.

"I left him a message but haven't heard back. He probably thinks I've let my imagination run away with me again."

"Again? What do you mean, *again*?" she snorted. "If they didn't have us to prod them along, the police here in Stone's Throw wouldn't have a clue!"

I had to admit she had a point.

"I guess you noticed Kemper didn't seem to think too much of Jeremiah Tansey," Ellis said. "I wonder if he had anything to do with all this."

"Nettie seems to think he runs around with that rough bunch at the Red Horse," I said, "but that doesn't mean he's a murderer."

"Hmm . . . I wonder if his dad knows he hangs around out there. Preacher Dave is as straitlaced as they come—or seems to be. I've never met Louella, though. Wonder what his wife's like."

"I don't know," I said, "but I'll soon find out. Grayson has ordered one of those huge Christmas baskets from that specialty shop over in Fort Mill and I told him I'd pick it up tomorrow and deliver it to the Tanseys. Says he feels kind of guilty because he hasn't done anything for them since they've been out there at Willowbrook."

"You're going to The Peach Stand? Wait up a minute, will you?" Ellis hurried away and returned with several bills that she stuffed into my hand. "How about bringing me a couple of jars of peach pickles and some blackberry jam?" She hesitated while I shoved the money into my purse. "You're not nervous about going out to Willowbrook again, are you? I'd go with you but Susan and I are shopping for the new baby tomorrow."

Ellis's daughter was expecting a boy after Christmas and Ellis's husband Bennett had already bought enough sports equipment to furnish a gym.

"Actually I'm kind of curious to see what Louella's like," I said. "Besides, Augusta's going with me."

"She was with us the other day when we found that body, too," Ellis reminded me. "You be careful out there, Lucy Nan."

The Green Cottage sat about a quarter of a mile from the plantation house at the end of a long gravel road in a grove of oak trees that had been huge even when I was a child. In the pasture across the road reddish-brown and white cattle grazed, and beyond that a hill of new pine saplings showed green against the brown December landscape. A couple of Herefords licking a salt block looked at us briefly through the barbed-wire fence as we turned into the drive. "Have you noticed how cows always look bored?" I said.

Augusta laughed. "Wouldn't you be?"

A rambling pyracantha bush stretched arms full of fiery orange berries against the pale yellow walls of the house and browning chrysanthemums, once purple, tumbled against the doorstep. Someone—Louella, I presumed—had hung a wreath of gold-sprayed cotton bolls on the front door. I had seen some like it earlier at the craft fair at the Baptist Church.

Preacher Dave himself met me at the door. He was a tall man with thinning hair and stooped shoulders. Keen blue eyes smiled at me from a weathered face. "Come in, come in!" Accepting the basket, he stepped aside to usher me in front of him. "And excuse the coveralls, please. Just got through waxing floors over at the church and haven't had time to change."

"That's quite all right . . . I don't mean to stay . . ." I found myself seated in a comfortable overstuffed chair, the arms and back of which were protected with crocheted doilies. "My cousin Grayson asked me to drop this by to thank you for looking after the property. He plans to get up here himself soon after the holidays but wanted to wish you and your family a merry Christmas."

Preacher Dave set the large basket on the floor. "My goodness, this looks wonderful, but it isn't necessary . . ." His voice trailed as he examined the contents of ham, cheese, jams, and pickles. "Louella! Come here, honey, and see what Santa Claus brought us!"

"Are those spiced peaches? My favorites! What a nice surprise!" At first glance Louella Tansey seemed to be all of one color—sort of a faded tan. Her thin brownish hair was pulled back in what would've been a bun if there had been enough of it and her eyes, behind bifocals, seemed to take on the tone of the beige housedress she wore. The only bright color, I noticed, was the green rickrack trim on the woman's apron. "Louella Tansey," she said, offering her hand. "Let me get you something to drink. I just made tea."

"Thank you, but I can't stay," I said, introducing myself. "I know it must be close to your supper hour." Augusta, who stood by the upright piano across the room, brightened at the mention of tea, but I could have told her it was probably iced tea our hostess was offering. Most people where we live drink it all year long. "I really must go," I said, rising.

"We're not going to hear of it are we, Louella?" Preacher Dave lifted the basket at my feet. "You just rest a minute while I take this to the kitchen and Louella'll bring you a nice glass of tea—or there's coffee if you'd rather."

"Coffee would be fine," I said, trying to avoid what I knew would be Augusta's envious expression. I've stopped counting the number of cups she drinks in one day. But Augusta, apparently oblivious to our conversation, was examining a large framed photograph on the piano.

I looked about the room while waiting, and although some of the furnishings seemed worn, the oval hooked rug in colors of green and rose looked bright and new as did the coordinating swag over the front windows. A burgundy Christmas candle sat in a silk arrangement on a lovely mahogany side table. Grayson should be pleased to have such caring tenants.

I wandered over to look at the photograph that had captured Augusta's attention. It was a studio portrait of a pretty young woman, whose wide sweet smile made me want to smile, too. Her dark hair was cut in a becoming page boy and her large eyes held a spark of mischief.

"She's lovely," I said, noticing that Louella had come back into the room. "Is this your daughter?"

She nodded, setting my coffee cup aside. "Dinah. But she's gone now. Dead."

"Oh, I'm so sorry!" How horrible! *Why couldn't I keep my mouth shut? Having children myself, I could only imagine how tragic it would be to lose them.*

Louella moved quietly past me and came to stand by the piano.

"This was hers, you know," she said, caressing the closed lid over the keyboard. "She did love to play."

I looked around to see Preacher Dave standing in the doorway. "Tell your cousin the vet thinks that little heifer we talked about is gonna be fine, and I mended that tear in the fence up there on the main road." And with that he turned and left the room.

I drank my coffee as quickly as I could, made my thanks, and left. Louella Tansey, looking frail and drab, a sad shadow of a woman, stood at the door gazing after me as if she wanted to follow.

Chapter Five

"Did you notice Preacher Dave's face?" I said to Augusta as we drove away. "He was as white as Logan's cat."

Augusta immediately turned on the heater. "Logan's cat?"

"It's a term my grandmother used," I explained. "Except nobody seems to remember who Logan was."

"How sad for their daughter to die so young," she said. "I can see it's been a hardship for them."

"I wonder how she died, but I didn't dare ask. I could tell they didn't want to talk about it. As far as I know, nobody even knew they had a daughter."

I pulled up to the stop sign before entering the main road, and as I did, a pickup truck turned in and passed us going in the opposite direction. The young man behind the wheel had straw-colored hair pulled back in a ponytail and he made the turn so quickly he almost went into the ditch. I waved because that's what just about everybody does around here whether we know the driver or not, especially out in the country, but the driver didn't wave back.

Augusta turned to look over her shoulder. "Who was that?"

"I'm not sure but I think it might have been Jeremiah Tansey.

Obviously in a hurry." In my rearview mirror I saw the faded blue truck disappearing in a cloud of dust.

As we passed the area behind the house at Willowbrook where we had found the tree I thought about stopping to get holly as we planned to decorate at Bellawood the next day, but it was already beginning to get dark and I didn't feel comfortable about going back there just yet—even with Augusta. Besides, there was always plenty of holly at Bellawood Plantation.

"I do wish we had some holly!" Genevieve Ellison said as she broke off a spray of pine. "This mantel just calls for it."

"I think they've used most of it in the other rooms," Nettie told her, "but we've plenty of cedar and spruce, and I think there's some hemlock down by the schoolhouse. That always looks graceful in an arrangement."

"I'll get it," I offered, glad of a chance to get some exercise. Several of us had congregated in the kitchen at Bellawood, which was separate from the main house, and a fire leapt on the great hearth blending the smell of wood smoke with that of the evergreens.

" 'It's beginning to look a lot like Christmas!' " Idonia sang as she heaped pine cones into a large wooden bowl. Idonia's idea of decorating doesn't stray too far from Opal Henshaw's, but you can't go too far wrong with a bowl of pine cones. Idonia had been singing since she arrived that morning, and had even attempted (with a hilarious jumbling of lyrics) "The Twelve Days of Christmas."

Melrose, she told us, had given her his Christmas present early: an antique gold locket in the shape of a dogwood blossom with tiny seed pearls in the center, and it dangled now against her forest green sweater. The locket had once belonged to Melrose's grandmother, she explained earlier, and she had hesitated about accepting anything so personal, but Melrose had insisted.

"It doesn't do a thing for me," he'd told her, laughing. "Who else is going to wear it?"

Idonia fingered it lovingly as she paused to admire her work. "Melrose said it had six pearls in it originally," she said, "but two of them are missing. Sometime after the holidays he's going to see if he can get them replaced for me." And with that remark she drifted into "Jingle Bells" and began to poke cedar boughs into a ceramic jar. The small room had become increasingly warm with the wood fire and I was glad I'd elected to wear a cotton shirt and jeans as had most of the others. Idonia must have been uncomfortable in her sweater as I noticed she stayed as far away from the fireplace as possible.

"Why don't some of you help me make a swag for the front doorway?" Genevieve asked with a critical eye on Idonia's attempts at arranging. "We can cut the greenery in lengths and spread them out here on the table to wire together."

I knew from experience that sounded easier than it actually was, so I put on my jacket and went outside for the hemlock. When I returned with the greenery, Nettie trailed it along the big pine mantel and tucked it behind fat red candles along with clusters of red nandina berries. Idonia, I noticed, was still attempting to make a swag while Genevieve worked quietly behind her repairing the damage. Still humming, Idonia apparently hadn't noticed, or if she had, she didn't care. I hoped this wasn't too good to last.

We spent the rest of our time at Bellawood in the main house, tucking sprigs of spruce and pine behind picture frames, putting candles in every room, and setting out bowls of nuts and apples. Someone with more artistic ability than I had made a feathery wreath of evergreens interspersed with fluffy white bolls of cotton for the front door. It reminded me of the wreath on the door of the Green Cottage back at Willowbrook, and for a while that put a bit of a damper on my Christmas spirit.

I told Nettie about my visit to the Tanseys on the drive home together. (Idonia was entertaining Melrose for dinner and had to stop for groceries.)

"Did you know they had a daughter who died?" I asked.

"No, but then I don't know them very well," Nettie said. "From all I've heard Preacher Dave seems to be a hard worker and everyone says he's doing a good job filling in at the church for Luther. I've only seen his wife once or twice—shy little creature."

"I think they go to Chandler's Creek Baptist Church out on Sawmill Road," I said. "Preacher Dave's a part-time minister there."

"Wonder where they lived before they came here?" Nettie said. "Nobody seems to know much about them."

"Maybe they're just trying to escape sad memories."

"Well, they'd better brace up because it doesn't look like they're going to escape Opal Henshaw and her fruitcake," Nettie said. "Reckon Claudia will work up enough gumption to tell her she's not going to help with the 'run'?"

I laughed. "I doubt it. Let's just hope nobody offers us any while we're caroling this weekend."

"I can't wait to meet Idonia's admirer," I said to Augusta that night after supper. "But I'm not quite sure what to think. She's known this Melrose about a month yet he's given her a locket he says belonged to his grandmother. Wouldn't you think a family heirloom like that would go to one of his children?"

"Maybe he doesn't have any children," Augusta said. With a smile she added a tiny gilded angel to an arrangement of hemlock and pine and stepped back to examine it. The caroling party was days away and the only Christmas decoration I'd put up was an evergreen wreath on the front door. Now the two of us were doing our best to make the house look festive with the leftover greenery I'd brought from Bellawood.

"If he has any, Idonia hasn't mentioned it," I said. "Ellis said he works part time for his cousin at the funeral home, but surely he didn't come to Stone's Throw just for that." I rummaged in the box of decorations until I found the stuffed reindeer with a bell around its neck that always spent the season on Julie's bed and set it aside. "I wonder what did bring him here?"

"Perhaps we'll know in time, but from what you tell me, your friend seems happy with things as they are, so it would seem advisable to let sleeping cats be," she said, refilling her coffee mug. Augusta rarely sips coffee; she *drinks* it, and she did that now. So fortified, she set the mug aside and with flying fingers went about weaving the remaining greenery into a fragrant swag. My giggle at her jumbled expression seemed to escape her completely.

"That's just the point," I explained. "Idonia's marriage wasn't very happy—only lasted a few years until her husband found somebody else and left her to raise their little boy alone. I don't think Idonia has ever gotten over the hurt, and I hate to think of it happening again."

The stones shimmered green and gold as Augusta twined her long necklace through her fingers. "Your friend is a grown woman, Lucy Nan, and she makes choices just as most people do. I'm sure you'll agree it's best to let her make her own decisions . . ."

I followed her as she carried the swag down the hall to the living room where she draped it over the mantel. It looked fantastic. "Everybody will think I hired a decorator," I told her.

". . . still," Augusta continued, "I don't believe it would be inappropriate if we looked into this fellow's background—inconspicuously, of course."

"Fine," I said. "He'll be coming here for the caroling party, and Augusta, I don't know of anyone who can be more inconspicuous than you!

"We'll have to do a rush job of decorating the tree before the party," I said as I swept clippings from under the kitchen table. "Ben and I are going out to Willowbrook tomorrow to cut one so I guess I'd better get the decorations down from the attic."

"What did your policeman friend think about the possibility of a hidden staircase?" she asked.

"Not much. He said they looked around inside to see if they could find where one might be but didn't have any luck." I shrugged. "There's probably nothing to it. Mimmer always did have a good imagination. She said all the Vances do."

"Oh, my goodness, that reminds me!" Augusta let the dustpan clatter to the floor. "I forgot all about the phone call. I don't suppose you've checked your messages."

I shook my head. "Hadn't had a chance. What phone call?"

"Your cousin Grayson called while you were out. It seems his grandson Vance and his young lady would like to see the old home place and asked if you might meet them there tomorrow. I believe he's expecting you to return his call."

I looked at the clock. It was a few minutes after nine. I hoped my cousin hadn't already gone to bed.

But he sounded wide awake when I reached him.

"My friend Ben Maxwell and I plan to go out to Willowbrook to get my tree in the morning—probably sometime after ten," I told him. "Would that be too early for Vance and Jamie to meet us there?"

"Should be fine," he said. "I gave them a key to the house, but they don't know Dave Tansey and he doesn't know them. Didn't want him to think they had a prowler about—especially after what happened last week."

"Good thinking," I said. "I'll phone Preacher Dave in the morning so they'll know what we plan to do."

"They never did find out what that fellow was about, did they?" Grayson asked. "Was there no kind of identification or any kind of transportation?"

"Not that I know of," I said. "The police seem to think he was probably a vagrant taking shelter there for the night—of course, there are things they don't tell me."

Ben showed up the next morning in time for coffee and some of Augusta's pumpkin bread before leaving for Willowbrook. Augusta won't admit it, but I think she has kind of a crush on Ben Maxwell. I noticed the bread was fresh-from-the-oven warm and the coffee strong and steaming hot just as he likes it. They've never met, of course.

"It's going to be weird going back to Willowbrook," I said as we got ready to leave. "I don't think I'll ever feel the same way about it again."

Ben kissed the top of my head as he helped me with my jacket. "You don't sound like you have much confidence in my ability to protect you. I'm crushed."

I gave him a quick kiss, then shoved him out the door before he got a notion to linger. Clementine, of course, wanted to go along, too, and jumped into the front seat between us. "I know exactly where the tree is so it shouldn't take too long to find it, but my cousin Vance and his girlfriend are supposed to meet us out there to see the house," I told him. "Nellie Virginia—that's Vance's mother—thinks he might have an idea of living at Willowbrook someday." I reached over the dog to touch his hand. "I hope you're not in a hurry."

"My time is yours," he said, giving my fingers a squeeze. "I'm not working on anything that can't wait."

Ben is a talented furniture craftsman who does a lot of work restoring antiques at Bellawood, which is where we became friends. His reddish brown hair and beard, now streaked with gray, are an indication of his Scottish heritage, and his blue eyes have the intensity to warm you through and through or pierce you with an icy glance, depending on the situation. I don't even like to think about how dull my life had become before Ben Maxwell ordered me out of his workshop at Bellawood along with the children in my grandson Teddy's kindergarten class. That was over a year ago and to tell the truth it could have been a disaster as a number of yelling children pursued several yelping puppies through his sacred domain, tracking sawdust, scattering nails, and upsetting tools along the way. Ben, I thought at the time, had been unnecessarily gruff. Now he and Teddy have become great friends—and he has a special place in my life as well.

Once at Willowbrook it didn't take long to locate the tree and Ben quickly sawed it down and carried it back to the van. The weather, although brisk, wasn't as cold as it had been the week before and while Ben trimmed the base of the tree and lifted it into the back of his vehicle I shed my heavy jacket to race with Clementine in and out among the evergreens while we waited for the others to arrive. It was almost eleven when I saw the approaching car.

"We were about to give up on you," I called as Vance and Jamie pulled up in front of the house.

My young cousin gave me a hug as we made introductions. "Sorry to keep you waiting," he said, "but I decided to drop by the Green Cottage first just to let the Tanseys know who we are." He smiled at Jamie. "Didn't want to get shot!"

"Did you see Preacher Dave?" I asked.

He shook his head. "Nope. Only his wife—Louella, isn't it? She was just leaving for work."

"Said her husband had already left for the church and their son works somewhere in Rock Hill," Jamie added.

"Right. When I phoned out there earlier this morning, Louella said they would probably all be gone. Works at that fabric shop on the other side of town."

Vance felt in his pocket for the key to the house. "Anybody ready for a tour? I haven't been inside since I was little but I remember thinking how beautiful it was. I'm curious to see it again."

"I hope you won't be disappointed," I said, knowing that time and neglect hadn't been kind to the old family home.

"I can hardly wait!" Jamie started walking a little ahead of the rest of us but she stopped suddenly and stood looking at the house. "Is somebody supposed to be in there?" she asked.

"Not that I know of," I said. "Why?"

Jamie pointed to an upstairs window. "I thought I saw someone up there. Looked like a woman. Didn't any of you see her?"

Vance frowned. "There shouldn't be anyone in there. Are you sure you saw somebody?"

Jamie hesitated before speaking. "I thought I did . . . I could swear it moved, but I guess it could have been a curtain or something."

I didn't want to tell her there weren't any curtains in the house. "Must've been poor Celia," I said and told her about the family ghost.

"Ghost or not, I think we should check this out," Vance said, turning to Ben. "What do you say we take a look inside? If there's anyone in there I'd like to know who they are and what they're doing here."

"Oh no, you don't!" I told him. "You're not leaving me out here. If you two go inside, I'm going, too."

Jamie nodded. "Count me in, too," she said.

I slipped back into my jacket as we huddled on the portico waiting for Vance to unlock the heavy front door. And that was when we heard it. Someone was playing a violin and the music was coming from inside the house.

Suddenly it seemed to have turned much colder.

Chapter Six

"This is ridiculous!" Ben said, wiping his feet before entering—as if a few extra clumps of dirt would matter to years' accumulation of dust. "There has to be a rational explanation for this."

Vance, who walked ahead of us, stopped so short I almost collided with him. "Can you hear anything now? It seems to be over," he said, putting out a hand to quiet us.

Standing there in a silent knot, we waited until my feet grew numb and I just had to shuffle a bit. "I think the concert's finished," I told them.

"Well, I'm going in search of the soloist," Ben said, striding into what had once been my grandmother's dining room. Vance chose to go in the other direction and began poking behind doors and into crannies in the drawing room leaving Jamie and me alone in the vast entrance hall, where even our whispers echoed around us. Clementine, who had chosen to chase a rabbit rather than accompany us inside the house, was of little or no use to us here.

"Kids!" Jamie said finally. "Has to be some kind of prank."

"Most likely," I said, hoping it was true. I didn't tell her that Ellis had heard similar music the morning we discovered the body beneath the balcony, and even Augusta had admitted to hearing a scuttling noise. Doors opened and closed and drawers slammed shut as the two men explored the rooms beyond, which included a large kitchen, small parlor, and two adjoining bedrooms in the back. Willowbrook was a solid square house built to last through the years, which it obviously had. The four rooms in the front shared two chimneys while the larger of the bedrooms in the back, the one that had been my grandmother's, had its own fireplace. The smaller room adjoining it had none.

Jamie and I wandered into the drawing room, which seemed to be the sunnier, and therefore the warmer of the rooms to wait while Ben and Vance stormed about like a dedicated SWAT team thumping and bumping about. "Don't worry," I told her, "I'm sure they'll be all right." She couldn't see that I had a death grip on the cell phone in my jacket pocket.

She managed a smile. "Vance has told me so much about this old place, I just had to see it—didn't expect such an adventure! It is beautiful, though—or it could be. I can see why he cares so much about it."

And I hope you care about him if you're planning to live here, I thought, sidestepping a pile of debris. The house smelled of mice and mildew.

"Come look at this." Vance appeared in the doorway and led us into the larger of the bedrooms. "Somebody has been using this fireplace." He kicked aside a couple of empty food cans and a crumpled bread wrapper. "It's a wonder this whole place hasn't burned to the ground."

We found the charred remains of a fire in the grate and a few pieces of firewood were stacked on the hearth along with an empty half pint of some kind of liquor I'd never heard of.

"Trespassers are getting in somehow," Ben offered. "Looks like you're going to have to start boarding the place up."

"I'll ask Granddad to speak to Mr. Tansey. I'm sure he makes an effort, but just locking the doors doesn't seem to be working." Hands on his hips, Vance stared at the clutter around the fireplace. "We can't have this kind of thing!"

"Preacher Dave says he's run off squatters from time to time, and I know he tries to keep an eye on the place, but with his other duties, I guess he can't check on things like he should." I found that I had trouble speaking through the knot in my throat. I was glad my grandmother couldn't see her precious Willowbrook now.

We went upstairs in single file to find a similar jumble of litter. The fireplaces had been sealed off in two of the four bedrooms but a pigeon, which had apparently flown in through a broken window, lay dead in a corner of one, and a dirty, tattered sleeping bag had been tossed in another. I wondered if it had belonged to the man who plunged from the balcony. Mouse droppings were evident everywhere and I glanced at Jamie to see how she was reacting to her tour of her boyfriend's ancestral home. Noticing the attention, she merely shrugged. "I think you might want to invent a better mousetrap," she told him.

Ben seemed to be taking careful note of the walls, paying particular attention to areas around the fireplaces. In one of the front-bedrooms, cabinets had been built on either side of the fireplace and he meticulously investigated both of them, tapping from every angle.

"Maybe there's a lever somewhere that makes it revolve," I teased. "That's the way it works in the movies."

"I did think we might find a tape recorder or something like that," Ben said, running his fingers along the sides of the cabinets. "That music had to come from somewhere."

Vance stood at one of the two long windows that faced the front. A shutter hung crazily to one side and pale winter sunlight cut a crooked pathway across the grimy floor. "There's a drainpipe loose out here," he said, "and the wind *was* blowing earlier. Do you think that might have been what we heard?"

"If it was, it was playing a tune!" Jamie told him. "And I think I've heard that song before."

It had sounded familiar to me, too, I said. "Did you recognize what it was?"

Jamie shook her head. "No, but I'm sure it didn't come from any drainpipe!"

I repeated the snatch of music in my head. The notes were from a few bars of a longer composition, and I knew they would haunt me until I learned what it was. During the drive home I hummed them aloud so I wouldn't forget, and Ben agreed that what we had heard at Willowbrook had been deliberately played for our benefit.

We had found nothing in any of the bedrooms upstairs or in the large room behind them that ran across the back of the house. Mimmer had told me that at various times that room had been a ballroom, a schoolroom, even quarters for a bachelor uncle, and later a storeroom for the family's discards. When we emptied the house after Mimmer died I rescued a perfectly beautiful Windsor chair that now sits in the corner of my living room from what my grandmother referred to as "the junk room."

"I hope Vance and his family won't waste any time closing up that house," Ben said as we waited at a traffic light. "The kids around here have obviously heard rumors of your family ghost, and some have even claimed they saw a woman in a hoopskirt on the balcony. That poor fellow's death out there just added fuel to the fire." He reached over to nuzzle Clementine's ears as she once again snuggled between us. "If anyone is injured in a fire out there—God forbid—your cousin Grayson would be held responsible."

"And I doubt if he even has insurance," I admitted. "It's almost impossible to get a policy on an empty house." Although I knew from my grandson that local students were out of school for a teachers' workday, I really didn't believe our mysterious violinist was part of a harmless prank. After all, Augusta herself had said we hadn't seen the end of the trouble at Willowbrook. And Augusta was usually right.

Ben had a meeting about an order for a cherry writing desk with somebody in Columbia that afternoon, but he took time to help me get the tree in a stand and put it in my living-room window before leaving. Later that evening my son, Roger, and his wife, Jessica, would drop by with Teddy to help me decorate. Meanwhile, Augusta got us started by stringing the lights and the delicate garlands that looked like miniature red apples. Charlie had brought them to me from a business trip several years before, and for a while after his death I couldn't bring myself to put them on the tree.

"I believe it's almost as pretty as the one we got for the church," I said as Augusta swirled strings of tiny white lights in a perfect pattern. I told her about the music we had heard that morning but didn't try to repeat the tune. Augusta loves to sing but her notes don't always ring true, and I knew it would be a waste of time to ask her if she knew it. Why, she told me herself she had never even been allowed to audition for the heavenly choir.

Now she stepped back to appraise what she had done, and apparently satisfied, sank onto the rose brocade rocking chair by the fireplace. I seldom keep a fire in there as we usually spent our time in the small sitting room, but since the family was coming tonight, Augusta had agreed to build one, and now a happy little blaze crackled in the grate.

"Did you ever find the source of that music?" she asked, trying to avoid rocking on Clementine's tail.

"No such luck, and believe me, we looked that whole place over, room by room. Ben took a lot of time checking those cabinets on either side of the fireplace, too, but he couldn't find anywhere that might be a hiding place."

"I don't suppose you heard anything else?" Augusta fingered her dazzling necklace, flashing gold and amber in the fire's light.

"You mean like the scuttling sound you heard?" I said. "No, but there must've been an army of mice in there! The whole place is a mess! Mimmer would just be sick if she knew."

"Well, she doesn't know, so don't worry on her account, but it is a shame to see a fine old home go to ruin." Augusta rose to check the macaroni and cheese she had made for supper and I followed to pop some corn for the tree. I'm hard put to come up with something to serve my daughter-in-law, Jessica, since she's a vegetarian and won't even indulge in an innocent hamburger now and then. Thank goodness she isn't one of those people who won't eat any animal products or I'd really be in a bind.

Corn popped in the microwave while Augusta sprinkled nutmeg over a bowl of homemade applesauce and I put together ingredients for a green salad. Supper was ready to serve and the two of us already had a good start on stringing the popcorn when Teddy burst in the back door and threw himself down to wallow with Clementine on the kitchen rug. Augusta, as usual, disappeared from view.

"Give Clementine a hug and then hurry and wash your hands. Supper's ready," I told him, knowing his mother would probably haul out the antiseptic wipes if she saw the dog licking Teddy in the face. Jessica has become adjusted to having Clementine around, but she's still having a problem with doggy hair, doggy slobber, and what she imagines to be doggy germs.

Roger waited until Teddy and his mother were stringing popcorn for the tree after supper before bringing up the subject of the unfortunate incident at Willowbrook. Augusta and I had been baking that week and now he snatched a Santa-shaped cookie and bit off its head as I arranged them on a platter. Jessica doesn't serve sweets in their home but I think she's finally given up on mine.

"So, Mom," he began, reaching for another, "you seem to be starting off the holly-jolly season with a bang—or should I say, a thud? Have you developed some kind of sinister detector that leads you to dead bodies? I'm beginning to wonder if it's safe for you to be about! Should we hire a bodyguard?"

Now, I'm proud of my son and love him all to pieces, but since he's been made chair of the History Department at Sarah Bedford, our local college, he's gotten obnoxiously bossy. I chose that moment to tell him so. "Look," I said, "the man was already dead when we found him. I doubt very much if he picked that morning to jump or fall or whatever from the balcony just because I was in the vicinity." (I didn't dare mention the notion that he might have been pushed!)

"Well, something's going on out there, and I hope you and Aunt Ellis will have the good sense to stay out of it. Let Cousin Grayson worry about it. After all, it's his house." Roger stood to clear the table while I scraped dishes at the sink. Ellis is the closest thing to an aunt my two will ever have since neither Charlie nor I had any sisters and my brother can't seem to stay married. "Preacher Dave seems to think the guy might've been a homeless person who probably had too much to drink," he said, stacking glasses on top of plates until they leaned precariously, "and I can't get a word out of Ed down at the Police Department."

Ed Tillman and Roger had been friends since kindergarten and I knew him well enough to know he could clam up tighter than a miser's purse. I wasn't having any better luck with my friend Kemper Mungo.

"Maybe he doesn't have anything to tell," I said, rescuing the tottering stack, "but if I learn anything, I promise I'll let you know."

"Just promise you'll stay away from there." He brushed my cheek with a kiss. "I worry about you, you know."

"I know," I said, giving his arm a damp pat. There was no way I was going to tell him about our experiences at Willowbrook that morning. I just hoped I could count on Ben to keep his mouth shut, too.

"I ran into Nettie at the library this morning and she told me you had made new window treatments for Julie's room," Jessica mentioned later as we finished decorating the tree. "When do I get to see them?"

"Anytime," I said, watching Roger boost Teddy up to put the star on top of the tree. It was a pitiful-looking star my great-grandmother had made by sewing gold oiled paper to cardboard but, dog-eared as it was, it was tradition, and traditions die hard in our family.

"What about now?" Jessica was already on her way upstairs so there was nothing I could do but follow.

Augusta had fashioned simple tab curtains from a heavy cotton blend, and since Julie loved purple, the pattern featured inch-wide vertical stripes in that color against a white background. At intervals, a scattering of fern fronds lent a bright touch of green.

Jessica fingered the fabric and inspected the lining. Naturally, she found it perfect. "This is absolutely lovely!" she exclaimed, turning to me with a new glow of respect. I know she must have been wondering how I learned to sew so well after the disaster of Teddy's Halloween costume—or what was meant to be Teddy's Halloween costume—but, of course, she was too polite to mention it. "I've been looking for something similar for that little upstairs bedroom. Bought those curtains in a hurry when we first moved in, and I never have liked them. Did it take you very long to make these?"

"Oh, not too long . . . I worked on them off and on, of course." I stiffened. I could *feel* Augusta standing behind me and I didn't dare turn around.

"Do you think you might show me how? I hate to pay somebody to make them, and I'd really like to learn if you think it wouldn't be too terribly hard." Jessica turned imploring blue eyes on me and I felt like the lowest kind of worm. My daughter-in-law seldom asks favors and I really wanted to do something special to please her.

"Great jumpin' Jehoshaphat! Don't tell me you *made* those!" Roger stood in the doorway, his eyes wide with shock—an expression, I thought, which was unnecessarily exaggerated. "When did you learn to *sew*?"

"I'm afraid I'm not a very good instructor, but if you'll measure your windows and decide on the fabric, I'll be happy to make your curtains," I said, turning to his wife.

Behind him in the hallway Augusta laughed silently.

"I guess I stepped into it this time," I told her after the others had left. "You are going to help me, aren't you?"

"Of course, but they really aren't all that difficult to make," she said. "I could show you how."

"When I was in high school, I made a C-minus in home economics—and I was lucky to get it," I said. "Our teacher, Mrs. Settlemyer, retired after that year. Everybody said she went to live in Alabama with her daughter but we always suspected the poor soul had a nervous breakdown. . . . You might be an angel," I told her, "but you're not a saint!"

The two of us sat in the darkened living room watching the lights of the tree reflected in the window while the fire burned low on the hearth. Since Teddy had done most of the decorating, a lot of the ornaments hung on the lower branches but that was fine with me. I closed my eyes, drinking in the fresh cedar smell. "Just two more days until the caroling party," I reminded Augusta, "and we'll finally get to meet Melrose DuBois!"

Chapter Seven

The next day was Friday and Weigelia Jones was coming to help me get ready for The Thursdays' caroling party the following night. Weigelia and I became friends when I was her tutor in the literacy program several years earlier, and when I'm in a bind she's good enough to work me in on her house-cleaning schedule. There's no spot of dirt that can elude Weigelia Jones's keen eyes, no cobweb too far from her reach, and when I see her coming I want to throw my arms around her and shout hallelujah. Instead, I put on a huge pot of coffee. Weigelia loves it almost as much as Augusta, only she fills her cup about halfway with cream.

I was hurrying through my breakfast of cereal and orange juice that morning when it occurred to me that Augusta was trying to get my attention. "Did you say something?" I asked, rinsing my bowl at the sink. I didn't want to be in Weigelia's way when she started working her miracles on my kitchen floor.

"Only two or three times," Augusta said. "You must have been a million miles away. Is something on your mind?"

"It's that blasted song!" I admitted. "That little snatch of melody we heard at Willowbrook yesterday. I can't get it out of my head and it's about to drive me crazy."

"The violin music?" Augusta tapped her slender fingers on the table. "Why don't you ask someone who might be familiar with the piece—perhaps someone at the college. Didn't you tell me there was a group who played—"

"The Fiddlesticks! Of course! Our postmaster, Albert Grady, plays the violin and so does his wife, Miranda. I have to buy Christmas stamps anyway, and today would be as good a time as any." And I bent to kiss her angelic cheek. "Augusta, you're a genius! Now, what was it you wanted to say?"

Augusta flushed, which meant she was pleased. Although she tells me vanity is folly, I've seen her admire her own reflection too many times to take her seriously. "I asked what you had in mind to serve for your caroling party tomorrow," she said. "I saw a recipe for individual meat pies in the newspaper the other day, and—"

"Perfect!" I said. "We'll probably be chilled when we return so I thought I'd have some kind of hot soup . . ."

"Hmm . . . that butternut squash soup would be good . . . with a bit of ginger and nutmeg and a dash of sherry, of course. We had it last Christmas, remember?"

"Good but troublesome. Too much stewing and brewing!" I told her.

"I don't mind stewing and brewing," she said in what I thought was just a hint of self-righteousness. (I didn't say so, of course.)

And so we decided on the menu—or Augusta decided on it. Not that I minded one bit. "Naturally, The Thursdays will bring finger foods," I said. And I could guess what most of them would be. Ellis would bring a chafing dish with her famous hot clam dip; Jo Nell, sweet-and-sour meatballs; Zee, chicken salad puffs; Claudia usually brought marinated mushrooms; Nettie made a wonderful cheese ball; and I could count on Idonia to furnish fresh fruit.

"Of course, we'll have sweets coming out of our ears," I said, thinking of all the Christmas cakes and cookies everyone would bring.

Augusta's eyes grew wide. "Out of your *ears?*" she gasped, and I laughed so, I hardly had breath to explain that it was merely an expression.

I was still laughing when I heard Weigelia's car pull up behind the house. Besides going to the post office, I had several other errands to run and I asked Augusta if she'd like to go with me as she usually preferred to be out of the house while Weigelia cleaned. "Sometimes I have a feeling she suspects I'm here," she once told me, "and I don't like to take any chances."

But this time she had other plans. "Ellis has decided she wants plum pudding for Christmas dinner," she explained, "and I promised to help her make it. If you're going by the library, however, I'm almost out of something to read." Augusta has been on a mystery kick for the past few months and has already worked her way to the M–P section in the Stone's Throw Library. I promised to see what I could do.

Weigelia hadn't even finished her first cup of coffee before I realized she knew something I didn't. She hadn't had much to say when she came in lugging that big old bucket with all the brushes and soaps she likes to use. (She turns up her nose at mine.) Today she wore the new Reeboks her sister Celeste gave her for her birthday and a long purple skirt that touched the top of her rolled-down socks. The "ten-gallon" red plastic handbag she carries had been duly deposited behind the pantry door along with her faithful green plaid coat.

"Okay," I said. "What is it?"

"I guess you want me to do Julie's room since she be comin' for Christmas," she said, pouring a second cup to go with her muffin.

"You might run the sweeper in there and flip the dust around a little." I sat across from her and stared until she had to look at me.

She hates it when I do that. "It's something about that man who died out at Willowbrook, isn't it? You've been talking to Kemper, haven't you?"

Weigelia's cousin Kemper Mungo is a sergeant with the Stone's Throw police and if anybody could worm information from him, it would be Weigelia Jones. Now it was up to me to get her to turn loose and tell.

It wasn't easy. "You know Kemper ain't supposed to be talking to me 'bout things like that—and he sure don't want me spreadin' it around," she informed me.

"And *you* know I'll find out eventually. Besides, *The Messenger* is going to get wind of it sooner or later." *The Messenger* is Stone's Throw's weekly newspaper, and when its editor, Josie Kiker, gets the scent of a story, she's like a hungry dog going after a bone. "After all," I reminded her, "Ellis and I did find the body. That should entitle us to something."

Weigelia finished her coffee, and in slow motion, rose, rinsed her cup, and put it in the dishwasher. "They found out that man's name," she said finally.

"The dead man? Who was he?"

She tied an apron around her middle and took her sweet time about doing it. "Last name Clark, I think . . . wait just a minute . . . I wrote it down."

I waited while Weigelia reached into her vast bosom for a scrap of paper and handed it to me. And then she laughed. *She* knew that *I* knew she was eventually going to tell me. The name *Dexter Clark* was printed in block letters on what had been the flap of an envelope. "Who's this Dexter Clark when he's at home?" she said.

I shrugged. "Beats me."

"Kemper say he got a record: breaking and entering, drunk and disorderly—you name it." She shook her head. "Not a very nice man."

"Not nice at all," I said, "but that kind of explains what he was doing at Willowbrook."

Weigelia grabbed her polish and dust rag and headed for the living room. "What you mean?" she asked, pausing in the doorway.

"Breaking and entering, and being drunk and disorderly," I explained.

According to Weigelia, the dead man didn't have a permanent address so nobody seemed to know where he came from or what he was doing here—other than taking shelter. And if my cousin Grayson didn't do something about securing Willowbrook, I was afraid he wouldn't be the last casualty there.

The lines in the post office reached to the door and I waved to Clarence Allen, one of the clerks, who waited patiently on a customer. He nodded in return, eyes glazed. It was mid-December and people were still mailing packages. The postmaster's door was closed and I knocked softly and called out to Albert. The Gradys are members of our church and I've always found him to be pleasant and even-tempered. However, as I said, it *was* the middle of December.

He looked up from his computer, glasses halfway down his nose. "Lucy Nan! How can I help you?" I noticed he didn't ask me to sit.

"I realize this is a bad time," I began, "but this tune is driving me crazy and I thought you might recognize it." I told him about the mysterious melody we'd heard at Willowbrook and even went so far as to hum a few bars.

His expression was blank. "Well, it does sound familiar, but I have no idea what it is. I hope you've told the police about this, Lucy Nan. It all sounds peculiar to me, especially after that fellow was found dead out there."

"My cousin thinks it's probably a prank, but I thought if I could just find out the name of the song it might have something to do with what's going on out there," I told him.

Albert pushed up his glasses and sighed. "If anybody might be able to tell you it would be Miranda. She has perfect pitch, you know—never forgets a melody—although to tell you the truth, I think you ought to leave it to the police."

"She still teaching at the middle school?"

He glanced at the clock. "Yes, but she has a free period in about an hour. Why don't you drop by and ask her? She'll probably be glad of a break."

I thanked him, stood in line for my stamps, and phoned the school to let Miranda know I was coming. By the time I collected Augusta's books at the library, I had five minutes to get to there.

Miranda is choral director at the school and I found her in the music room surrounded by stacks and stacks of sheet music. "We're as ready as we're going to be for our holiday concert tomorrow night," she said when I came in. "Now, I have to decide what we need to work on for the spring!"

"Albert said you never forget a song and might be able to identify something for me," I said, explaining the reason for my visit.

"Why don't you hum a few bars and we'll give it a try," she said, sitting at the piano.

When I finished, she repeated the notes on the piano, adding even more of the melody. "That's it!" I said. "Please tell me you know what it is!"

Miranda laughed. "Of course. It's Romanian Rhapsody no. 1 by George Enescu. I played it in a concert once when I was in college. Beautful piece."

I nodded. "It has a haunting quality, don't you think? Maybe that's why whoever's doing this chose that particular song." I told her the story about the family ghost and how some have even claimed to see a figure in a period gown.

She frowned. "And this was supposed to have happened when?"

"Sometime during the War Between the States," I said. "Probably around 1863."

"Then they need to go back and do their homework," Miranda said. "Enescu wasn't born for more than a decade after that!

"I don't want to scare you, Lucy Nan," she added, "but it sounds as if somebody might be trying to frighten people away. They could easily use a CD or a tape of the music to give the ghostly effect—but why? What's going on out there they don't want anyone to know about?"

I had been thinking the same thing, and the more I thought about it, the madder I got. In fact, I was practically seething by the time I pulled up behind the Stone's Throw Police Department. The grocery store could wait!

Weigelia's cousin Kemper wasn't in but I was lucky enough to catch Captain Alonzo Hardy in an idle moment, and by the time he saw me coming, it was too late to run and hide.

"I want to know what's going on at Willowbrook," I demanded, telling him of our experience the day before. "First, a man is killed out there, and now this! Are you sure you searched that place thoroughly? And just who was the man we found?" I didn't want to get Kemper in trouble by admitting I already knew the dead man's name.

He sighed and motioned for me to sit, then proceeded to tell me what I already knew. "I've spoken with Dave Tansey and he's promised to board up the more accessible windows and do more to discourage vagrants out there. That old house is practically an open invitation to trespassers, I'm afraid. As far as we could tell, this man who was killed hadn't been drinking—fellow by the name of Dexter Clark. Had a record, though—petty stuff mostly. Didn't seem to have a permanent address." The captain picked up a pencil and rolled it between his palms. "No tellin' how long he'd been camping there. Reckon he knew a good thing when he saw it, and others, no doubt, have followed suit."

"But the music—"

"Shoot, everybody around here knows that crazy old ghost tale! Somebody rigged that up to scare people away." He tossed the pencil aside. "I'm telling you, we looked over every inch of that place, checked very nook and cranny where they might hide something like that, and came up with zilch!"

I told him Ben and Vance hadn't had any better luck.

"Well, we'll try to give it another look-see. Maybe we can surprise them, find out what this is all about . . . could be just some kids with nothing better to do, but if you'll take my advice, Ms. Pilgrim, you'll stay away from there."

I told Augusta about our conversation that night as I helped her make the small meat pies for the party. I browned the ground beef and combined it with onion, spices, and other ingredients while Augusta made the pastry and cut circles for the pies. She planned to make the soup the next morning, she said, and we had decided to serve hot spiced punch when everyone returned from caroling.

"You mentioned that Louella Tansey was at home when your cousin arrived yesterday," she reminded me. "Do you think it might have been her?"

"I don't see how she could have gotten to the house before Vance and Jamie. They hadn't been there more than a minute or so before we heard the violin. Besides, I'm sure we would've seen her. And she said Jeremiah had already left for work."

Augusta's hands flew as she spooned filling onto circles of pastry, folded them over, and crimped the edges. In what seemed only seconds, neat rows of pies lined the baking sheets ready to pop into the oven. I watched in silent amazement as she whisked an egg together with a spoonful of water for the glaze. "Once this party is behind us, perhaps I can do a bit of investigating on my own," she said, sliding the pastries into the refrigerator to be baked at the last minute.

"We really won't have that much to do tomorrow," I said. As usual, Weigelia had left the house spotless.

"What carols do you plan to sing?" Augusta gave her Christmas apron a jaunty flip and hung it in the pantry. She had made one for both of us, and hers was a patchwork creation of stars and bells in silver, lavender, and blue, while mine featured a similar pattern in red, green, and gold.

It would have been hard not to notice the wistfulness in her voice. "Oh, the usual songs, I guess. Why don't *you* come, Augusta?"

"Do you think I might?" I am not exaggerating when I say her smile was radiant. "I wouldn't sing, of course."

"Of course you might! It'll be fun! Weigelia's coming, too." Weigelia had offered to help with refreshments the next night, but I persuaded her we'd much rather have her company and her voice. Weigelia has this deep, rich contralto that sounds like the soul of an angel is breaking free from somewhere deep inside her. I guess it's kind of like Augusta should sound, if only she could.

Chapter Eight

"Are they here yet?" Ellis whispered, standing in the doorway.

"Not yet! Hurry and come inside—it's freezing out there!" I knew who she meant without asking, as I was just as eager as she was to get a look at Idonia's mysterious Melrose DuBois.

Ellis's husband Bennett crowded in after her, beating his gloved hands together. "You picked a dandy night for caroling. Must be twenty degrees out there!"

"Actually, it's twenty-six," I informed him. "Ben has a bar set up in the kitchen if you need some antifreeze."

"Everybody else is here," I told Ellis. She had brought her clam dip over earlier and now hurried into the dining room to adjust the heat under the chafing dish. Claudia's husband Brian hovered over the table competing with Zee for the sweet-and-sour meatballs, while Jo Nell's Paul kept Ben company in the kitchen. Bennett, I noticed, soon joined them.

Nettie, who stood at the living room window nursing a glass of red wine, held aside the curtain to peer into the street. "Seems they should be here by now . . . you don't suppose she's forgotten the time?"

"Oh, dear! What if they don't come?" Jo Nell looked over Nettie's shoulder. "Do you think something's happened?"

"*I think* I'm going to have some of these appetizers everybody's wolfing down with a nice glass of wine," Ellis said, warming herself by the fire.

"Sounds like a plan to me." Weigelia set a dish of mixed nuts on the coffee table and stretched out her hands to the blaze. "Only I'm gonna warm my insides with some good hot coffee before I go out in the cold." She shook her head. "I think the whole lot of us are crazy—that's what I think!"

Weigelia has cleaned for most of The Thursdays at one time or another, and not only knows about the dust balls under the sofa, but our other secrets as well. Ellis finally admitted to me that she'd given Weigelia her grandmother's treasured recipe for frozen fruit salad years before she gave it to me.

Claudia moved among us, a glass of wine in one hand and a tray of her marinated mushrooms in the other. "Well, I wish they'd hurry and get here before I lose my nerve to go out and face the elements. I don't know how I'll manage to sing if my teeth are chattering!"

"Have another glass of wine," Zee advised her, lifting her own.

"Has anybody ever *seen* Melrose?" Jo Nell asked. "I wonder what he looks like."

Nettie turned from her vigil by the window. "You'll soon find out—they just drove up!"

"Everybody hush, now! Just act natural," Zee advised.

"And how's *that*?" Ellis said.

Jo Nell crossed over to admire the tree, examining each ornament as if she'd never seen them before. "How pretty!" she exclaimed, fingering a fragile glass bird. "Where did you find this one, Lucy Nan?"

"Jo Nell Touchstone! You gave it to me yourself when you drew my name last year," I reminded her.

All of us were laughing when Idonia and Melrose made their entrance, somewhat hesitantly, through the dining room from the kitchen, so I suppose we did present sort of a laid-back front.

"It was much easier coming in the back way," Idonia said, slipping out of a tan suede jacket I'd never seen before, and I'll swear she looked as if she'd lost at least five pounds! Melrose, of course, was at her side to receive it, along with her muffler, hat, and gloves. "I'd like all of you to meet my friend, Melrose DuBois," she said, beginning introductions all around.

I stepped up to relieve Melrose of his burdens and welcome him to my home, and after a few minutes of awkward chatter, Ben and some of the other men whisked him away to the kitchen. That devil Ellis Saxon smiled at me from across the room, and I turned quickly away to steer Idonia toward the refreshments. The two of us had discussed earlier what we expected Melrose to look like, and I'll be darned if he didn't fit the description down to his holiday bow tie and trim mustache!

A good four inches shorter than Idonia, who towered over him at five feet nine, Melrose DuBois was a round sturdy man with ruddy cheeks and a fringe of graying brown hair, who looked as if he might have stepped right out of the early nineteen hundreds. If he had plucked a pipe from inside his coat and sported a pocket watch, I wouldn't have been a bit surprised.

While the others gathered around Idonia with assurances of her new friend's welcome, I found a spot on the table for her fruit tray and put a cup of hot punch in her hand. Idonia doesn't care for alcohol, but she has finally gotten used to seeing the rest of us indulge now and then.

"He's every bit as nice as you said he was," Claudia said. "And so polite, too."

"And such a pleasant smile," Nettie added. "I'll bet he has a good sense of humor."

I agreed with Zee that Idonia's gentleman friend was a brave soul to take on all of us at once, and Idonia seemed to relax and bask in the glow of the pleasantries. And pleasantries were what they were. Melrose DuBois didn't have the charm of a Cary Grant, the wit of a Robin Williams, or the sex appeal of a George Clooney—but then, who does? He was simply a Melrose, through and through, and if that was enough for Idonia Mae Culpepper, it was enough for me.

Tonight Idonia wore a sea green turtleneck tunic with beige wool pants and brown suede fur-trimmed boots. The gold locket with the two missing seed pearls glowed softly against her sweater. I don't think she'd gone out without it since Melrose gave it to her a few days before.

Later, as we left to go caroling, I saw Augusta for just an instant out of the corner of my eye as she stood in the hallway wrapping herself in her "forty miles" of cape before stepping outside with the carolers. She pulled a plum-colored hat over her radiant hair before disappearing from my vision completely.

Everyone else was bundled to the teeth as well. In fact, most of us wore so many layers it was hard to tell one person from another. Claudia's husband Brian, who claimed to be tone deaf, elected to stay and keep the home fires burning, but the rest of us waddled out looking like so many penguins. "If I fall, promise you won't let me roll away," I said to Ben as we maneuvered the front steps together. He pressed my gloved hand close against him as we started out. "Just try and get away," he whispered, making me feel warmer at once.

"Where to?" called Ellis, who, with Bennett and Weigelia, led the way.

"Why not start with the Johnsons next door?" Zee answered, throwing the beam of her flashlight along the low stone wall that led to our neighbor's house.

Our neighbors huddled politely in the doorway listening to our rendition of "Oh, Come All Ye Faithful," and even braved the cold to hear a couple of verses of "Jingle Bells." We declined their invitation to come in for eggnog and fruitcake and hurried along to the next house. Melrose's tenor, we discovered, blended beautifully with Ben's baritone, so we urged the two of them to the front of the group with Weigelia after that. Augusta, I noticed, stood at a discreet distance mouthing the words, and I ached for her, knowing how she wanted to sing.

Since they both sang alto, Idonia dropped back to stand next to Nettie at the rear of the carolers, but her eyes were only for Melrose, and the pride in her face was obvious as she listened to him sing.

"Couldn't we just skip the Willoughbys?" Zee asked as we hurried across the street. "You know good and well Myrtle will pass around those awful cookies."

"I don't know how we can ignore them," Ellis told her. "Besides, you don't have to take one."

But that, we found, was easier said than done. "I'm so glad you came around tonight—been baking all afternoon!" Myrtle Willoughby quickly threw a wrap about her. "Quick, Wilbur, bring me the cookie jar! I have plenty for everybody," she called, hurrying to meet us. "Now, don't be shy . . . take two—more if you like." She shoved the container at each of us in turn. "Now, don't tell me you're dieting," she said to Zee. "Nobody diets at Christmastime."

"I'm glad we didn't sing that song about the figgy pudding," Paul Touchstone commented as we left. "She might've made some of that, too!"

Ben burst forth with his booming laugh. "That reminds me of this little maiden lady who lived over in Sweet Gum Valley, where I grew up," he began. "Seems she was interested in the new preacher in town, and somebody told her they'd heard the fellow liked a woman with a big mouth . . . so she invited him over for dinner. 'Won't you have some **HAM, TATERS, and APPLE**

PIE?' she said, stretching her mouth as large as she could. Well, that didn't do the trick," he continued when the laughter died down, "so she reckoned he must favor the opposite. Well, the next time he came to dinner she made up her mind not to open her mouth any bigger than a keyhole. 'Preacher,' she said, 'help yourself to some of them prunes, and please pass the pudding.' "

Nettie prodded him with her flashlight. "Do law, Ben Maxwell, I believe you made that up!"

"Did *not*! It was one of those McGaritys—Ruby Lee, I think it was—lived just down the road from my grandmama—ugly as homemade sin, the lot of them!"

We had decided to serenade the last two families on the block and call it a night, and were congregating on the Dorseys' front walk when somebody jostled me from the rear and I turned to find Idonia practically breathing down my neck.

"Jo Nell, will you please stop crowding me? You're stepping on my heels," she complained.

"I don't know how, since I'm standing over here," Jo Nell said from a couple of feet away.

"Well, somebody keeps bumping into me. I can't take a step without being shoved from behind," Idonia insisted.

"Don't look at me," Nettie said. I noticed that she had moved up beside Claudia and Zee in an effort to move things along. "Let's sing 'Rudolph,' that's a lively one," she said, beating her mittened hands together.

"How about 'The Twelve Days of Christmas'?" Bennett joked.

"And how about we leave you here to sing a solo?" Ellis suggested.

My feet were so numb I could hardly feel them as we sang "Deck the Halls" to Amelia Kimbrough at the house on the corner, ending with "Silent Night," and if I hadn't been so cold, I could have listened to more. The voices of Ben, Melrose, and Weigelia, with others blending in harmony, were so sweet it brought tears to my eyes. I quickly wiped them away before they could freeze on my face and walked ahead of the others to get a start on warming the soup and pastries.

Idonia caught up with me as I hurried up the front walk. "Lucy Nan, I think somebody's been following me," she said, panting to keep up.

"You mean tonight? Idonia, we were all out there together. It was probably just somebody in our group."

She glanced behind her as we went inside together. "I thought so, too, at first, but the whole time we were caroling, I heard footsteps a few steps behind me, and once, when we sang at the Dorseys', I'm sure somebody tried to grab my arm."

"Are you sure it wasn't Melrose?" I smiled, trying to make light of the situation, but Idonia wasn't amused.

"You know good and well he was with Ben and Weigelia. He wasn't even near me!"

"Were you able to get a look at this person at all?" I asked, thinking it was probably Nettie or one of the others.

In the kitchen, Idonia slipped out of her coat and tossed her gloves onto a chair. "Everybody was so bundled up, it was hard to tell who was who, but I really don't think it was one of us. Whoever it was had a scarf wrapped over his face, and whenever I turned around, he seemed to move away. I'm sure I saw somebody slip into the shadows of that big magnolia in the Dorseys' front yard."

"But why? What do you think they wanted?"

"I can't imagine, but it made me feel uncomfortable, and, Lucy Nan, you know me well enough to know I'm not easily excitable." She peeked inside the slow cooker. "Mm . . . soup smells good! Butternut squash?"

I nodded. Upon our return to the house we had found our fire keeper, Brian, watching a football game in the sitting room while the fire burned to ashes on the living-room hearth. Somehow,

I noticed, Augusta had managed to slip back inside and turn up the heat on the cooker, and checking the oven, I found foil-wrapped meat pastries warm and ready to serve.

Voices and laughter in the living room alerted us the others had returned, and Idonia drew me aside as we went to greet them. "I'd rather you not mention this to Melrose, Lucy Nan. I don't want him to think I'm one of those hysterical women who gets upset over nothing."

I gave her a reassuring hug. "I won't," I said, "and you aren't."

In the living room a shamefaced Brian added wood to the fire and Nettie settled into the closest chair to pull off her boots and warm her feet. "I'm not moving," she announced, "until I can feel my toes again."

With Weigelia's help I set out trays of pastries and mugs of soup to have with the fruit Idonia had brought earlier, and Ellis arranged a huge platter of cookies, jam cake, and lemon bars for dessert. Seated on the sofa, Idonia, her cheeks still flushed from the cold, laughed with Melrose at something Bennett was telling them.

"Remember the first time we were served vichyssoise?" Bennett said, winking at Ellis.

Ellis made a face. "How could I forget when you keep reminding me?" She laughed. "We were just out of college," she explained, "and were invited to a progressive supper. The first course was vichyssoise served like this—in mugs." She glanced at Bennett, who took up the story.

"It was cold, of course, with chives sprinkled on top, and neither of us had ever had it before . . ." Bennett waited for a signal from his wife before continuing. "On the way home, I asked Ellis how she liked the soup, and she said she reckoned it was okay once you got used to the cold, but she had an awful time straining those pine needles through her teeth!"

"Idonia tells us you're staying over at the Spring Lamb," Paul

Touchstone said to Melrose, after the laughter died down. "Getting enough to eat over there?" he added, ignoring his wife's warning frown.

Melrose patted his round stomach and laughed. "Obviously, I'm getting enough somewhere, but I take most of my meals out."

"Working over at the funeral home, I guess you get the news firsthand when anybody around here dies," Zee said.

Melrose nodded solemnly. "Sooner or later, that's where we all end up, only I'd a whole lot rather it be later."

Nettie washed a lemon bar down with coffee. "I don't reckon Joe Harris Carlisle's been around lately?"

"Joe Harris Carlisle . . . ?" Melrose looked puzzled at the laughter that followed. "Don't believe I've met the fellow."

"You will," Nettie told him. "Comes in every so often to get measured for his coffin."

"Must weigh over three hundred pounds," Zee explained, "and just keeps on getting bigger, so Joe Harris has Al Evans measure him now and then just to be sure he'll fit."

"That's right," Weigelia told him as she helped herself to coffee. "And there ain't no way you be missing him when he comes in, either."

Claudia laughed. "If I don't stop eating, I'm afraid I'll be in the same fix! These pies are wonderful, Lucy Nan. Where do you get all these great recipes?"

"Must be heaven sent," Ellis said from across the room, and I could plainly see Augusta standing beside her. The two of them were obviously enjoying their little joke.

"It was a very nice party," Augusta said after everyone left. "Everyone seemed to enjoy the caroling and the singing was lovely. Your friends are fortunate to be blessed with such lovely voices."

"I know," I said, putting the last plate in the dishwasher. "It was fun, wasn't it?"

Augusta gave the dog a treat. Poor Clementine had been banished upstairs for the duration of the party and was now basking in the attention being showered upon her. "I'm afraid I didn't last long enough to hear most of it," Augusta admitted, teasing Clementine with a dog biscuit under her apron. "As you know, I'm not fond of the cold."

I nodded. "Did you last long enough to notice if someone was following Idonia?"

"Following Idonia? Why, no, I didn't see anyone, but then everyone had on so many wraps, it would have been difficult to tell them apart."

Augusta rewarded Clementine with the biscuit and went to the closet for the broom. I watched in amazement as she twirled it about the floor in so many loops and whirls, before putting it back in its place. After all the guests who had passed through our kitchen that night, not a crumb or a speck of dirt remained. "I wish I could do that. Do you think you could teach me?" I joked.

But Augusta didn't smile. "Why does Idonia believe someone was following her?"

"She has no idea, but she was truly frightened, and she isn't the high-strung type."

"I did notice one thing that rather bothers me," Augusta said. "That locket Idonia was wearing—the one shaped like a flower—is exactly like the one the Tanseys' daughter wore in that photograph on their piano."

Chapter Nine

"Are you absolutely *sure?*" Ellis asked Augusta the next day. "Could you really tell that much about a photograph? Maybe Idonia's locket isn't absolutely identical to the one Dinah Tansey wore."

"There could be several like that," I said. "How do we know the Tansey girl had the only one of its kind?" Unlike Augusta, I hadn't paid much attention to the locket in the photograph and held on to the hope that Melrose DuBois wasn't a liar and that our good friend wouldn't be hurt because of him.

Augusta continued putting away dishes from last night's party and her silence seemed to go on forever. When she spoke, her voice was so soft I had to move closer to hear. "The seed pearls are missing in the same places," she said, turning to face us. "I'm sorry, but it seems that something's not right."

Ellis had dropped by after church that Sunday to collect her chafing dish and had surprised us with a huge red poinsettia for the dining room. "I would've brought it in time for the party yesterday, but I don't know where you'd have put it with all that food," she said.

Frowning now, she traced with her finger the Z-shaped scratch on my kitchen table where Roger had tried to build a picture frame from scrap lumber for his Boy Scout project. "So where did Melrose get the locket he gave Idonia? You don't suppose he stole it, do you?" Her face turned almost as red as the plant she brought. "And I was beginning to like him, too!"

Augusta spoke calmly. "Let's not accuse anyone until we know the truth. No purpose is ever served by hopping over the firearm."

Ellis rolled her eyes at me and shrugged. "Jumping the gun," I mouthed when Augusta wasn't looking.

"Isn't Claudia supposed to visit the Tanseys this afternoon to help deliver that fruitcake?" I said. "Maybe we can catch her before they leave."

"That chicken! I knew she'd let Opal Henshaw browbeat her into going, but now I'm glad she did." Ellis reached for the phone. "I'll give her a call and ask her to try and get a good look at that photograph."

"Just tell her not to mention it to Opal," I reminded her. "The less she knows about this, the better."

"Didn't you say the police planned to have another look around your grandmother's old home?" Augusta asked while Ellis made her phone call. "I wonder if they'll discover anything."

"Captain Hardy said he'd let me know if something turned up, but if I don't hear from him by tomorrow, I'll give him a call," I said. "There was a small mention about the man falling from the balcony in the Columbia paper today, but it still didn't identify him as Dexter Clark."

Augusta looked thoughtful. "Perhaps the authorities aren't ready to release the man's identity."

"They must have a reason for keeping it quiet," I said.

Ellis finished her phone call and told us that Opal planned to come by for Claudia promptly at two o'clock to deliver their Christmas baskets. "Poor Claudia!" she said. "It's probably going to take them most of the afternoon. Can you imagine spending all afternoon with Opal Henshaw?"

"You did remind her to make a point to look at that photograph, didn't you?" I asked her.

"I reminded, and Claudia promised. Let's just hope she isn't too obvious about it."

"Well?" I asked Ellis later that day when she came over to dress for Bellawood's candlelight tour. "Have you heard anything from Claudia?"

Ellis nodded. She didn't look happy. "Called a few minutes before I left. She said the locket in the picture looked like the same one to her and that Opal was curious about it, too. Said she was sure she'd seen one just like it."

Please don't let this be happening to Idonia! "What are we going to do?" I said. "Should we say anything to Idonia?"

"Say anything about what?" Nettie came out of my bedroom snapping the elastic in her long skirt. "This blasted thing's about to cut me in two. If you hear a loud pop, you'll know what happened."

The planners of the event had asked The Thursdays, as hostesses, to dress in period clothing and allowed me to bring several items home for Nettie, Ellis, and me. "Try that blue gingham. It might be more comfortable," I said, and while Nettie was getting into the dress, Ellis and I told her what we suspected about Idonia's locket.

"I wouldn't want to be the one to tell her," Nettie said. "This is not good! It might be better to speak directly to that rat Melrose." She finished buttoning her dress and tied an apron around her plump middle. "Ah, that's better! At least I can breathe."

We dressed in layers because, except for fireplaces in some

rooms, the areas at Bellawood weren't heated. Ellis chose an ankle-length black skirt with a high-necked white blouse, and draped a blue knitted shawl about her shoulders. Her dark curls, now streaked with gray, looked becoming tied back with a black ribbon. "I'll be darned if I'm going to look like that woman in the *American Gothic* painting with my hair pulled back and parted in the middle!" she informed us.

I wore a mop cap to cover my short straight hair and slipped on a purple-flowered dress large enough to have room for all the layers underneath.

"Are we supposed to bring anything?" Ellis asked as the three of us climbed into her van.

"Nettie's punch bowl is already there and the docents are taking care of refreshments," I said. "All we have to do is meet and greet."

"I wonder what the others are wearing," Nettie said, spreading her skirt about her.

"Idonia said she was going to borrow something for herself and Jo Nell from the high school drama department," Ellis said. "Her niece teaches over there, you know, and Zee told me she was wearing a dress she had in college."

"Not that Southern belle hoopskirt thing!" I said. "Bellawood's a farmhouse, not Tara."

Nettie laughed. "Didn't she wear that in some kind of pageant one time? Remember when Stone's Throw put on that bicentennial play? That dress was cut so low I thought surely her bosom was going to bounce right out of it!"

"Genevieve Ellison will have apoplexy," I said, but I couldn't help but feel a little jealous. There was no way I would be able to fit into a gown I'd worn in college!

It had turned dark by the time we arrived and someone had already lit the luminaries that lined the long drive up to Bellawood. A man dressed for the cold in muffler and cap directed us with a flashlight into the meadow across from the house where several other vehicles were already parked.

I parted reluctantly with my wrap at the door, while Ellis was whisked immediately to the building that housed the kitchen, and Nettie to the schoolhouse, where, we were told, Jo Nell waited. A quartet from the Baptist Church, scheduled to entertain guests with carols, was assigned there as well. I obediently took my place in the drafty entrance hall and watched them hurry away to spend a toasty evening in their allotted places.

The old house looked festive and welcoming from the wreath on the front door and banks of greenery on the mantel to the pungent smell of wood smoke and pine. I spoke briefly to Andy Collins, known to most of us as the Dulcimer Man, who was setting up in the parlor where candles glowed in hurricane lamps and firelight flickered on the hearth. Zee would be stationed in the upstairs hall, I learned, and Idonia in a second-floor bedroom, and every time I heard footsteps cross the porch, I braced myself for Genevieve's outburst when she saw Zee's revealing gown. I could hardly wait!

It served me right, I suppose, to be disappointed. The rose taffeta had faded over the years and Zee had even sewn a lace insert at her throat. Still, she managed to look trim and youthful with an antique brooch at her neck and her hair piled high on her head. Zee had chosen a dark auburn as her hair color for the season and it really was becoming.

"Zee, you look beautiful! Scarlett would be jealous," I said, ushering her into the hallway. "But where's the hoopskirt?"

She laughed. "I let Melanie borrow my hoop for a party one time and never saw it again." Melanie was Zee's daughter by her first husband—or maybe it was her second. "Anyway," she added, "can you imagine trying to *drive* in one?" She twirled, showing off dainty slippers. "Consignment shop—aren't they adorable? Of course, my feet are freezing! And how about this fancy brooch I found at a flea market? They have the most fascinating things in there."

Genevieve came along to hurry Zee upstairs before I could answer, and soon afterward a great swirl of frigid air ushered in Idonia stamping her feet and hugging her new suede coat about her.

"Good heavens, it's cold out there! And Zee just ran off and left me as soon as she parked the car. Had to hike all the way from across the road by myself in the dark, and I'd give my right arm for something hot to drink." Idonia pulled off her gloves and stuffed them into her pocket as she glanced upstairs. "I hope there's going to be some heat up there."

I told her Genevieve had put space heaters in some of the upstairs rooms and that Zee was probably in a hurry because she said her feet were cold.

"Well, of course they're cold since she insisted on wearing that sorry excuse for shoes." Idonia slowly unbuttoned her coat and passed it over to a waiting docent. She wore a prim gray silk with tucks down the front and a lace collar. The infamous gold locket was her only adornment.

"They're serving cranberry punch in the dining room," I told her, "but I don't think it's hot."

"What's Melrose doing with himself tonight? Is he planning to drop by?" I called after her as she made her way upstairs.

She gave me a backward wave of her hand. "He was going to, but his cousin needed him to help out at the funeral home, so I guess he won't be coming."

Fulton McIntyre, of course. Our minister announced in church that morning that Fulton had died, which was no surprise since the man was ninety-three and ailing. *So that's why Idonia's so crabby*, I thought. I knew something must have gotten her dander up. If Idonia was upset over playing second fiddle to a dead man, what would she think if she knew what we suspected about her locket?

I didn't have time to think about it, however, as guests began to arrive and I stayed busy guiding them from one room to another. From the parlor came the strains of "What Child Is This?" and "Away in a Manger" played sweetly on the dulcimer and for a second I thought I saw Augusta sitting in a corner by the fireplace listening. A closer look proved me right: it *was* Augusta and her expression was so blissful and serene it made me forget for a moment just how bossy she can be. I had mentioned to her earlier that the Dulcimer Man was scheduled to play, so I wasn't surprised to see her there. Augusta had attended one of Andy's concerts with me earlier in the year and I knew she was fond of his music. When I glanced in there a few minutes later she was gone.

"Augusta was in here a little while ago," Ellis whispered when I dropped by the kitchen during a break later that evening. "Didn't stay long . . . guess she came to hear the Dulcimer Man."

"I saw her in the parlor," I said, sipping gratefully on the hot spiced cider served from a pot on the hearth. "Aren't the Fiddlesticks coming back? I passed Albert and Miranda leaving with their instruments."

"Nope. I believe a flute trio from the high school band is next on the agenda," Ellis said as she added more ginger cookies to the tray on the table.

I turned in front of the fire to get thoroughly warm before crossing back across the yard to the main house. "Better let me have a cup of that punch to take back to Idonia," I said. "She was asking for something hot to drink."

Ellis laughed. "She's already been in here. Drank two cups in here and took one back with her."

"Did she seem upset?"

"No, just thirsty. I thought she was going to drink the punch bowl dry. Why?"

I told her about Idonia's earlier behavior. "I guess she's just disappointed that Melrose couldn't join her tonight."

"If there's anything shady going on about that locket he gave her, Melrose DuBois had better get a running start!" Ellis said.

In keeping with the period, we had been asked not to wear watches that night, but because long sleeves covered my wrists, I could keep mine well out of sight. It was almost eight-thirty when I returned to my post in the hallway, and every room in the old house seemed to be filled with visitors. It was easy to imagine the home as it had been in the past with friends, music, and laughter, and if a building has a spirit, this one must have been happy. Plans were for the open house to end at nine, but some of the musicians stayed longer, and several of the town's older citizens settled down to exchange tall tales by the dining room fireside, so it was closer to ten before everyone cleared out.

I was helping some of the docents clear away the clutter downstairs when Zee rushed into the room on the verge of tears. "Lucy Nan, something's wrong with Idonia! You've got to come quick! I can't wake her up."

We all raced upstairs behind her to find Idonia seated at a small writing desk in a rear bedroom, her head upon her chest. The room was close and warm because of the space heater, and Idonia, who was unaccustomed to late hours, had been out caroling the night before.

"She's probably just worn out," I said, calling her name. "Idonia! Wake up! It's time to go home." I got no response.

"I felt her pulse," Zee said. "She's breathing okay, but she seems to be out like a light."

By that time Nettie and Jo Nell had joined us. "She's not on any medication, is she?" Nettie asked. "Sometimes antihistamines can make you drowsy."

"Nothing but a low-dose thyroid pill," I said. Idonia was usually as healthy as a horse.

Jo Nell sniffed at a punch cup beside her. "What's she been drinking?"

"Just hot spiced punch, and so have I," I told her. "There's nothing in there to harm her."

"Wait a minute . . . I think she's waking up," Zee said as Idonia blinked her eyes. "Is it time to get up?" she mumbled before closing them again.

"That does it!" I said. "Who has a cell phone? I'm calling nine-one-one."

Chapter Ten

"No, wait! Don't!" Nettie said. "We might be able to catch Glen Smiley before he gets away. He was talking with somebody out front just a few minutes ago. Idonia would hate it if we made a big issue of this."

Genevieve rushed into the hallway and hollered downstairs in her loud demanding voice for somebody to run and find the doctor. Glen Smiley graduated from high school in the class just ahead of ours and has been practicing medicine in Stone's Throw for close to thirty years. Although his name is somewhat of a misnomer, as his bedside manner leaves something to be desired, you won't find a better diagnostician, so I was relieved to hear the doctor's monotone muttering in the hallway below.

"What's going on here, Lucy Nan?" he asked, taking the stairs in great loping strides. But I could only shake my head. I was too frightened to speak.

"Idonia Mae, I want you to look at me," he said, kneeling beside her chair. "Look at me and tell me where you are."

Idonia's eyelids fluttered and her head rolled to one side. "Don't feel so good . . . leave me 'lone." She sounded more like herself in spite of the slurred words.

"Have you had anything to eat or drink tonight?" the doctor persisted, examining her more closely. Idonia slumped forward until her head rested on the desktop. She didn't answer.

"She drank a lot of that spiced cider," I told him, gesturing toward the cup.

"Is this it?" He picked it up and sniffed it. "You-all didn't slip any vodka in there, did you?" He directed the question at Genevieve without so much as a flicker of a smile.

"Certainly not!" she answered, looking from one to the other of us. I could tell she wasn't quite sure about the rest of us.

"I can't do anything for her here," he told us, taking a cell phone from his pocket. "She needs to go to the ER, but first we'll have to get her out of that chair before she slides onto the floor."

"It'll take them about five or ten minutes to get here," Dr. Smiley said, after making his phone call. "Meanwhile, let's get her over on that bed so the EMTs can take a look at her."

I heard somebody gasp behind me and turned to find Genevieve with a fist rammed into her mouth. "That bed's almost two hundred years old," she said. I honestly thought she was going to faint.

"Then it oughta hold up a few minutes longer," the good doctor said. "And we don't need all of you in here, either," he added. "At least one of you can go outside and watch for the ambulance."

"I—I will! I'll wait for them out front." Jo Nell's voice trembled. "Only I'll need to borrow a flashlight. I don't—can't remember where I put mine."

"Take mine. I left it by the front door," I said. I could tell she was about a sniff and a swallow away from crying.

"And somebody needs to find Ellis," Jo Nell said. "Oh, Lordy! What if something's happened to Ellis, too?"

"Nothing has happened to Ellis. She's probably still straightening up out in the kitchen," Nettie assured her. "Don't worry, Jo

Nell, we'll find her." And giving Genevieve's arm a jerk, she propelled the startled woman from the room.

Zee and I stayed to help Glen Smiley move Idonia to the bed, and I must say she didn't cooperate one bit.

"Like picking up a big sack of chicken feed," Zee said.

I couldn't imagine where that analogy came from because as far as I know Zee St. Clair has never lifted a sack of chicken feed in her life.

"You better hope and pray Idonia didn't hear you say that," I told her.

The doctor frowned as he took her pulse. "Does anybody know how to get in touch with Nathan?"

Idonia's only son lives somewhere in Georgia but I couldn't remember the city. "Is it that serious?" I asked him. "What's the matter with her, Glen?"

"I'll know more about that when we get her to the hospital and have whatever's in that punch analyzed. Are you sure Idonia's not on any medication? Has she been having trouble sleeping lately? Look in her purse—see if you can find anything in there."

"She came with me. I don't even know if she brought a purse," Zee said.

"Yes, she did! I saw her take it upstairs," I said, "so it should be somewhere in here."

Zee found Idonia's gray leather handbag in one of the bureau drawers but there was no medication in there, only a comb, a package of tissues, and a tube of her favorite shade of lipstick, tawny rose.

"Is there anything you can do to help her?" Zee asked, kneeling by the bed.

"To be on the safe side, they'll probably have to do a gastric lavage," the doctor said.

I've watched enough medical shows on television to know that meant washing out the stomach and that Idonia wasn't going to like it one bit. Now she sighed as she shifted her position on the bed and made a face as if she smelled or tasted something bad.

"What's the matter with Idonia?" Ellis's breathless question accompanied her frantic footsteps on the stairs. "It's not her heart, is it?" she asked, grabbing Glen Smiley by the arm.

"I'm inclined to believe it's possibly something she ingested," he said, freeing himself from her grasp. "You were in the kitchen, weren't you? Do you know if anyone else suffered an adverse reaction to something they may have consumed tonight?"

Ellis looked at him as if he'd asked her if she'd served up rat poison. "Well, of course not! It was only spiced apple punch and ginger cookies. Idonia did drink a lot of it, though. Said she hadn't had time for supper."

"She's going to be all right, isn't she?"

"Glen thinks we should get in touch with Nathan," I said before he could answer. "Do you know where he's living?"

"No, but Jennifer should," Ellis said. Jennifer Cole is Idonia's niece, who teaches at the high school.

"Then I think you'd better call her." Glen moved to the doorway at the sound of a siren in the distance. "That must be the ambulance, so let's clear out and give them some room. You can follow us to the hospital if you like, but the sooner we get there, the better."

Taking his advice, I hurried into the hallway, but Ellis still stood in the middle of the room looking like she just remembered she'd forgotten to put on underwear. "Wait a minute!" she said.

"Wait for what?" Zee asked. "Hurry up, Ellis, we have to get out of here."

Ellis turned and walked resolutely to stand over Idonia's inert body. "It's gone," she said, turning to look at us.

"What's gone?" I said.

"The locket. Her locket's not here." Ellis's searching fingers traced Idonia's neckline, felt beneath her head and shoulders. "Did one of you take it off?"

"Of course not," Zee said. "That locket was the last thing on my mind."

"But not Idonia's," I said. "If that locket doesn't turn up, we'll have another emergency on our hands."

"She didn't appear to be wearing anything like that when I examined her," Glen said, "but if she is wearing jewelry, they'll remove it at the hospital for safekeeping."

"Well, it wasn't anywhere on the floor," Ellis said as we followed the ambulance to the hospital. "I searched that room on my hands and knees."

"Genevieve promised they'd comb that whole area tomorrow," I said. "It might have fallen off somewhere between the house and the kitchen, so it would be almost impossible to see it in the dark."

"Right now that's the least of our worries," Nettie said. "I phoned Jennifer and she's going to meet us at the hospital."

"What about Nathan?" I asked. "Did she know where to find him?"

"She said she'd try, but he travels a lot in his work, and it's not always easy to catch up with him." Nettie whistled through her false teeth as she sighed. "Do-law! Won't we be a sight parading into the hospital in these long-tailed outfits? It must be close to midnight already."

"The drunks in the emergency room will think they're hallucinating," Ellis said in an attempt at humor.

But the three of us were quiet for the rest of the ride. I'm sure the others were hoping and praying, as I was, that our friend was going to be all right. We Thursdays made up a strange motorcade, I thought, noticing Zee's headlights following closely behind us, and Jo Nell's behind her. Because of the late hour, we decided not to call Claudia unless Idonia's condition worsened. After all, what could she do? What could any of us do?

Ellis's gaze met mine in the rearview mirror as we finally turned into the hospital parking lot, and I knew we must be thinking the same thing. *Where was Augusta when we needed her?*

There was a time when I considered anyone in their forties to be ancient. Not anymore! If I remembered correctly, Idonia's niece Jennifer was at least forty-three, and she still looked young to me in spite of her lack of makeup and red-rimmed eyes. She greeted us all with hugs as we filed into the waiting room and led us to an area that was comparatively unoccupied.

"They won't let me back there yet, but they sent a sample of whatever she drank to the lab for analysis," she told us, shoving a strand of brown hair from her face. "I guess all we can do now is wait. I'm so glad you're all here! It would be awful to have to go through this alone." She had left a telephone message at Nathan's home in Savannah, Jennifer told us, but he hadn't returned her call. "I left my cell phone number and asked him to get back to me as soon as possible, so he must be out of town," she said.

"He'll probably check his phone messages in the morning," I said, seeing her downcast face.

We had received curious stares from most of the people in the waiting area—at least those who weren't asleep—but it wasn't until Ellis rose to get coffee that Jennifer seemed to realize we were dressed a bit out of the ordinary. "Have you all been to a costume party or something?" she asked.

We laughed when Zee explained about the candlelight tour, and that seemed to help everyone relax at least for a little while.

Several of us wanted coffee so I volunteered to help Ellis with the errand, glad of a chance to do something other than sit and wait. The receptionist pointed out a small snack room at the end of a hallway and I saw Ellis, who walked ahead of me, hesitate in the doorway. "I should've known you'd be in here," she said to someone inside.

The room seemed empty at first until I noticed a lone figure drinking coffee at a small table in the corner. Augusta.

"Where in the world have you been?" I asked, taking the vacant chair across from her. "Idonia's really sick, Augusta. We don't know what's the matter with her."

"I know." She reached across the small table and took my hand. Her hand on mine was light and calming, and although it didn't relieve my anxiety about Idonia, I drew a sense of serenity from her touch.

"I became a bit chilled at Bellawood," she said, "and so I came on home. When you didn't arrive by midnight, I sensed something was terribly wrong."

"But how did you know where I was?" I asked.

"I saw all your friends' cars here in the parking lot." Augusta took a swallow of coffee and wrinkled her dainty nose. "This coffee is really quite dreadful!" she said.

"The menu is limited, so I'm afraid we don't have any choice," Ellis said. Inserting money in the machine, she waited for the cup to fill. "Augusta, can't you do something—*anything*—to help her?"

"I'm sure you're aware, Ellis, that I can't interfere in matters—" Augusta began.

Ellis filled another cup and set it down with a slosh. "Why not?"

"It's not in her contract," I muttered. I was fed up with platitudes. I wanted action.

"It has nothing to do with a contract, Lucy Nan. Your friend is under the care of excellent doctors who are doing their best for her. I am here for both of you, and will continue to be if you need me. And I will pray." Augusta's sea green eyes looked almost gray and she fingered her necklace as she spoke. The stones were a clear blue like a rain-swept sky.

"Well, if you see Idonia's guardian angel, I wish you'd tell her to get cracking," I said.

The angel spoke softly, slowly lifting her eyes to mine. "She already has," she said.

"I think we hurt Augusta's feelings," Ellis said as we started back to the waiting area. "Lucy Nan, you're *crying*! And I feel awful, too. I think we should go right back in there and tell Augusta we're sorry."

"The coffee spilled over and burned my fingers," I told her. "It hurts—that's all." That wasn't true, of course, and Ellis knew it as well as she knew me. *I* hurt. I hurt all over from the inside out. My friend might be dying and I had been rotten and mean to my own guardian angel, who was as close as a sister to me. What was the matter with me?

I swallowed the knot in my throat, sniffed back the tears and put on a cheerful false face for the others. As soon as Ellis and I distributed the coffee I would go back and admit to Augusta that I was a royal pain.

But an intern chose that moment to summon Jennifer into the emergency room.

Chapter Eleven

"It was some kind of sedative," Jennifer explained later. "Starts with an e and sounds like a prehistoric animal, and it was in her punch."

We'd waited over twenty minutes wondering if Idonia was going to make it, and Jo Nell had already started making a list of the people we'd have to call if she didn't when Nettie marched up to the desk and demanded to know what was going on. Intimidated, no doubt, by a bunch of nutty women in long dresses, the clerk phoned back to the ER to explain the situation, and a few minutes later Glen came out to tell us they had pumped Idonia's stomach but she was going to be all right.

"But how did . . . whatever that drug is get in her punch?" Zee wanted to know.

"That's something we need to find out," Glen said. "The dosage was more than the amount needed to make her sleep. I doubt if it would've killed her, but at her age, it's best not to take any chances."

Beside me, Jo Nell drew in her lips and grunted. She always gets her hackles up at the mention of age.

Glen sat on the edge of a chair looking every one of his fifty-seven years with tired eyes and rumpled clothes. "I've phoned the police and they're sending someone right over to talk with all of you, so please don't leave until they get here."

"Surely they don't think one of us might've done it!" Jo Nell, who had been nodding off herself a few minutes before, grew wide-eyed and bushy-tailed at the thought.

Glen managed a feeble attempt at a smile. "Jo Nell, I'm sure no one would ever think that of you, although I'm not too sure about the rest of this motley crowd. The point is, however, somebody did drug Idonia's drink and one or more of you might have noticed something that would help us find out who it was." He looked at his watch. "Now, after I fill out this report, I'm going home to bed. As soon as you give the police the information they need, I suggest you do the same."

"You won't have to twist my arm," Nettie said, covering a yawn. "But why in the world would anybody want to hurt Idonia?"

That's what Kemper Mungo wanted to know when he arrived a few minutes later. Idonia had been taken to a private room where Jennifer planned to stay with her overnight. If her condition improved as expected, we were told, she might even be released the next day.

One of the residents at the hospital herded us into a small meeting room on the first floor for our session with Kemper, who kindly apologized for keeping us up so late. "It's imperative," he explained, "that we try to find the reason behind this before too much time passes."

"You mean before we all forget," Zee said.

"The medication must have been in the third cup of punch," Ellis told him. "She drank two in the kitchen right there in front of me. I would've noticed if somebody slipped something into her drink."

"It could've happened in the main house where the Dulcimer Man was playing," Nettie said. "I saw Idonia talking with somebody in there while I was taking a break from the schoolhouse and I'm almost sure she had a cup of punch with her then."

"Good. Good." Kemper was silent for a minute. "Now, try to remember if she set the cup down. Was there a table nearby? And do you know who she was talking to?"

"It was a woman—one of the docents—can't think of her name, but I've seen her there before . . ." Nettie smiled. "Now, I remember! The docent offered Idonia some refreshments, shortbread cookies, I think, and Idonia put her cup aside to serve herself from the table."

Kemper frowned. "And the docent? What did she do then?"

"Several people came into the room just then and she went over to speak to them." Nettie shook her head. "Oh, I wish I'd stayed around longer, but I had to go and give Jo Nell a break!"

Zee patted her arm. "How could you have known?" She turned to Kemper. "What's in this stuff that was in the punch? Where did it come from?"

"From what I understand it was a prescription drug for insomnia," Kemper said. "Dr. Smiley thinks it was probably dissolved in some kind of harmless liquid before being added to the punch."

"And the punch was hot, so that would probably make it even less noticeable," Nettie pointed out.

"But why Idonia?" I said. "And why would somebody want her to sleep?"

Ellis spoke out with the voice of reason. "So they could steal her locket."

"Her locket! Of course. I'd almost forgotten about that," Jo Nell said, shaking her head. "Why would anybody want Idonia's locket?"

"It might be a good idea if somebody would tell me about this locket," Kemper said.

"It was an early Christmas gift from Melrose," Jo Nell said. "It belonged to his grandmother, and Idonia's going to hit the ceiling when she finds out it's gone."

"Melrose is Idonia's gentleman friend," Zee explained, seeing the expression on Kemper's face.

We took time about describing the locket, and then, of course, Kemper wanted to know when we first discovered it missing.

"When was the last time any of you saw Idonia before the drug took effect?" he asked.

"I guess I saw her last," Zee said, "since I was hostess in the upstairs hall and she had that room up there in the back. She spoke to me as she came upstairs that last time."

"Can you remember what she said?" Kemper asked.

"She said I should go downstairs and listen to Andy Collins—he plays the dulcimer, you know—and . . ."

Kemper frowned. "And what? Anything else?"

Zee flushed. "Just that whoever made the shortbread cookies stinted on the shortening. Idonia's shortbread is always a best-seller at bake sales, you know. It's her grandmother's recipe."

Kemper tried to cover a smile. "Did you see anybody upstairs who might have had an opportunity to put the drug in Idonia's punch?"

"I went down a little while after that to listen to the dulcimer music," Zee said, "and I guess two—maybe three—people passed me on the stairs. Later, when it was time to leave, I couldn't wake her up."

"Can you remember who these people were?" he asked.

"Two of them were our minister and his wife, Pete and Ann Whittaker, and the other person was one of the docents, I think. She was wearing a sunbonnet and a long dress."

"Sunbonnet? Is that the usual dress for a thing like this?" Kemper scribbled something on a notepad.

"There were a few of them around," I told him. "They left it up to us about what we wore as long as it suited the period."

Kemper sighed and sneaked a look at his watch. "Tell me about this . . . what's his name . . . Melrose? Has Idonia known him long? Does anybody know where he came from?"

Nettie explained that Melrose was staying at the Spring Lamb and worked part time for Al Evans. "He seems harmless enough," she added. "Idonia brought him to our caroling party last night and he sings a pretty good tenor."

"And by the way," I added, "Idonia seemed to think someone was following her last night."

Zee frowned. "You mean while we were caroling? Wouldn't we have seen them?"

"Has anyone else mentioned this?" Kemper asked.

I shook my head. "Not to me. Of course we were all bundled to the nines and it was dark as pitch out there."

Kemper made a note of this, shaking his head. "Any of the rest of you notice an extra person?"

Nobody answered.

"I'll take that as a no," he said, covering a yawn.

"You don't think Melrose had anything to do with what happened to Idonia tonight, do you?" I said. "If he was working over at Evans and Son like Idonia said, he wouldn't have had the opportunity."

"*If* can be a big word," Kemper said.

"If Melrose DuBois was at Bellawood tonight, one of us would've seen him," I said after Kemper left.

"I'm sure Kemper will check with Al over at the funeral home to make sure he was where he said he'd be," Nettie said.

"And *who* he said he *is*," Jo Nell added. "He might not be kin to Al at all."

Zee's once-elaborate hairdo was tumbling over one eye and she shoved it back carelessly as she buttoned her coat. "Now that we know Idonia's going to be all right, I'm going home and sleep for a week!"

"I'm with you," Jo Nell said. "I can hardly keep my eyes open."

"Not me." Ellis stood and stretched, earning sleepy-eyed glances from stragglers in the waiting area. "I was so tired just a while ago I thought I'd drop, but now I've gotten a second wind." She looked around. "Anybody else for coffee?"

"Ellis Saxon! Do you realize what time it is?" Nettie pointed to the clock. "It's time to take me home—that's what time it is, and then you two can stay up all night if it suits you."

"I'll bet I know who has a pot going," I said to Ellis after we dropped Nettie off next door. And then I remembered: *Augusta!* I had meant to go back to the hospital snack room and apologize for being such a miserable creature, but Jennifer had been called to the inner sanctums of the ER and I had forgotten all about it.

"If I were Augusta, I'd tell us to brew our own coffee after the grief we gave her tonight," Ellis reminded me.

And that's what I was afraid of. A light shone from the kitchen window as we hurried up the steps and across the back porch, but I hesitated with my hand on the doorknob. *What if Augusta wasn't there?* The very thought of it made my insides turn to slush. I had lived for fifty-five years before Augusta Goodnight entered my life, and I could manage without her again, but it would be like saying good-bye to a part of me. A part that was sometimes direct to the point of being blunt, but was also warm and kind and endearingly funny.

"What's wrong with you? It's cold out here! Move it, will you, Lucy Nan?" Ellis stomped her feet.

The kitchen was empty except for Clementine, who looked up from her sleeping place on the rug and reluctantly came to greet us. The coffeepot stared at us with a cold eye.

I stooped and took the dog's big, shaggy head in my arms. I wanted to cry. "Hey, girl," I said, stroking the soft fur on her neck. "Where's Augusta?" But I wasn't sure I wanted to know.

"In here." She stood in the doorway of the sitting room wrapped in a ratty old throw I keep on the back of the sofa, only on Augusta it looked almost elegant. From the television behind her came familiar voices from one of those old movies she loves to watch. Augusta adores Cary Grant. She glanced at the kitchen clock and then at us with something akin to relief on her face. It was almost three A.M. "Idonia?" Augusta spoke softly.

"She's going to be all right," I said. "There was something in the punch she drank that made her sleep and they had to pump her stomach . . . Augusta, I meant—"

The angel nodded. "I stayed to hear what the physician said about your friend's condition, but didn't find it necessary to linger. Do they know how something like that happened to be in her drink?"

Ellis, with a yearning look at the coffeepot, told her about our conversation with Kemper. "It must have been put in Idonia's cup when she set it down for a few minutes in the parlor. I think Kemper believes it was Melrose.

"Lucy Nan and I are sorry we were rude and obnoxious to you back at the hospital," she added, "but does this mean you aren't going to make us any coffee?"

When Augusta Goodnight laughs, as she did now, it clears the air like an April breeze and makes you forget, at least for a little while, your nagging little doubts and fears. "Cinnamon or vanilla? Or how about a dash of chocolate?" she asked, adding coffee to the pot. Augusta never measures and it always tastes just right.

We all agreed on chocolate and I got out mugs and plates for the apple cake Augusta had made earlier.

"I hope Bennett won't wake up and look at the time," Ellis said, helping herself to the coffee. "I phoned from the hospital and told him I'd be late, but not this late."

Augusta sat at the table across from us turning her coffee mug in her hands. "Why Melrose?" she asked.

I swallowed a forkful of apple cake. It was warm, moist, and spicy. "Why Melrose what?"

"Why does your policeman friend suspect Melrose?"

"I don't know that he *suspects* him," I said. "It's just that we really don't know much about him. Melrose was supposed to be working at the funeral home, but I guess he could've mixed in with the rest of the crowd. Maybe he wore a beard or something."

"And Idonia's locket was missing," Ellis added. "Looks to me like whoever drugged her punch did it so they could steal the locket."

"It's beginning to look that way," I said. "She's worn it all over town since she got it, and last night she seemed to think somebody was following her while we were caroling."

"Do you think we should've told Kemper about the locket in that photograph at the Tanseys?" Ellis asked.

"I thought about that, too," I said. "But we're not really sure it's the same one, and Idonia would never forgive us if we got Melrose in trouble over nothing."

Augusta fingered the stones in her necklace. "Why not ask your friend Idonia if there might be something significant *inside* the locket—something the thief might consider important? I can't imagine why Melrose DuBois would give Idonia a special piece of jewelry like that if he was going to take it back."

Ellis shrugged. "Beats me, but I suppose anyone could have done it. Idonia made a big fuss over that hot spiced cider, said she'd be back for another cup later. Several people came in after that because Idonia told them how good it was."

She stood to take her plate to the sink. "And I didn't mention this earlier because I didn't want to get him in trouble, but there was somebody else there tonight who might want Idonia's locket."

"Oh, for heaven's sake, Ellis, just tell us who!" I demanded. It was too late and I was too tired for my friend's theatrics.

"I'm surprised you didn't recognize him, Lucy Nan. He was the one who showed us where to park the car. He was all wrapped up, of course, but I'm almost sure it was Preacher Dave."

"Dave Tansey? How could you tell? It was dark and that man wore a hat pulled down over part of his face." *But if the locket really had belonged to his daughter, Dave Tansey would naturally want it back,* I thought. Louella had said it was a family keepsake.

"I recognized his voice," Ellis said. "Besides, I've seen Preacher Dave do that kind of thing before. Remember when we went to that big wedding last summer when Claudia's cousin married and they had the reception at somebody's estate? He was helping to park cars then. Guess it earns him a little extra money."

Augusta hadn't spoken during this time and now she seemed to be regarding her empty cup as if she expected to find an answer there.

"So, what are you thinking, Augusta?" I asked, preparing for her quiet words of wisdom.

"It seems to me," she said with a whisper of a smile, "that both Melrose and this Preacher Dave have got a lot of 'splainin' to do."

Augusta has been watching entirely too many *I Love Lucy* reruns.

Chapter Twelve

"Melrose was a little out of sorts that you all didn't call him last night," Idonia said when I dropped by to see her the next day. "I really believe it hurt his feelings."

After observing her all night, the doctors had dismissed her with instructions for rest and diet, so I made my customary boiled custard run and found Jo Nell there ahead of me with the same. It must be a family thing, but as soon as somebody sneezed at our house my grandmother was already heating up milk in a double boiler.

We hadn't been there long before Zee popped in with some of her chicken noodle soup and a big bottle of ginger ale. "I didn't think you'd be in the mood for spiced apple punch," she joked. Idonia didn't think it was funny.

"Where is Melrose, by the way?" Jo Nell asked. "Did you tell him about the locket?"

Idonia nodded. "No way I could keep it secret. Everybody in town probably knows it by now, and the police have been all over me like white on rice. They seem to think somebody drugged me to steal it."

"So what did he say?" I asked.

"What did who say?" Idonia sprinkled nutmeg over some of Jo Nell's custard and took a tentative taste.

"Melrose. What did he say when you told him about the locket being stolen?"

"He was most upset, of course. Wanted to hurry right over, but to tell the truth, I'm not feeling up to snuff just yet—you know, to put on makeup and all that. Besides, Nathan's due in later this afternoon. I do wish you hadn't called him, though. It nearly frightened the poor boy to death."

Idonia's "poor boy" was close to forty years old. "Of course it frightened him, Idonia," I said. "You're his mother and he loves you."

"Well, I hope he doesn't start in on my going back to Savannah with him for Christmas. I've been rehearsing with the choir since October and I'm not about to miss out on Lessons and Carols next Sunday. Besides, dress rehearsal's tomorrow night."

"Do you think you'll be strong enough for that?" Zee asked.

Idonia smiled. "I feel stronger already. This boiled custard just hits the spot, Jo Nell. What kind of extract is that?"

"Oh, I put in a little of this and a little of that," my cousin said. I knew very well she used blackberry wine but what Idonia didn't know wouldn't hurt her.

"Idonia, can you think of any reason somebody would want that locket?" I asked.

"The police asked that same question, and the answer is no. It isn't especially valuable except in a sentimental way, of course, and Melrose is as much in the dark about it as I am."

"Maybe it will turn up yet," Zee said. "I know they planned to retrace your steps at Bellawood. Could've been a faulty catch or—"

"I don't think so, Zee, or they would've found it by now." Idonia set her empty bowl aside. "I think somebody wanted that locket for a reason. Remember when I said somebody was following me when we went caroling?" She shuddered. "Every time we passed along where those big oaks are on Heritage Avenue, I felt like somebody was waiting behind them, and I could've sworn I saw somebody dodge under the limbs of that magnolia in the Dorseys' front yard."

"If they meant to snatch that locket it would've been impossible to reach it under all those wraps you had on," I said, "unless . . ."

"Unless they intended to grab me along with it," Idonia added. "Remember how dark it was that night? And we were all bunched together and bundled so, who would've noticed?"

"I'm sure Nettie would," I told her, in an attempt to put her at ease. My neighbor had admitted she couldn't follow the harmony unless she was standing next to Idonia.

"Maybe it wouldn't be a bad idea for you to go home with Nathan," Jo Nell said, with a look that had *trouble* written all over it.

"Fine, if he'll wait until after the program Sunday. Now, could I have a little more of that custard, Jo Nell?" Idonia held out her bowl.

"I don't have a good feeling about this," Jo Nell said as we walked outside together. "If I were Idonia, I'd be scared to death."

"I guess she feels that whoever drugged her cider was after the locket and not her," Zee said, "but it makes me furious to think what could've happened. I certainly hope they'll hurry and find who did it."

But *whose* family keepsake? I wondered. In all the worry and excitement of the night before, none of us had thought to relate our suspicions about Idonia's locket to the rest of The Thursdays. And I'd rather have a root canal than mention it to Idonia just yet.

"Well, I hope Nathan will put his foot down about Idonia staying here through Sunday," Jo Nell said. "I just don't think it's safe for her here."

"You know good and well Idonia's going to do what she darn well pleases," Zee said. "And what makes you think it will be any safer when she comes home after the holidays?"

Augusta and Clementine were waiting for me on the back steps when I got home, and naturally Augusta wanted to know about Idonia.

"She's doing better than I thought she would," I told her, surprised to see her waiting in the cold. "You haven't been out here all this time, have you?"

"I took another little tour of your grandmother's old home," she said, following me inside. "They've boarded up the place to discourage intruders."

"Good. As long as it didn't discourage you," I said. "Find anything interesting?"

She smiled. "It's what I *didn't* find that seems curious."

"What do you mean?"

"I believe we've all been looking in the wrong places to discover where that music is coming from," Augusta said. "Everyone's been concentrating on those cabinets in one of the front bedrooms upstairs, so I did a little experimenting to find out if they're being tampered with."

"What kind of experimenting?"

"I strung a very fine hair across the area where there might have been a panel or other opening," she explained. "It was almost invisible to the eye, and if anyone disturbed it, it's doubtful they would have noticed it."

"And did they?" I asked.

Augusta curled up on the sitting room couch and took Clementine's head in her lap. "It hasn't been touched," she said.

"But where else could it be? It has to be coming from somewhere."

"I don't know," Augusta said, "but I intend to find out. I'm not ready to toss in the dishrag yet!"

"Uh-huh," I said, as her meaning sank in. "And where did you learn about that clever little experiment?"

"I have my sources," she said, reaching for the TV remote. "If there's nothing you want to watch right now, I really should catch up on my exercising. I'm afraid I've been remiss all week. Do you mind getting it started for me?"

"Of course not," I said, feeling a slight twinge of guilt for my own slackness in that area. Augusta had learned to insert a videotape, but she has yet to master the DVD, which she referred to as BVDs until Ellis told her that was an old-fashioned term for men's underwear.

I left her there, bending and swaying as gracefully as a ballet dancer to the tune of that old song, "The Continental," and went upstairs to change. Ben was picking me up for dinner in less than an hour and I hoped I wouldn't fall asleep at the table after getting to bed so late the night before.

I showered quickly, smiling as I thought of Augusta's method of detecting, learned, no doubt, from one of the many mysteries she'd read, and of her funny, upside-down expressions, and I wished I could share them with Ben.

Later, over dinner, I did tell him what Claudia had observed of the photograph in the Tanseys' living room. "The same pearls were missing in the locket their daughter wore as in the one Melrose gave Idonia," I said.

Ben hesitated with his coffee cup halfway to his mouth. "Surely you don't think the man gave Idonia the jewelry then drugged her to steal it back."

"Zee told me she heard his alibi checked out," I said. "Al Evans said Melrose was helping him at the funeral home until after ten o'clock. Idonia was already deep in 'la-la land' by then, but somebody did it, Ben. They did it deliberately."

His hand reached for mine across the table. "My God, it might've been you, Lucy Nan."

"I don't think so," I said. "I wasn't wearing the locket. Idonia thinks somebody was following her the night we went caroling . . . somebody who wanted that locket!"

During dinner I had toyed with the pork tenderloin, a favorite of mine, and then refused an offer of dessert. The red carnation in a bud vase on the table began to blur in front of my eyes and the room seemed much too hot.

Ben called for the check. "Time to get you home. Guess I shouldn't have ordered that wine."

"And tired as I am, I should've had better sense than to drink it." Thankfully, I let him help me with my coat and practically crawled into the passenger seat of the car. Afterward, at home in bed, I remembered something else I meant to tell him. I was going to ask Ben if he thought I should mention to the police about Preacher Dave being at Bellawood the night before.

I wasn't surprised when Idonia showed up at dress rehearsal for Lessons and Carols the next night looking, as my granddaddy used to say, like she'd been jerked through a knothole backward. Nathan had personally escorted her into the church and promised to return for her as soon as rehearsal was over.

"He's going to stay with me tonight, then come back for the service on Sunday," she told us, beaming. "And Sara and Millicent are coming, too!" Sara and Millicent are Nathan's wife and teenaged daughter who, much to Idonia's distress, rarely visit Stone's Throw, so at least something positive came of our friend's ordeal.

Although we customarily wear black choir robes, Cissy Sullivan, our choir director, had decided white would be more fitting for the occasion and the small choir room was filled with the flurry of flapping sleeves as we tried them on.

"I look like Moby Dick in drag," Nettie whispered as she studied her reflection in the mirror. "I'm sure angels don't look anything like this."

Ellis looked at me and grinned. "I think you can take that to the bank," she agreed, which naturally reminded me of Augusta and what she had suggested the night before.

"Has anyone thought to ask Idonia if she looked inside the locket her friend gave her?" I asked. "Somebody might be after what's *in* the locket instead of the locket itself."

It hadn't, of course, because up until the night we discovered it missing, most of us admired it for what it was—an interesting piece of jewelry and a thoughtful token of affection. After that, Idonia's alarming experience at the hospital and our concern for her welfare took precedence over everything else.

I had promised Augusta I would ask Idonia at the first opportunity, and that opportunity was now. I found her sitting at the back of the alto section studying her music. "I hope I can still hit that low F," she said, looking up. "My throat's still a little froggy."

"Just fake it," I said. "Who's to know?"

She made a face. "Cissy."

She was right, of course. Our choir director can zoom in on a false note as if she has built-in radar.

I sat beside her. "Idonia, do you mind telling me what was inside that locket Melrose gave you? It might have something to do with why it was taken."

She shook her head. "I don't see why. It was just an old picture, a photograph of a man and woman. Looked like it might've been made back in the twenties sometime. It was rather sweet, really. Melrose said they were his grandparents."

"Was there anything else?"

"No. I don't know why there should be."

"I don't suppose you've heard anything more about it," I said.

"Nothing encouraging, and Lucy Nan, the police have even been questioning poor Melrose—as if he might have something to do with it. Can you imagine? The man wasn't even there that night!"

"I guess they have to cover all their bases," I said. "I'm sure he understands."

At that moment we were interrupted by Cissy banging several loud chords on the piano, our signal to take our places, and we spent the next hour or so going over the music for the following Sunday.

When Cissy was more or less satisfied we were as good as we were going to get, we were told to line up to rehearse the processional.

"I wish we didn't have to process," Zee complained as we walked through the Fellowship Hall and up the stairs to the back of the sanctuary. "Cissy always puts me between two sopranos and I can't hear my notes."

"That's called harmony," Ellis reminded her as we lined up to process. Ellis, one of our stronger sopranos, took her place to lead us down the center aisle to the choir loft in the front of the church, and I stepped in line between Idonia, an alto, and R. G. Strickland, a tenor, and tried to remember to start off on the left foot—and the right note.

Large white candles in feathery wreaths of evergreens were arranged beneath the stained-glass windows on both sides of the sanctuary and a graceful swag of magnolia leaves intertwined with burgundy and gold ribbon scalloped the choir loft behind the pulpit. I thought of all the Christmases the century-old building had marked, of faithful hands, long gone, that had decorated as we still did with magnolia, holly, and pine; of voices, silent now, that filled the church with praise and song. The place smelled of dust and candle wax and cedar, and a little of the spicy scent of R. G. Strickland's aftershave, and I basked in the warmth of just being there.

I knew Augusta planned to attend the service Sunday and was looking forward to the music. I hoped she wouldn't be disappointed.

Cissy took her place at the great pipe organ and the first few bars of "Hark the Herald Angels Sing" resounded through the empty sanctuary. I felt a thrill as I always do at the joy and excitement of it and took a deep breath to begin.

Ahead of me Idonia took one step into the sanctuary. *Glory to the newborn King!* we sang. And then somebody screamed. It had to be a soprano because it was shrill enough to shatter glass, and it seemed to go on forever.

And—oh, God, it was Ellis!

Chapter Thirteen

Had something happened to Ellis? I pushed my way down the aisle through a flock of white-robed choir members to find a knot of people hovering over something or someone in the center of one of the back pews.

"Is she breathing? Let me through!" Margaret Moss demanded, and we parted like a billowing white sea. Margaret has been Glen Smiley's nurse for as long as he's been in practice and we meekly bowed to her authority. I saw Ellis's face as she stepped aside to make room for her and if she hadn't blinked, I'd have thought it was carved in marble.

"She's not moving." Zee reached out a tentative hand.

Who's not moving? I couldn't see over the snowy mountain of shoulders.

"Don't touch her! Somebody call nine-one-one!" Margaret barked, and I maneuvered my way to a pew in front of her to see the nurse feel for a pulse on a limp wrist. Behind me I heard Cissy calling for help on her cell phone. Margaret soon abandoned the wrist and began CPR by breathing into the patient's mouth. It wasn't until she tilted the injured person's head back that I saw who was lying on the pew in such a twisted manner. It was Opal Henshaw!

Jo Nell crowded against my shoulder. "Oh, my goodness! What happened? She's not dead, is she?"

By the way Margaret, her face set in a grim expression, continued with her chest compressions, I thought it very likely that was the case.

White-faced, Cissy hurried toward us. "The rescue squad is on the way," she said, and then caught sight of poor Opal knotted pretzel-like in the pew. "Dear God in heaven! What happened to Opal?"

Ellis glanced at the balcony above us. "She must've fallen from the balcony. You know how she is about having everything just so. The swag up there is way off-center. Opal probably went up there to put it right."

"But it was perfect yesterday when I was here going over the music," Cissy said. "Opal was putting on the finishing touches and she seemed pleased with everything then."

"Do you suppose somebody moved it?" Jo Nell asked in a small voice.

Why would anyone do that? No one spoke it aloud but I could guess what the others were thinking. Although Opal Henshaw wasn't well liked, I couldn't imagine why anyone would wish her dead.

Nettie turned away from Margaret's attempts at resuscitation. "That's a long way to fall. If only Opal had just left well enough alone! She probably went up there to make one last adjustment and lost her balance—bless her heart."

"Looks like it was her last adjustment, all right," Zee muttered.

"Isn't she breathing *yet*, Margaret?" somebody asked, breaking what seemed like eons of silence. But Margaret didn't answer.

In one of the pews across the aisle I saw Opal's familiar green jacket and the large wicker basket she usually carried that contained extra ribbon, tape, wire, and scissors among other items used for decorating.

Somewhere somebody started to cry and I moved as far away as

I could get and sat near the front of the church. My legs gave about as much support as those pine boughs in the window and I didn't feel so pert myself.

"Maybe we should pray," Jo Nell suggested. That made sense to me, but at the sound of the approaching EMTs Margaret looked up and bellowed for us to clear out and wait in the choir room.

"Poor Opal!" Ellis sighed, plopping down beside me. "I can't imagine how helpless she must have felt when she fell."

"She was usually so careful," Cissy said. "Opal always had someone with her when she was decorating the balcony. It doesn't make sense that she would go up there and try to adjust things on her own."

"Who?" Ellis asked.

Cissy frowned. "Who what?"

"Who was with her when she hung the swag in the balcony?"

"Oh . . . different people." Cissy paused for a minute. "This time I believe it was Preacher Dave."

"Opal's seemed a bit despondent since Virgil passed away so suddenly from that heart attack last summer," Idonia said. "You don't suppose she—"

Zee pulled off her choir robe and tossed it over the back of a chair. "If Opal Henshaw wanted to kill herself, I doubt if she'd jump from the church balcony.

"Besides," she whispered, "everybody knows that sorry husband of hers flirted with every woman in Stone's Throw. She had to have known it, too."

"Virgil Henshaw was annoying, but harmless," I said. "Still, I doubt if Opal would deliberately end her life over him."

"At least not until she'd straightened that lopsided swag," Ellis said.

Jo Nell dug in her purse for a tissue to stem her tears. "I don't see how you all can be so catty and hateful with poor Opal squashed like a melon out there in our own church—and right here at Christmas, too!" And she blew her nose with a loud blast.

Cissy sat facing us on the piano bench, her cell phone still open in her hand. Now she flipped it shut. "She used a cane," she announced. "Opal used a cane."

I had never noticed her needing one. "I didn't know she'd been injured," I said.

"No, no! I mean she sometimes used a cane to reach down from the balcony and center the swag on the hooks," Cissy said. "That was how she made adjustments without having to lean over so far."

"Then where is it?" Nettie asked.

"Maybe we should look for it," Idonia suggested. "Not that it matters now."

Margaret came in a few minutes later to tell us the medics hadn't been able to save Opal Henshaw. "Her neck was broken. They said she'd probably been dead several minutes before we found her." Margaret shook her head and eased into a chair on the first row. "I was afraid of that all along, but I had to try . . . I just had to try."

We all sat silently for a while, not knowing what to do or say, and I, for one, was depressed. *What would Augusta do?*

Tea, of course. In emergencies like this one, Augusta would brew hot, bracing tea. We kept a large electric percolator and a supply of coffee and tea bags in the choir closet. At least I could do that much. I rose abruptly and almost stumbled over Ellis's feet.

"Where are you going?" she said.

"To make tea, of course."

"Good," Margaret said. "We had to notify the police about Opal, and I look for them any minute. I expect we'll be here for a while."

"What about Opal?" I asked. I would never be able to look at that pew again without thinking of Opal Henshaw's unfortunate tumble.

"Well, they couldn't move her yet—not until the police get here," Margaret said. "We had to leave her where she fell."

"I don't suppose you noticed a cane?" Cissy said, explaining about Opal's method of decorating from the balcony.

Margaret nodded solemnly. "You're right. I've seen her use that, too, but I didn't notice it anywhere around. I think she usually keeps it in that little alcove behind the last pew in the balcony."

A couple of the other choir members who had served on the decorating committee with Opal said they, too, had seen her put the cane away in there.

Then why hadn't she used it today?

I was dismayed a few minutes later to hear the grating voice of Stone's Throw's Police Chief Elmer Harris, and the irritating squeaking of his shoes as he approached from the hallway outside the choir room. Thank goodness Ed Tillman, a childhood friend of Roger's and a lieutenant in the Stone's Throw police, came along as well.

"Miss Lucy Nan, Miss Ellis, Miss Nettie," Ed began, acknowledging most of us by name, "why don't we step into the classroom next door for a few minutes while Chief Harris talks to some of the others?"

We clamored to follow him, leaving the chief to growl his questions to the remaining choir members. And I must admit, Ed didn't seem at all surprised to see us there.

As Ed made notes, Ellis began by telling him how she had first discovered Opal's body, when she led the procession down the aisle.

"And prior to this, did any of you see or hear anyone in the balcony or anywhere else in that area?" Ed asked, pausing in his scribbling.

"I guess we were so busy rehearsing—and talking, too," Jo Nell admitted, "we probably wouldn't have heard anyone if they'd been there." She frowned. "Why? Surely you don't think somebody *pushed* Opal from that balcony, do you?"

"For heaven's sake, Jo Nell, he's just being thorough," Zee said. "I mean, I suppose you have to cover all possibilities, don't you, Ed? And I for one find it the tiniest bit peculiar that nobody's seen hide nor hair of that cane Opal used!"

Ed, of course, was not aware of the cane or its purpose, and everyone tried to explain it to him at once until he insisted, rather sharply I thought, that we speak one at a time, and then only when called upon.

After Ed was satisfied with our answers, we were told to wait in the choir room while he and Chief Harris searched the balcony and the sanctuary for any sign of the missing cane. Meanwhile, we were relieved to learn that Opal Crenshaw's body had been removed.

"This is awful!" Ellis said as we sat sipping a second cup of tea. "It's hard to believe this is really happening."

Zee groaned. "Leave it to Opal to take all the joy out of Christmas."

"I'm sure she didn't die on purpose, Zee," Jo Nell said. "But at least she's gone to a better place."

I supposed that was true; at least I hoped it was, but to tell the truth, I couldn't think of a better place than Stone's Throw, South Carolina. I had been raised in this church and Charlie and I were married here, as were my parents and grandparents before me, and now Opal Henshaw had gone and bashed herself in the very pew where my great-aunt Edith and great-uncle Davis had worshipped for at least forty years.

Finishing my tea, I was startled by the sudden racket of three loud chords on the piano. "Come on, everybody and take your seats," Cissy directed. "We might as well use this time to go over the music."

We had just finished the "The Cherry Tree Carol," our third

selection, when Chief Harris squeaked back to announce they had been unable to find Opal's cane.

"Could this be it?" Hugh Dan Thompson, our baritone soloist, returned from the men's room just then waving a wooden walking stick with spiral carving.

"Sure looks like the one," Cissy said. "Where did you find it?"

"It was propped behind the john in the men's room." Hugh Dan passed the stick along to the chief. "I remember Virgil Henshaw using this cane or one like it when he had that knee surgery a few years back," he said. "This must be the one Opal kept in the balcony."

Chief Harris turned the cane in his hands. "Then what in tarnation was it doing in the men's room?"

"Looks to me like somebody didn't want Opal to find it," Nettie said.

"Idonia's been awfully quiet," Jo Nell said as we hung up our choir robes before leaving. "I wonder if she's feeling all right."

"I saw her go into the restroom a little while ago," I said. "Maybe I'd better go and check on her."

Only a couple of days ago Idonia had been close to literally sleeping her life away, and for all I knew she might have passed out in there. I hurried down the hallway and pushed open the door of the ladies' room, dreading what I might find. Our church had recently benefited from improvements to our kitchen and bathroom facilities and as a result just about everything in the ladies' room was mauve. I found Idonia sitting in the room's one upholstered chair, a somber figure against a floral pattern of mauve and green, clutching her pocketbook on her lap. She looked as if she'd been told to make her own funeral arrangements and not to take too long about it.

"Idonia, what's going on? Are you all right?" When I drew

closer I noticed the tearstains on her face. "Do you want me to call Nathan?"

She looked up at me with eyes as bleak as the dark December sky. "I don't know what to do, Lucy Nan. I just don't know what to do."

"About what?" I knelt beside her and took her hand. It was cool and trembled at my touch. "Idonia, I'm afraid this has all been too much for you. You'll feel better when you get home where you can rest." I wondered if there was any hot water left in the percolator. "Do you think you might be able to get down some tea?"

She shook her head and threw aside my hand. "There's nothing wrong with me! It's not that—I'm fine."

"Then what?" I stood and rubbed the cramp in my leg. She didn't seem fine to me.

"It's . . . well, it's Melrose."

"What about Melrose?" I wet some paper towels and passed them along to her. "Here, maybe you'll feel better if you wipe your face. I really think you're trying to do too much too soon, Idonia."

She accepted the towels and made a couple of token dabs. "He was here. I saw him."

"Melrose? When?"

"Earlier, when we first got here. I saw him leaving as Nathan and I were walking into the building, and I thought maybe he'd come to watch us rehearse and changed his mind." Idonia wadded up the paper towels and aimed them at the trash can. She missed. "I called to him, but he didn't answer. Pretended like he didn't even see me."

"Maybe he didn't," I said.

"You should've seen him, Lucy Nan. He couldn't get away from us fast enough." Grim-faced, Idonia looked up at me. "And what in the world was he doing here in the first place?"

Chapter Fourteen

Augusta was waiting up when I got home.

"I kind of halfway expected you to drop in on rehearsal," I told her.

She smiled. "I'd rather wait and be surprised."

"You would've been surprised all right if you'd been there tonight," I said, and told her what had happened to Opal Henshaw.

Augusta's hand went immediately to her necklace, which caught the light from the fire, and I felt as if I could lose myself in its shimmering twilight depth.

"And how is Idonia?" she asked, setting down a tray with two glasses and a bottle of red wine.

"Close to being a basket case, I'm afraid." I poured a glass for both of us and took a sip. It tasted of wood smoke and cherries and late summer sun—not at all like the inexpensive wine I usually buy at the supermarket, although the label was the same. "Why did you ask about Idonia?" I said.

"Because this all seems to center around her." Augusta's loose garment trailed the floor as she sat on the hassock, glass in hand. "Think about it, Lucy Nan: Idonia's gentleman friend, Mr. DuBois, is living in Opal Henshaw's home. The locket he gave her, which may or may not have belonged to the Tanseys' daughter, has been stolen and Idonia drugged. Now Opal herself has been killed." She paused to study the contents of her glass, turning it so that it, too, caught the fire's light. "But that's not where the trouble began." Augusta looked up at me as if she expected an explanation.

"I suppose it began at Willowbrook when that vagrant fell from the balcony," I said, "but I don't see how that could possibly have anything to do with Idonia."

Augusta went to the kitchen and returned with a small plate of gingersnaps. Now she broke one in two, gave part of it to Clementine and ate the other.

"Now, why did you do that, Augusta?" I asked. "You're always telling me not to feed her and you've gone and broken your own rule. Clementine will be begging all night."

Augusta laughed. "No, she won't, will you, Clementine? Be a good girl now and lie down."

The dog did as she was told without so much as a beseeching look.

Augusta took another cookie and passed the plate to me. Clementine put a paw over her eyes and whimpered but she didn't move. Augusta ignored her.

"I'm afraid your friend, however innocent, has been caught up in a dangerous web of wickedness and deceit," she said.

"Idonia had nothing to do with whatever's going on!" I said. "And now Opal Henshaw's death has everybody scared. I'm worried, Augusta. I'm beginning to think this Melrose DuBois isn't all he's cracked up to be. Idonia admitted she saw him leaving the church tonight before Opal fell from the balcony . . . and frankly, we're not all that sure Opal's death was an accident." I told Augusta where the missing cane was found.

"Still," she said, "we have to consider the possibility that

Mr. DuBois might have had other reasons for being there. Perhaps he only wanted to hear the choir rehearse."

"Then why didn't he stay? And why did he pretend he didn't see Idonia when she called to him?" I shook my head. "No, I think there's something fishy going on there, and I'm afraid poor Idonia's going to be the one who pays for it."

"You said the police were there tonight. Did she mention this to them?"

"You see . . . that's another thing. She admitted that she didn't, and now she's all upset for keeping quiet about it," I said.

Augusta cupped her wineglass in both hands. "There must have been other people about as well," she said.

"Zee said she saw Preacher Dave cleaning in one of the Sunday school rooms, but that's not unusual. He often works there at night and had been helping Opal with the decorations earlier. Chief Harris was talking with him when we left."

"Preacher Dave . . . his daughter wore an identical locket in that photograph on the Tanseys' piano . . ." Augusta sat quietly for a while, wondering, no doubt how Miss Jane Marple or Hercule Poirot would approach the situation. "Do you think the authorities believe Opal Henshaw's death was deliberate?"

"It looks that way," I told her. "And so do I."

"It would help," she said, "if we knew more about the man who was killed out at Oakcreek."

"Huh?" Maybe I had missed something.

"Your family home. Isn't that what you call it?"

I laughed. "I think you mean Willowbrook. And I agree it all seems to stem from what happened there. The police aren't talking, but I'll see if I can't get Weigelia to find out if Kemper knows any more about it."

"Do you know where the Tanseys lived before they came here?" Augusta asked.

"No, but I can find out," I said. "The deacons are in charge of buildings and grounds so I'm sure they did some kind of background check before they hired Preacher Dave to fill in for Luther. Claudia's husband Brian is on the Board of Deacons. I'll give him a call tomorrow." I yawned. "Right now I'm going to bed . . . and you might as well go ahead and give Clementine that other gingersnap you have in your hand. I know you're going to do it as soon as I leave the room."

Augusta only smiled.

"Lucy Nan, tell me it isn't true about Opal falling from the balcony!" Claudia called the next morning before I had a chance to finish my first cup of coffee. "You were at choir rehearsal last night, weren't you? I heard Ellis was the one who found her."

"The answer is yes to all of that," I said. "Are you still at home? I was going to call Brian later to ask if he might have any information on where the Tanseys lived before they came here."

"I'm just getting ready to leave, but Brian's in the shower. I'll tell him to give you a call." Claudia works several days a week in the dean's office at Sarah Bedford, our local college. "Oh, Lord, Lucy Nan! Do you think this has anything to do with what happened to Idonia and the locket the Tanseys' daughter wore in that picture? And I know I should feel awful about the things I said about Opal Henshaw, but I can't help it. I just plain didn't like her!"

"I don't guess we're supposed to like everybody, Claudia. And let's face it, Opal didn't make it easy."

"Have you talked with Idonia this morning?" Claudia asked. "I called a little while ago to see if she was okay, and she wouldn't give me the time of day. Sounded pretty upset."

I didn't doubt it. "I'll check on her later," I said. "And don't forget to ask Brian to give me a call."

I was putting away the breakfast dishes when Brian phoned a little later. "That was quite a shock about Opal Henshaw," he began. "Police have been questioning Preacher Dave, I hear, and I understand he's kind of upset."

"I can see why," I said. "This has shaken everybody up. Brian, weren't you on the committee that hired him when Luther fell and broke his hip? Do you happen to remember where the Tanseys lived before?"

"You'll have to ask your cousin about that, Lucy Nan. The family was already living out there on his property when he came with us. I do remember he gave us a written recommendation, though, from some little place in Georgia."

"Do you know where it was?"

"No, but it's in the files. I can look it up, or you can ask Frances."

Frances Smith was secretary of the diaconate and one of the few people I knew who wouldn't be embarrassed if she were hit by a bus and strangers came to poke about in her refrigerator.

"Sure," Frances said, when I phoned her at home a few minutes later. "I remember exactly where Preacher's from because it's such a peculiar name for a town. He comes from a little place in Georgia called Soso—worked for a lumberyard there." She paused. "I suppose you were at the church last night when they found poor Opal. Preacher Dave's all torn up about it. Blames himself for not going up in the balcony to help her, and from what I hear, that idiot Elmer Harris isn't making him feel any better grilling him like he did."

I agreed with Frances's opinion of Stone's Throw's police

chief, but I didn't think it was out of line to question anyone who might have been in the church when Opal was killed. "He was probably in another part of the building when that happened," I said. "Preacher Dave shouldn't feel guilty about something he couldn't help."

Unless he had reason, I thought.

Augusta began looking up Soso in the encyclopedia as soon as I got off the phone. "I wonder why they named it Soso," I said, looking over her shoulder. "Guess they decided it wasn't all that great, but it wasn't too bad, either—just soso."

"Here it is, right below Milledgeville. Is that very far from here?" Augusta held a finger in place on the map.

"If we started early we could probably make it in a day," I said. "I'll ask Roger to drop by and let Clementine out while we're gone, but first I want to see if Weigelia's learned any more from Kemper."

But Weigelia Jones was more interested in what she could learn from me.

"What about that Henshaw woman they say fell from you-all's balcony?" she bellowed. "Sounds like somebody done pushed her to me!"

I told her I suspected pretty much the same thing and had she managed to learn from Kemper any more about the dead man we found out at Willowbrook.

"I believe I'm gonna be staying away from any balconies," she said. "Getting to be downright dangerous if you ask me—bodies falling all over the place! Why you so bent on knowing 'bout that man?"

"I have my reasons," I said. "Just tell me, Weigelia. Do they know what he was doing there or not?"

"Not," she said. "Kemper did say somebody had seen him on a motorcycle when he stopped at a convenience store somewhere in North Carolina the day before he was killed, but ain't no motorcycle turned up around here." She frowned. "That's all I know. Besides, I don't think I'd tell you if I did know anything more. And don't you and those Thursdays you run around with go poking your noses where you got no business! It would just plumb ruin my Christmas if I had to go to your funeral this week!"

I thanked her for her thoughtful concern and promised to remain upright and breathing.

It was a little after nine before Augusta and I got on our way, and we had been on the road for about an hour before I remembered I had meant to go by and check on Idonia.

"You brought that funny little folding telephone along, didn't you?" Augusta said. "I happen to have a Thermos of hot chocolate, and my strawberry muffins are still warm. Why don't we stop up there on the other side of that bridge and you can call her?"

Augusta is fascinated by the tiny size of cell phones but I can't get her to use one to call me. She says her fingers are too big. "My old friend Mr. Bell would be amazed if he could see what has come of his fascinating invention!" she'd exclaimed when she first saw one.

"You mean Alexander Graham Bell?" I said.

"The very same."

"You *knew* Alexander Graham Bell, the inventor of the telephone?"

"And why ever not? That gentleman had his problems the same as everyone else. More than his share, in fact." Augusta got almost testy.

"You've never mentioned that before," I reminded her.

"I don't like to brag," she said.

This morning the idea of hot chocolate and muffins sounded tempting and it *had* been a long time since breakfast. I parked under a large pine tree in a grassy area beside the road and punched in Idonia's number while Augusta poured steaming chocolate into two Christmas mugs. It smelled wonderful!

The phone rang four times before she answered, and Idonia's voice sounded muffled.

"Are you all right?" I said. "I'm worried about you, Idonia. Did you get any sleep last night?"

"Not much," she said. Or at least I think that's what she said.

"Is Nathan still there?"

"Had to leave for some kind of meeting," she said. "No reason for him to stay anyway."

I took a sip of chocolate. And then another. "I don't guess you've spoken with the police."

That was met with silence. "Idonia," I said, "why don't you just phone Melrose and talk with him about this instead of letting it worry you this way? I'm sure he must've had a reason for being at the church last night."

"Can't. He's gone." If a voice were a color, Idonia's would've been black.

"Gone? Gone where?"

"I don't know, Lucy Nan. The police were here asking about him earlier. Somebody told them they saw him leaving the church last night. They couldn't find him at Opal's and Al Evans said he hasn't seen him since yesterday."

This didn't sound good. "I'm going to call Ellis," I told her, "so don't do anything until you hear from her. And, Idonia? Lock your doors!"

"We might have to turn around and go back home," I said as I explained the situation to Augusta. "I don't like leaving Idonia alone, and if I can't reach Ellis or one of the other Thursdays, we'll have to leave Soso for another day."

But Ellis picked up on the first ring. "North Pole," she said. I could hear carols playing in the background.

"You sound awfully chipper after your gruesome discovery last night. What are you doing?"

"I know. I'm awful, aren't I? But everybody's coming here for Christmas and I'm getting ready to make Susan's favorite cookies . . . I found the prettiest little Christmas dress for Beth, and that game she's been asking for . . . and, oh, blast it, Lucy Nan, don't ask me not to be merry! I'm not letting Opal Henshaw ruin the holidays for me!"

I laughed. Ellis's granddaughter, Beth, was almost seven and her daughter, Susan, was expecting her second child, a boy, the first of the year. "Do you think you might share some of that Christmas cheer with Idonia?" I told her about Melrose's conspicuous absence.

"That little jerk! Don't worry, I'll get her over here if I have to drag her, and I'll call Zee and Jo Nell, too. Good excuse to bring out the wine."

"You know Idonia doesn't drink wine," I reminded her.

"Well, maybe it's time she started." The music in the background shifted into secular with "Santa Claus Is Coming to Town." "Say, what are you and Augusta up to anyway? Where are you, Lucy Nan?"

"Tell you when we get back," I said, and helped myself to a muffin.

"Idonia will be in good hands with The Thursdays," I told Augusta, but we'd better get a move on if we plan to get to Soso and back in one day."

She packed the remaining muffins away. "I do hope we're not just running around in pursuit of wild ducks," she said.

Chapter Fifteen

Augusta drew in her breath sharply as we drove through a small country crossroads before turning onto Interstate 26. "Dear heavens, what is that?" she asked, staring at a large looming figure in one of the yards to our right.

I laughed. "An inflatable snowman," I said. "It's made out of vinyl."

"Why?" Augusta continued to look over her shoulder as we passed.

"It's a Christmas decoration," I explained. "See, here's a big Santa on the lawn up ahead."

"My goodness." Augusta sighed, and adjusting her cape about her shoulders, took needlework from her huge tapestry bag to begin working what can only be described as magic. I glanced at her from time to time to see what looked like a winter landscape emerging as she drew threads in glorious colors in and out of the fabric. I've never seen her use a pattern nor have to remove a stitch.

I turned the radio to a station that featured semiclassical holiday music and Augusta turned up the heater. Almost every house we passed had some token of the season: wreaths on doors, swags along fences, mailboxes decorated with evergreens and red ribbon.

If our trip to Soso had been for some other reason, I would have felt positively festive, but in spite of The Thursdays and all their TLC, I couldn't help worrying about Idonia. Someone had deliberately shoved Opal from that balcony, and if they felt it necessary, I didn't think they would hesitate to kill again.

"Oh, dear," Augusta moaned when we turned onto Interstate 85 at Spartanburg, South Carolina. It was as close to complaining as she would allow herself and I knew she preferred to observe the scenery from the smaller side roads but today we needed to reach our destination as quickly as possible.

"They have good barbecue in Georgia," I told her. "We'll stop somewhere for lunch."

Augusta perked up considerably. "And Brunswick stew?"

Barbecue and Brunswick stew are two of Augusta's favorite things. "Of course," I assured her. "Where do you think Brunswick stew got its start?"

But it took longer than I had remembered to reach the state line and by the time we crossed Lake Hartwell into Georgia it was after one o'clock and my stomach was growling. "If you can wait until we turn off at Commerce," I told Augusta, "there used to be a good place to eat between there and Athens."

She looked up briefly from her needlework. "I'm not the one with the noisy stomach," she said.

Less than an hour later I turned onto Highway 441 and hurriedly purchased our late lunch to go at a place called Pig in a Poke, eating my barbecue sandwich as I drove. The two of us rode in companionable silence as we passed the little towns of Madison and Eatonton before branching out onto the two-lane road that would eventually take us to Soso. On either side of the road, winter-bare trees stretched dark limbs against a gray sky, and now and again a strong wind swept dry brown leaves across the road in front of us. In the pasture on our left, white-faced cattle huddled together, looking up to stare as we passed by. I glanced at my watch to find it was three-fourteen. Soon we would lose daylight and a storm was coming up.

"Here! Turn left!" Augusta suddenly directed, pointing to a sign a few miles down the road. "Soso must be over this way."

"Don't blink," I said a few minutes later as we came into a smattering of stores and houses scattered along both sides of the road.

"Why not?" Augusta asked.

I laughed. "It's just an expression. It means the place is so small, if you blink you might miss it."

Augusta didn't answer. Her attention seemed to be fixed on something on the opposite side of the street and she turned to look back as we drove past.

"What is it? Did you see any sign of the lumberyard?"

She shook her head. "No, it's just that for a minute I thought—"

"Thought what?"

"It's nothing, really." Augusta waved her elegant hand. "Now what are we supposed to be looking for?"

"We need to find the lumberyard. Sandy said Preacher Dave had a recommendation from a man named Martin Shackelford of Shackelfords' Lumber."

"Perhaps we should ask—" Augusta suggested.

"No need. Can't you smell it?" The pungent scent of raw pine and sawdust grew stronger as we came to the end of the third block. "There it is, just down the road on the right."

"It appears to be closed," Augusta said as we drew up in front of a head-high chain-link fence. "The gate's locked."

I parked and got out of the car to see if I could find a sign of life, but the only living being I aroused was a mutt about half as big and ten times more ferocious-sounding than Clementine, which came bounding out, teeth barred. This dog was not in a good mood. I backed quickly away.

"Come now, we're not here to harm you . . . that's a good fellow." Augusta spoke calmly from somewhere behind me and the dog grew quiet and sat, tail thumping. He seemed to be smiling.

"Well, I'll be doggone! I ain't seen nothin' like that since Christ was a corporal!"

I turned to find a middle-aged man in sweat-stained overalls and a John Deere cap approaching from across the street. He snatched off the cap as he drew nearer. "Old Skeeter here must've taken a likin' to you, ma'am. He acts like he's gonna eat most folks fer supper."

I smiled and introduced myself. He couldn't see Augusta, of course. "I was hoping to speak with a Mr. Shackelford. Martin Shackelford. Do you know where I might find him?"

He scratched his head before replacing the cap. "I reckon he's done gone on over to the church. Tonight's the Christmas covered dish and Martin always helps them set up fer it. We've done closed for the day, but if there's anything I can help you with, ma'am, name's Buster—Buster Shackelford. I'm Martin's cousin."

We shook hands. "Our church has hired a sexton who, I understand, used to work here, and I just wanted to get some information about his background," I said. "Maybe you knew him—Dave Tansey?"

He frowned. "Don't know as I did, but I haven't been back long. Just retired from the army last summer, and it sure is good to be home!" He grabbed his hat as the wind picked up. "It's a-fixin' to come up a pretty bad storm, and we need to get out of this weather. Why don't you come on over to Aunt Eula's where we can talk without gettin' wet?" He pointed to the house across the street.

What was I going to do? I hated to turn around and go home after having come this far. "Is there any place I can stay tonight?"

I asked. "Maybe I can come back and speak with your cousin tomorrow."

"Lord, don't you worry none about that! I'll bet you could use a good hot cup of coffee about now and Aunt Eula always keeps a pot on. She just took her lemonade cake out of the oven, too, and I reckon she might even spare us a piece." And with that Buster Shackelford turned and started back across the street, expecting me to follow. As I stood there wondering what to do, a large woman in a big pink apron waved to me from the porch and motioned for me to come on over, so I did. Augusta, I noticed, followed at a distance.

As soon as I introduced myself and began explaining the purpose of my visit, Aunt Eula whisked me into the kitchen, sat me at the table, and served me coffee in a mug with gingerbread men painted on it. "My grandson did that in kindergarten," she said proudly. "Harry's almost seven now."

I told her I had one the same age and we became instant friends. The coffee was almost as good as Augusta's and not only was the cake warm, moist, and tangy, but the slice she gave me could have fed the entire state of Georgia. Augusta, I noticed, lingered in the doorway with a pitiful look of yearning, and I knew she was practically tasting that cake and coffee, but there wasn't a thing I could do about it. When Aunt Eula wasn't looking I broke off a good-sized chunk of cake, wrapped it in a paper napkin, and stuck it in my purse.

Buster finished his cake in double time, washed it down with coffee, and helped himself to another cup. "Bet you never tasted cake as good as this," he said, and I took one look at Augusta and said it was even better than my mother made. I'll bet my mother hasn't made a cake from scratch in thirty years, and even then they weren't anything to brag about.

"I hate to intrude on your family at a busy time like this," I said to my hostess, "but I was trying to get some information on a man who was hired to fill in temporarily with maintenance at our church. His name is David Tansey but everybody calls him Preacher Dave."

"Oh, sure, I knew Preacher Dave, but they lived out a good ways and we didn't see a whole lot of him in town—at least I didn't, but I think he was a good, hard worker over at the lumberyard. I never heard anything against him. It was sad, though, about their daughter. Dinah was a friend of Carolyn, our youngest, and such a pretty girl."

The chair creaked as Aunt Eula plopped down beside me. "Lord, it's good to take a load off! Been on my feet all day." She fanned herself with the bright apron. "Made two chicken pies, two pecan pies, that lemonade cake, and a couple of loaves of dilly bread, and honey, I'm about done in!"

I told her I could certainly understand why. "Your daughter Carolyn," I said, "does she live nearby?"

"Oh, honey, I wish she did! Carolyn and her husband moved to Florida last year, but they'll be here for Christmas. They have the sweetest little girl now—just learning to walk, and we just can't wait to see her!"

I said I didn't blame them, thanked her for the refreshments, and rose to go. I wanted to ask her more about the Tanseys' daughter, but I could see this wasn't the time. "I really must go, but do you think it will be all right with your cousin Martin if I come back and talk with him in the morning?" I asked Buster.

"Go? Go where?" Aunt Eula clamped a big red hand on my arm. "You gotta eat somewhere, honey, and you're not going to find anything half as good in one of those fancy restaurants in Milledgeville or Macon as what we'll be serving up tonight. And then, you'll *have* to stay for the pageant afterward. Our Harry's one of the wise men."

Now, how could I refuse an offer like that? I glanced at Augusta, who waved a few fingers and disappeared.

It was beginning to rain when I went across the street and moved my car into the Shackelfords' backyard. Augusta joined me there and I gave her the cake I'd saved for her.

"So you're going?" she said, pinching off a crumb to taste.

"To the church supper?" I shrugged. "I don't think I have a choice, and then there's the pageant afterward. We'll have to find some place to stay tonight."

Swaddled in her endless emerald green cape, Augusta leapt from the car and lifted her face to the rain. She did a quick pirouette, skirt whirling. "I do love Christmas pageants!" she said.

"Maybe I'll have a chance to talk with Martin Shackelford or someone else who knew the Tanseys," I said.

I rode to the church with Aunt Eula and her husband, Ed, along with Buster, his niece Mae Edna, and two of the Shackelford cousins Annie Lou and Fannie Sue. Annie Lou, who wore her graying brown hair in a bun on top of her head, was freckled and tall and so skinny you'd have trouble seeing her if she turned sideways. Her cousin Fannie Sue was as round as a beach ball with a rollicking laugh and a head full of short red curls. All had the surname Shackelford, and all, including me, balanced a cake, pie, or casserole on their laps. The car smelled so good I think I gained weight on the ride over alone.

Martin Shackelford was up to his elbows in flour when we stepped inside the fellowship hall of the Light and Life Baptist Church a while later. "Be sure and try his biscuits," Buster advised. "But you better get in line because they go fast. Makes them with whipping cream."

Earlier I had phoned Roger to let him know I wouldn't be home until the next day and asked him to please take care of Clementine. Of course, he wanted to know what I was doing in Soso, Georgia, so I told him I was there for a little last-minute Christmas shopping at the outlet in Commerce. Now, to stay honest, I would have to stop and buy something on the way home.

Aunt Eula introduced me to so many cousins, nephews, nieces, and siblings I lost track after the first three or four. Everyone had brought something to eat and the women scurried about placing the food on long tables and setting out dinnerware while the men set up tables and chairs for the meal. I was glad when one of the women (I think it was Mae Edna) accepted my offer of help and allowed me to place red candles and freshly cut evergreens on every table. A cedar Christmas tree surrounded by wrapped gifts stood in the corner of the room. The gifts, I was told, were for the children and would be given out later.

I sat during the meal with Aunt Eula and Ed, Ed's sister Ruby, Buster, and Mae Edna, and although we take pride in our fare in Stone's Throw, I'll have to admit, these people had us beat. They had chicken cooked every way imaginable, plus casseroles, bread, cakes, pies, and pickles of just about every kind.

During dessert, I managed to ask Mae Edna, who sat on my right, if she knew anything about Dave Tansey.

"Not much," she said, after finishing a generous wedge of apple pie. "They didn't belong to our church, but their son . . . Joshua, isn't it?"

"Jeremiah," I said.

"Well, he was a couple of years ahead of me in school, and it seems like he stayed in trouble most of the time."

"For what?" I asked.

"Oh, just different things . . . smoking pot . . . cutting class . . . stuff like that."

"What about Dinah, his sister?" I said. "She must've died awfully young. What happened?"

"From what I heard, she married the wrong man. Just ran off without a word. It was awfully hard on the Tanseys."

"But what hap—" Before I could learn anything more, somebody came around to ask if we wanted coffee, and people started moving tables to the side to make room for the pageant to follow.

Somebody turned out the lights except for those in the front of the room illuminating a small makeshift stage. The room grew quiet as the minister began to recite the familiar passage from Luke: *And it came to pass . . .*

The pageant had begun. Everyone had turned their chairs to face the stage and there happened to be an empty one next to me. It didn't stay empty long. I soon felt the light touch of a hand on my arm and knew Augusta was beside me.

Watching the scene unfolding in front of me I forgot about what had happened to Opal Henshaw the night before; forgot about the elusive Melrose; and forgot about Idonia's brush with danger. And when we rose at the end to sing "Silent Night," Augusta sang as well. And this time she almost managed to stay on key.

Afterward, the kitchen was filled with the crinkle of plastic wrap and the crackle of aluminum foil as people hurried to cover what was left in their dishes for the trip back home. I grabbed a sponge and helped Ruby Shackelford wipe off the tables, then overwhelmed, tried to stay out of the way. But as the bustle died down, I grabbed the chance to jump in to renew my conversation with Mae Edna.

"You were telling me about Dinah Tansey's husband," I began. "What happened? Why did she die?"

"I'll tell you why she died."

I turned to find Martin Shackelford standing behind me. "She died because that worthless man she married didn't get her to a doctor in time," he said.

"Tubal pregnancy," Mae Edna whispered. "Tube ruptured and the poor thing died from internal bleeding. I've heard it near about destroyed her husband. They say he hadn't been the same since."

"Huh! Crocodile tears if you ask me! All that caring came a little too late for that poor little gal," Martin continued. "And what's more, he didn't even have the decency to tell her folks what had happened until she was dead and in the ground.

"Dexter Clark!" Martin spat out the name as if it left a bad taste in his mouth, and looked at me sharply. "Not worth killin', if you ask me. You're not kin to him or nothin', are you?"

Without waiting for an answer, he began lining up empty containers on the table. "Mary Lynne, this one's yours! Got your name on it. And, Elaine, I know this pan belongs to you. I seen you when you come in with it."

"Did you say, Dexter *Clark*?" I asked, dogging the man's heels. "The man Dinah married was Dexter Clark?"

He nodded. "She married him, all right, but he wasn't much of a man."

I looked around for Augusta and saw her standing close by. It was obvious from the expression on her face the angel had heard every word.

Dexter Clark was the name of the man who had died at Willowbrook.

Chapter Sixteen

By the time we started back to Soso, the temperature had dropped and an icy wind blew in gusts that chilled me to the bone. We didn't waste any time crowding into the family van, and Ed Shackelford drove slowly to avoid sliding on black ice in the road.

"There is no way I'm gonna let you drive in this mess tonight to any hotel," Aunt Eula informed me when I brought up the subject of a place to stay.

"You've already been so kind, I don't want to crowd you," I said—although I really didn't relish the idea of driving on slick, wet roads, especially since I didn't know where I was going.

"Honey, one more is nothing to me. I won't even know you're there. You can have Arabella's room. She's not due in until the weekend." Arabella, I learned was the Shackelfords' oldest daughter, who taught at an elementary school in Covington.

"Hope you don't mind sharing with Cousin Fannie Sue," Eula continued. "She just drove down from Atlanta to see Harry in the pageant tonight. She'll be leaving in the morning."

Fannie Sue and I had worked together clearing tables earlier that evening, and although she seemed pleasant enough, the woman must have weighed over two hundred pounds. I hoped we didn't have to share a bed, but I was so tired, I felt I could probably sleep anywhere.

But that seemed out of the question just then because the Shackelfords wanted to discuss the events of the evening and all of them began to talk at once. Naturally everyone thought Harry was the star of the show. We congregated in the kitchen, where Aunt Eula heated a big pot of spiced apple cider and passed around a tray of fruitcake and sugar cookies. I didn't see how anybody could possibly eat another thing after what we had put away at the covered dish supper, but the refreshments soon disappeared. I sipped the cider slowly, grateful for its warmth, and wondered if I should bring up the subject of the Tanseys again, but decided it would be best to wait until the next day when I could speak with Martin Shackelford alone.

Just as I finished my drink one of the cousins suggested a game of charades. This was met with boisterous approval and the whole family filed into the living room where they gathered in front of a huge Christmas tree and began to choose sides. I hung back in the kitchen, hoping I wouldn't be noticed.

"I hate to be a party pooper," I told Aunt Eula, "but I have a long drive ahead of me tomorrow so I'd better get some sleep."

"I guess I should've warned you about these folks," she said. "They'll stay up all night sometimes, and be no worse for the wear for it the next day." She patted my arm. "I expect you're tired, as well. Come on upstairs and I'll show you where you can sleep."

"Count me in, too. I have an early day tomorrow." Overnight bag in hand, Cousin Fannie Sue followed along behind us.

To my relief, Aunt Eula opened the door to a pleasant, inviting room with crisp white organdy curtains, colorful hooked rug, and *twin beds*. I thanked her and said my good nights, then washed my face, and slipped into the soft flannel gown she left out for me. I was asleep as soon as my head hit the pillow.

I didn't even think about Augusta until I woke the next morning at a little after eight, but she usually takes care of herself in situations like this, so I wasn't worried. The house was quiet when I came downstairs, Fannie Sue having risen earlier, and the charade-players still asleep. And although I had thought I couldn't possibly be hungry again this soon, I found myself devouring crisp bacon with coffee and orange juice and the best waffles I've ever put in my mouth.

Because I hadn't planned to stay overnight, I had nothing to leave with Aunt Eula as a hostess gift to thank her for her hospitality. I would stop at the outlet in Commerce on my way home and have something sent from there, I decided. I was rinsing my dishes at the sink when Aunt Eula came into the kitchen and planted a kiss on my cheek.

"Guess what I just found on the hall table—and with my name on it, too? Lucy, are you sure you want to part with this? Please tell me you are, because I can't bear to give it back!"

I tried not to act surprised when she held out Augusta's beautiful hand-stitched needlework of a small country church in the snow. It looked amazingly like one we had passed during our drive over the day before.

"Of course I want you to keep it," I said. "I can't think of another person I'd rather have it than you."

"Well, I'm going to take it over to Milledgeville this very morning and have it framed. I don't believe I've ever seen anything like this—it's absolutely perfect!"

Of course it was. "Why, thank you, Aunt Eula," I said, and smiled.

I found Augusta waiting in the car when I left a few minutes later. "Thanks for leaving the needlework, Augusta. It was a thoughtful thing to do and a perfect gift for Aunt Eula. She loved it! . . . And by the way, where were you all last night?"

"I found the sofa most comfortable after the Shackelfords

finally tired of their game. Have you ever played charades, Lucy Nan? All those signals—it was most enlightening."

I laughed and assured her that I had as I drove across the street to the lumberyard. This morning the gate was open and the unfriendly dog was nowhere to be seen.

"I wonder if I might find a cup of coffee in there," Augusta said.

"I'll bring you some if they have any, but on second thought, maybe you'd better come with me, just in case our friend Skeeter is anywhere about," I said as I got out of the car. A man who looked vaguely familiar—probably one of the cousins—pointed the way to Martin Shackelford's office and I found him at a makeshift desk covered with blueprints and a disarray of papers.

He didn't seem to recognize me at first glance so I introduced myself again, reminding him we had met briefly the night before.

"Right. You were asking about Dave Tansey. Might I ask why?"

"My cousin hired him to take care of the family property just outside of Stone's Throw, and he's also filling in for our church sexton for a while. I understand you wrote a recommendation for him, and I wanted to find out a little more about his background." Taking the chair he offered, I told him there had been several puzzling incidents since the family's arrival.

He frowned. "Like what?"

I told him about finding Dexter Clark's body at Willowbrook and what had happened to Opal Henshaw at our church. I really wanted to learn more about the Tanseys' daughter Dinah but couldn't think of a way to approach the subject tactfully.

"Dexter Clark? So he's dead, huh? Well, I hate to say it but that ain't no great loss!" Martin Shackelford threw back his head and laughed. "You don't think Preacher Dave had anything to do with all that, do you?" He shook his head. "Ugh-uh. That dog won't hunt! I wouldn't be surprised if Dexter was mixed up in selling drugs or something. Ran around with a bad bunch. Now,

Dave Tansey—he's a good man and a hard worker. I hated to see him go."

"Then why *did* he leave?" Nothing ventured, nothing gained, as Mimmer used to say.

Martin Shackelford stood and poured coffee for himself in a thick white mug and some in a Styrofoam cup for me. I took a sip before I remembered to save the rest for Augusta, who was sending frantic signals from across the room.

"He never came out and said so, but I think he just wanted to get away from bad memories . . . The Tansey boy got into some trouble in school here, and then the girl married that sorry son-of-a—Sorry, ma'am—and then her dying like that. It like to broke her mama's heart. Poor woman! Louella Tansey was always quiet, shy, you know. Wouldn't say boo to a goose, and this girl's death like to done her in."

"When Dinah married, did they live around here?" I asked.

"No, he took Dinah to live somewhere in North Carolina if I remember right. Far as I know, they never came back here, and I was glad to see the back of him. Some say he changed, tried to turn his life around, but he sure as hell had a long way to go."

The telephone on his desk rang just then and I took the opportunity to thank him for his time and excused myself. He stood and shook my hand before picking up the receiver. It was good to know some men still had manners.

I waited until we got back in the car to give Augusta the coffee. "I guess that settles it," I said. "The man who died at Willowbrook was the Tanseys' son-in-law Dexter Clark. But the Tanseys claimed they didn't know him, and if the family disliked him so, what was he doing out there?"

Augusta drank her coffee before answering. "It does seem suspicious, but it could have been a coincidence, I suppose. Perhaps the Tanseys didn't know he was there."

I drove slowly through the town of Soso and turned right toward

Eatonton. "Martin Shackelford said Dexter wasn't worth killing," I said. "Obviously, somebody thought otherwise."

Augusta was quiet for a while and I knew she was thinking. "Did Mr. Shackelford plan to go hunting this morning?" she asked finally.

"I don't think so. Why do you ask?"

"He said the dog wouldn't hunt."

I laughed. "Oh, Augusta! That's just an expression. It means the same thing as barking up the wrong tree."

Augusta shook her head and turned up the heater. "Never mind," she said.

Just before getting back on the interstate, we stopped at the outlet mall in Commerce. Weigelia needed some decent gloves and Julie had been asking for pajamas. For her main present I was giving my daughter a check to buy clothes. She works for a small newspaper in north Georgia, and although she loves her job, I know she has a hard time making ends meet on her small salary.

I made my purchases and was taking my time browsing in the boys' department considering just one more thing for Teddy when Augusta caught my attention. I looked up to see her standing by the window waving both arms. Her honey-gold hair had slipped over one eye and her long necklace danced and bounced in the sunlight.

"What is it?" I asked, hurrying over. Did angels ever have fits?

Augusta pointed out the window. "It's him! At least I think it is. See . . . he's going into that store over there."

I looked over her shoulder. "Who? Where?"

"Idonia's gentleman friend. What's his name? Melrose! Isn't that him just down the street?"

I shoved aside a display of toddler-size holiday dresses and pressed my face against the glass to see where she was pointing, and was just in time to catch a glimpse of a man's back as the door of a shop closed behind him. The man was of similar shape as Melrose: sturdy and round and a little less than medium height, and the coat looked vaguely familiar, but I couldn't be certain. "Are you sure?" I asked Augusta. "What would Melrose be doing here?"

She gave me a not-so-angelic push toward the doorway. "That's what we want to find out, but you'll have to move faster than that or we'll lose him."

Clutching my shopping bags in one hand and my purse in the other, I careened out the door and skidded wildly into a stunned group of elderly women who were trying to decide where to meet for lunch.

"So sorry. P-please excuse me!" I stammered, giving Augusta the look I usually reserve for people who talk on cell phones during a movie.

Racing down the sidewalk, I followed my impatient angel into a store that sells cookware and kitchen gadgets to find her waiting for me behind a display of spatulas. "Well?" I demanded. "Where is he?"

She nodded toward the back of the room. "He was looking at those aprons back there. He can't have gone far."

"*Aprons!* How can the man possibly be interested in aprons at a time like this?" I said. "Weigelia says the police want to talk with him about what he might have seen at the church the other night, but if he's made Idonia unhappy, they'll have to get in line after me!" I hurried to the area Augusta had pointed out, but Melrose DuBois wasn't there.

Parting an array of dish towels, I glimpsed the back of a Melrose-like head hotfooting it up the coffeemaker aisle. "I'll head him off at the pass," I whispered to Augusta. "You keep watch at the door."

She smiled and nodded, moving quickly into position. I knew Augusta had watched enough cowboy movies to understand the vernacular. Unfortunately, a very large woman who was obviously shopping to equip several kitchens for a school of the culinary arts picked that moment to wheel her loaded cart in front of me, blocking both my view of Melrose and the aisle.

I was getting out of breath by the time I reached the checkout counter and Augusta, who simply shook her head and shrugged. Melrose, or the man who looked like Melrose, was nowhere to be seen.

To tell the truth, at that point I was just about ready to give up. After all, we really weren't sure we were on the trail of the right person, and I had spied a couple of fascinating kitchen aids I was certain would turn me into a gourmet cook and wouldn't have minded spending a little more time in the shop.

But that was not to be. "There he is in the parking lot!" Augusta said, grabbing my arm. "Oh, do please hurry, Lucy Nan!"

I gave the bewildered cashier an apologetic smile and rushed out the door behind her.

Weaving in and out among parked vehicles, I followed Augusta, who followed Melrose. Now and again she paused to wave me on with a swirl of her cape until we ended up on the other side of the mall. Cheeks flushed with excitement, and possibly from the cold as well, Augusta posted herself in front of a bookstore. For once, I noticed, the cold, damp December wind didn't seem to bother her in the least.

It bothered me. "It's freezing out here, Augusta! I don't see anybody out here that faintly resembles Melrose DuBois."

"That's because he's in the bookstore," she said, calmly folding her arms. "All we have to do is wait."

"Well, I'm waiting inside where it's warm," I told her. "And I suggest you do the same."

"But what if he sees you? We don't want him to slip away again."

"I know he can't see *you*," I said, "but do you think he's aware that *I'm* following him?"

"I wouldn't want to take a chance." Augusta shaded her eyes against the glare of the window and looked inside. "He seems to be taking his time browsing among the books. Let's give him a little time, Lucy Nan. He'll have to come out again soon."

"If I have to stand out here in the cold, at least I'm going to be sure it's worth the wait," I said, looking in my purse for dark glasses.

Augusta shivered the slightest bit and tried to pretend she hadn't. "What do you mean?" she asked.

I put on the glasses, pulled my hat over my ears and wrapped a muffler around the bottom of my face. "I just want to be sure it's Melrose DuBois in there," I said, trying to peer through the window without being obvious.

"But, Lucy Nan, I told you it was."

How could I put this gently? Augusta looked so crestfallen I hesitated to mention that she had been becoming more and more nearsighted in the past few months. Why just last week she'd mistaken our neighbor for a mailbox. Nettie had been standing at the corner in her long blue winter coat waiting for the traffic light to change when Augusta, who was watching out the window, drew in her breath.

"What's wrong?" I asked.

"Oh, nothing," she said. "It's just that for a moment, I thought I saw the mailbox move."

But as it turned out, I didn't have to remind her, because Augusta Goodnight was right. One quick glance was all I needed to assure me that the man in the bookstore was indeed Idonia's slippery "gentleman friend," Melrose DuBois.

Chapter Seventeen

"Don't let him see you looking," Augusta warned. "Perhaps we should step over there and wait. It's out of the wind and we'll still be able to keep an eye on the door."

I followed her to a sheltered spot in front of a nearby shop where we huddled miserably, eyes on the bookstore next door. Augusta wrapped herself mummy-style from head to toe in her limitless velvety cape and I stuck my gloved hands under my arms and stamped my feet to keep them warm, ignoring the curious looks of passersby.

"How many books is the man going to buy?" I complained at last. "Seems he's been in there for an eternity!"

Augusta laughed. "Not quite, but maybe we'd better take another look." She gave my arm a comforting pat. "If you're up to waiting a few more minutes I'll go in there and see what's holding him up."

It didn't take her long. When Augusta emerged from the store, I knew with one look our quarry had given us the slip again. The angel looked so disappointed I almost forgave her for making me stand outside in the cold. "He must have left by another door," she said. "I couldn't find him anywhere."

"Then he knows I was following him," I said as we hurried back to the car and blessed warmth. "But what in the world is he doing here? Do you think Melrose might be following *us?*"

Augusta waited until the heater warmed up before answering. "I think it's possible he was there ahead of us," she said.

"Where?"

"In that little town—Soso. When we first arrived yesterday I thought I saw him coming out of a building there."

"What building?" I asked.

"The post office, I think, but I didn't get a good look at him."

Taking my life in my hands, I merged into the traffic on the interstate heading north and home. "Why didn't you say something?" I asked when I was able to breathe again.

"I only got a glimpse and I wasn't sure it was the same man I saw at the caroling party." Augusta fingered her necklace as she watched the landscape rush past. "It puzzles me, Lucy Nan. What was he doing in that town? And if he means well, why did he avoid you back at the shops?"

I thought about that for a minute. "He must be aware that the police in Stone's Throw want to talk with him, and that doesn't stack up too well in his favor. It's all beginning to seem suspicious to me." I gripped the wheel as if it were Melrose DuBois's neck. "What I wouldn't give to have just five minutes with that little snake!"

"Let's wait and cross that stream when we come upon it," Augusta said primly. "After all, we don't have enough evidence yet."

"How much evidence do you need?" I asked.

"Right now what I *need* is another cup of coffee. Perhaps I'll be able to think more clearly then." Augusta loosened her wrap and tucked a stray strand of reddish-gold hair into place. "The cup I had earlier seems to have left me wanting."

I laughed. "My sentiments exactly. There's a place this side of Spartanburg where we can stop for coffee and pick up a couple of hamburgers, too. I'll be ready for a break by then."

I tuned in Christmas music on the radio and both of us were quiet for the next hour or so, Augusta with her thoughts, I suppose, while I concentrated on the traffic and wondered how The Thursdays were dealing with the situation back in Stone's Throw.

Later, we ate our burgers in the parking lot of a fast-food restaurant and shared an order of fries, while reviving on steaming coffee.

"About Melrose DuBois," Augusta began after I returned from disposing of the wrappers. "He and the people who live on your family's property—the Tanseys—seem to be key figures in this series of unfortunate events in Stone's Throw."

"Right," I said. "We just need to find the connection."

Augusta finished her coffee before speaking. "It's beginning to be plain that the connection is the locket."

I nodded. "I think you're right on the money there, Augusta. The locket belonged to the Tanseys' daughter, then Melrose came in possession of it somehow and gave it to Idonia. *Somebody* wanted it badly enough to drug Idonia and steal it that night at Bellawood. Dexter Clark, who had been married to the Tanseys' daughter, ended up under the balcony at Willowbrook with his neck broken, and Opal Henshaw, who rented a room to Melrose at the Spring Lamb, died in a suspicious fall from the church balcony. Melrose DuBois seems to be in the middle of all of this." I started the car and eased back onto the highway. "What is it that's so important about that locket? I wonder if Melrose knows?"

"If he doesn't, he must have guessed by now," Augusta said. She turned to me solemn-eyed. "And didn't your friend Claudia say that Opal Henshaw seemed unusually interested in it? Lucy Nan, I believe it's imperative that we find that locket—and soon."

But how will we do that if we don't even know who has it? I wondered. *Why would Melrose give Idonia the locket only to steal it back and risk her life in doing it?*

Augusta must have come to the same conclusion. "I think we

should begin with the Tanseys," she said, almost as if she were thinking aloud. "Didn't you say Dave Tansey was helping to park vehicles at Bellawood that night?"

"Yes, but one of us would have noticed if he came upstairs—unless it was while we were taking a break in the kitchen."

"If he were in costume, however, he'd be less conspicuous," Augusta said.

Somehow the idea of Preacher Dave dressing up in period clothing made me laugh. Tall and lanky with a timeworn face, he would certainly suit the concept of a hardworking farmer of the 1800s, but I couldn't imagine him going to the extent of securing the proper costume, then scurrying to change into it after a night of directing parking.

"What about Louella?" I said. "Some of the women wore bonnets that night. It would've been easier for her to go unnoticed than either of the men. But how are we going to find out where she was during that time?"

Augusta smiled. "Where there's a will, there's a . . . well . . . a course of action," she said.

A perfect challenge for The Thursdays.

I found several of them keeping Idonia company at her place when we arrived in Stone's Throw later that afternoon. While others in the group watched *A Wonderful Life* on television, I snatched Ellis away for a whispered conference in the kitchen.

"Where in the world have you been?" she asked. "We were getting worried."

"Never mind! I'll tell you about it later. Has Idonia heard anything from Melrose?"

Ellis shook her head. "Not a mumblin' word, the little twerp! What do you think that old fool's up to, Lucy Nan?"

"I'm beginning to think it's nothing good." I told her about Melrose giving us the slip at the outlet mall. "And Augusta says she saw him in Soso yesterday, too."

Ellis laughed when I told her about our adventurous stay with the Shackelfords, but grew serious when she learned the man whose body we had found at Willowbrook had been married to the Tanseys' daughter, Dinah.

"But didn't they tell the police they didn't know him? And Preacher Dave made no bones about how he felt about the man she married. Do you think one of them gave him a shove?"

I shrugged. "Beats me, but it all seems to center on that locket. Augusta and I believe one of the Tanseys has it and that it's important for us to find some way to get a better look at it."

Ellis helped herself to an apple and polished it on her sleeve. "And how do we do that?"

"That's what we have to discuss. Who's not here? I didn't see Nettie or Claudia."

"Nettie's over at Claudia's helping her make a Japanese fruitcake for the staff party at Sarah Bedford tomorrow."

"That's quite an undertaking! I think I'd volunteer for something simpler than that," I said.

Ellis laughed. "She probably didn't have a choice being the new kid on the block. Remember, Claudia's only been working at the college a few months."

"Do you think everyone might be able to get together for a little while tonight? Maybe we can put some of these pieces together."

Ellis swallowed a bite of apple. "I guess so, but what are we going to do about Idonia?"

"What's this about Idonia?"

For a few seconds I froze, then turned to find Idonia standing in the kitchen doorway.

Ellis and I stood there looking at each other for what seemed like minutes, waiting, I suppose, for the other one to speak. "Oh hell, Idonia, I guess the jig is up," Ellis said with a backward glance at me. "Maybe you'd better sit down. We have something to tell you." Ellis steered her back into the living room and switched off the television set.

"I guess we'd better start with the locket," I said after we settled Idonia in her favorite chair. "We're almost sure it's the same one the Tanseys' daughter is wearing in that photo of her on their piano. It even has the same seed pearls missing."

Idonia twisted her hands in her lap. "Then why would Melrose tell me it belonged to his grandmother?"

Ellis sat on the arm of our friend's chair and put a hand on her shoulder. "Maybe he thought it would make it seem even more special," she said, forcing a smile.

"Do you think he was the one who—who stole it?" Idonia bit her lip. "*Somebody* drugged my punch, but it wasn't him! I know Melrose wouldn't do that to me. Besides, he seemed most upset when I told him what had happened."

"It couldn't have been Melrose," I assured her. "Al Evans confirmed that he worked until after ten that night at the funeral home."

Zee frowned. "Then who?"

"Probably one of the Tanseys," I said, and told them what I'd learned from Martin Shackelford. "Remember that man we found out at Willowbrook? Died from a fall from the balcony out there? Well, he had been married to the Tanseys' daughter, Dinah."

Ellis made a rude noise. "Fall nothing! I'll bet one of those Tanseys pushed him."

"But which one?" Jo Nell asked. "I can't imagine Preacher Dave or that mousy Louella doing anything that bold."

"What about that boy—that Jeremiah? I wouldn't put much of anything past that one!" Zee said.

Idonia sat up straighter. "Seems if Jeremiah Tansey was at Bellawood, one of us would've seen him."

"Wait a minute!" I said. "Somebody had a video camera that night—remember? Genevieve wanted to get a record of the festivities and it seemed that every time I turned around, they had it in my face."

"Ralph Snow. He filmed for a while in the schoolhouse, too, until Nettie had enough of it and ran him off," Jo Nell said. "If any of the Tanseys were there, maybe they'll show up on film."

"I'll give Ralph a call," I offered, "if one of you will get in touch with Nettie and Claudia." I looked at my watch. "It's a little after five o'clock now. I'll be serving up soup and corn bread in a little over an hour for anybody who's interested."

"Sounds good," Idonia said. "But how can you manage, Lucy Nan, in such a short time?"

Ellis looked at me and smiled. She knew who would be making the soup and corn bread.

"Ralph's going to drop his camera by in a little while," I told them as we all gathered around my kitchen table later that evening. "Of course I had to swear in blood I'd have it back by tomorrow."

Idonia, who had barely touched her food, shoved her plate aside. "It's not that old locket I worry about, it's Melrose! I haven't heard from him since day before yesterday, and it just isn't like him not to call. I'm so afraid something's happened to him."

Something *would* happen to him if I had my way, I thought, but instead, I said, with some conviction, that I was sure Melrose was just fine.

"I expect he'll show up before too long," Zee said. "After all, it's only been a couple of days."

Nettie stood as we heard a car in the driveway. "I'll bet that's Ralph with the camera now. I can't wait to see what's on that film."

Jo Nell frowned. "What if we don't find anything there? Then what?"

"Then we'll have to figure out some way to get our hands on that locket," Ellis said.

Chapter Eighteen

"Now, what do you call this apparatus?" Augusta asked the next day, inspecting Ralph Snow's camcorder without daring to touch it. We had eaten an early breakfast of oatmeal, cinnamon toast, and freshly squeezed orange juice and the camera sat on the kitchen table ready to be returned to its owner.

"A video camera," I said, "only it records sounds and voices as well. I promised Ralph I'd have it back before noon as he'll be going out of town for Christmas."

Augusta laughed and clapped her hands. "Mickey Mouse!"

"What?"

"Mickey Mouse. Cleveland Tarver."

I shrugged. "I guess you're going to explain that," I said.

"Cleveland Tarver. I was assigned to him for a brief period during the war. He was a widower going through some difficult times just then. His only son was in the service overseas and his daughter-in-law and grandson came to live with him for a while—sweet little boy about three—Sonny, they called him. The son's wife was constantly worried, of course, so Cleveland bought this camera—a movie camera they called it then. With it she recorded Sonny's activities so his father wouldn't miss so much of his childhood, and once in a while they would show cartoons on their home screen—most were about Mickey Mouse." Augusta smiled. "How Sonny loved watching them . . . and so did I!"

"What happened?" I asked, expecting the worst. I knew Augusta was referring to World War II as that had been her last period on assignment as a guardian angel until recently.

"What happened to whom?"

"To Sonny's father, and to—Cleveland—what's-his-name?" I asked.

"Sonny's father came home after the war and went on to become a physician, I believe. Cleveland eventually married again and lived well into his nineties." Augusta examined her cup and seemed surprised that it was empty. "Any more of that coffee?"

I rinsed our dishes in the sink and put them into the dishwasher. All this chasing around and worrying was starting to get to me. I could use a little Mickey Mouse myself. "Augusta, what are we going to do? We seem to have come up against a brick wall and I don't know where to go from here. Ellis is right. We have to find out who has that locket!"

Augusta wiped off the table in one wide, circular swoop, and it gleamed as if it were new. "I was hoping something would turn up on that camera last night, but that doesn't mean any of those people weren't there."

"We know that Preacher Dave was in the vicinity, and Ellis was going to phone the fabric shop where Louella works and make up some story to find out if she was working there that night, but then we realized the drop-in at Bellawood was on a Sunday and they wouldn't have been open then," I said.

"Then where do you think she might be on a Sunday night?" Augusta asked, teasing Clementine with a doggy treat.

"Well . . . I suppose she could've been at her church, especially since her husband's the minister. But he was at Bellawood parking cars, so they must not have had a service."

"Maybe not a proper service, but there could have been choir rehearsal or some other kind of meeting," she said. "Do you know anyone who belongs to that congregation?"

"Not right offhand," I said, "but I'll ask around. Frankly, Jeremiah's the one who concerns me. I wish I knew where he was the night Idonia's locket was taken."

Augusta stood at the window as if she might find an answer somewhere in the clouds. "I'm sure the boy keeps company with someone. Perhaps some of his companions might be able to help."

"According to Kim who does Nettie's hair at the Total Perfection, Jeremiah hangs out with that bunch at the Red Horse Café and I'm not about to go in there! And even if I did, I doubt if they'd tell me the truth."

I remembered how Kemper had reacted when I first mentioned Jeremiah that morning at Willowbrook. "We've heard nothing more from the police about their investigation into what happened to Idonia. I guess Opal's death sort of put it on the back burner, but I think I'll give Kemper Mungo a call. They may or may not know about the Tanseys' connection to Dexter Clark, but I have a feeling the police know a lot more about what goes on with Jeremiah Tansey than they're letting on."

Augusta rode with me to return the camcorder to Ralph Snow, and afterward I dropped by the library to return a couple of her books and check out enough mysteries to last her until after the holidays. "I don't know what to do about Idonia," I confessed on the way home. "She's worried about Melrose DuBois—afraid something's happened to him, when I know good and well he was alive and kicking when we saw him in Georgia yesterday."

Augusta was reading the jacket copy on one of the mysteries. "If it were you, would you want to know the truth?" she said, setting the book aside.

I considered the question. "Yes, I think I would. But Idonia's been through a rough time, Augusta. She seems especially fragile just now. Do you really think I should tell her?"

"She seems an intelligent person to me, and she's certainly mature enough to deal with adversity. I believe your friend might consider it an injustice to be treated in any other manner."

"In other words, you think it's insulting to protect her?"

"Idonia's free to make choices just as you are, Lucy Nan. I'm sure she's capable of facing the situation if necessary."

I wasn't so sure about that, but I didn't have time to think on it longer because we reached home to find two cars parked in our driveway, and Nettie, wrapped in her old brown sweater, scuttling over from next door, house shoes flapping.

My first thought was that something was wrong with Idonia. "What's going on?" I asked Zee, who happened to be the first person I reached.

"Have you seen *The Messenger* this morning?" she asked.

"Not yet," I said. "Has something happened to Idonia?"

"No, no! Wait until you see this!" Claudia rattled the weekly newspaper in my face. At the same time, Nettie called out something I couldn't understand, probably because she was still putting in her teeth, and I ran to help her recover the fuzzy slipper she'd lost under the azalea bush.

"I had a feeling there was something peculiar going on there," Nettie said, panting to keep up.

"What? Where? Will somebody please tell me something?" I trailed after them into my house where Claudia spread the newspaper on the kitchen table, smoothing it with her hand.

"Read this," she demanded, poking her finger on what was obviously the lead story on the front page. I didn't need my reading glasses to make out the bold headline: LOCAL MATRON DIES IN FALL FROM BALCONY.

Silently I read the first few paragraphs describing what had happened at the church that night. I didn't see anything new.

"Well, we knew this already," I said, wondering why they were so excited.

Zee leaned over my shoulder. "Skip to the obituary information at the end," she said.

Services will be held, Sat., Dec. 22, at Stone's Throw Presbyterian Church . . . I read aloud. "Gosh, that's tomorrow!"

"Never mind that," Zee said. "Check out where it tells about her family."

I cleared my throat. *Mrs. Henshaw was preceded in death by her husband, Virgil Henshaw, and a sister, Maisie Clark of Raleigh, North Carolina. She is survived by a brother, Terrance Banks, of Knoxville, Tennessee, and a nephew, Dexter Clark . . .*

"Dexter Clark! Do they mean Dexter Clark as in *dead* Dexter Clark?"

Nettie nodded. "One and the same."

"Whoever put this in the paper obviously didn't know he wasn't still alive," Claudia said.

"So Opal's nephew was married to the Tanseys' daughter, Dinah," I said. "That's why she was so curious about the locket Dinah wore in the photograph. But wouldn't she have known about the marriage?"

"Not necessarily," Claudia said. "We were talking about families, holiday customs, things like that, the day we delivered the fruitcakes and Opal told me her only sister died several years ago and she rarely spoke to her brother. She didn't mention a nephew."

Zee frowned. "Even if Dexter married the Tansey girl after his mother died . . . still, you'd think Opal would've been invited to the wedding," she said.

"Maybe they eloped," Nettie suggested.

"Wait a minute!" Claudia, who had been sitting, suddenly jumped to her feet. "If Opal didn't know about her nephew's marriage, why did she take such an unusual interest in that picture while we were at the Tanseys' place that day—especially about the locket Dinah wore? Wanted to know all about it."

"Do you remember what she said?" I asked.

"Something about her mother—or maybe it was her grandmother—having one like it. Louella told her it was a family heirloom. She hurried us out of there right soon after that. You could tell she didn't want to talk about it."

"Melrose must have shown the locket to Opal before he gave it to Idonia," Zee said. "Do you remember if Opal mentioned Idonia having one like it?"

Claudia nodded. "I'm pretty sure she did . . . Yes, I'm positive because Louella said she guessed there must be more than one."

"But not with two seed pearls missing in the exact places," I said. "And that very night somebody drugged Idonia's drink and stole it."

"But they must've known about Idonia's locket earlier," Zee pointed out. "She swears somebody was following her while we were caroling."

That didn't surprise me because Idonia had taken every opportunity to show off her gift from Melrose. "It had to have been one of the Tanseys," I said. "Do any of you know somebody who goes to their church?"

"I think Helen does," Claudia said. "Helen Harlan. She's a student at Sarah Bedford, works part time in the office to help with her tuition. Helen's kind of quiet and serious—keeps to herself, but she mentioned going to Chandler's Creek. I think she sings in the choir."

"Do you know how to get in touch with her?" I asked. "Maybe she could give us an idea where Louella Tansey was last Sunday night."

"Sure. I'll probably see her tonight at the staff Christmas party . . . but what'll I *say?*"

"You'll think of something," I told her, "just let us know what you find out—"

"As soon as you can!" Zee added. "And shouldn't somebody check with Al Evans about Idonia's slippery boyfriend? After all, Melrose is supposed to be working there."

"And claims to be related, too!" Nettie clicked her teeth. "You reckon Al knows what that little varmint's been up to?"

There wasn't but one way to find out, and I was about to volunteer when Ellis came bursting in, almost tripping over Clementine, who was stretched out in her usual place.

"I've left two messages! Don't you ever pick up?" she said, then realizing we were all gathered around the story in *The Messenger,* pulled out a chair and joined us.

"You're just in time. You're nominated," I told her after the others took time about telling her what we had discussed.

Ellis stooped to pet Clementine as an apology for almost stepping on her tail. "Nominated for what?" she asked.

"To see what you can find out about Melrose from Al Evans," I said. "Surely he must have some idea what the man's about."

I could tell by her expression Ellis was going to balk. "You want me to go to the funeral home? By myself? And I can never tell when Al's looking at me. He has a glass eye, you know."

"Oh, for heaven's sake, I'll go with you, but we'd better get on with it," I said. The day was over half gone, I realized, and I still hadn't spoken with Kemper Mungo although I had left a message earlier asking him to get in touch. No doubt he thought I wanted to bug him to tell me what he knew.

"Has anybody seen Idonia?" Ellis asked as we left. "I've been trying to reach her all morning."

Nettie suggested she'd probably gone to the grocery store and Zee promised to check on Idonia on her way home, but I still felt uneasy as Ellis and I drove the few blocks to Evans and Son. If the person responsible for the other two deaths thought Idonia might know too much, our friend could be next.

Al Evans greeted us cordially and seated us on a Victorian love seat upholstered in purple velvet. Now he shook his head and fastened his gaze on the huge decorative vase in the corner—at least that's where he seemed to be looking. "I wish I could help you, but I declare, I don't know what Melrose has gotten himself up to. I'm sure the police would like to know, too, but unfortunately, he didn't see fit to tell me."

"Do you know where Melrose lived before he came here?" I asked.

Our host pondered that silently for a minute. "Melrose spent most of his life in a small town in Mississippi working in his father's hardware store, then later, for somebody else. After his wife died a few years ago, he moved from here to there—didn't seem to know what to do with himself."

"Did they have children?" Ellis asked, and Al shook his head. "No, and I think it might've made a difference if they had. He's been lonely, I know, and I expect that's why he came here to work with me. As far as I know I'm the only relative Melrose has left. Our mothers were sisters, you know. I just wish I knew what was going on."

Suddenly he rose and went to a large metal urnlike vessel on the table behind him. "My goodness, where are my manners? Can I offer you ladies some coffee?"

I could feel Ellis stiffening beside me. "Um—no, thank you," we chorused.

Ellis leaned forward. "He didn't leave any word at all?"

Al Evans shook his head. "That incident with his friend Mrs. Culpepper really bothered him, I could tell. Seemed to blame himself. Of course I tried to tell him it wasn't his fault . . . I just wish I knew where he was."

I looked at Ellis and she nodded. "I know where he is—at least he was there yesterday," I said, and told him about my experience seeing Melrose DuBois at a north Georgia outlet mall.

"Well, if that doesn't beat all!" Al sighed. "I shouldn't be too surprised, though. Melrose seems to have developed some strange habits lately."

"Like what?" Ellis wanted to know.

"Secretive little things—like he'd go off by himself and not bother to say where he was going, what he was doing." Al shrugged. "Not that it really mattered. He's a grown man and it's his business how he spends his time. But I guess you could say Melrose made an issue out of not making an issue."

"I guess we'll have to tell the police about your seeing Melrose at the mall," Ellis said as we left.

I agreed. I was sort of holding out for Idonia's sake to see if he turned up. I had left another message for Kemper earlier, asking him to call my cell phone number, and when it rang, I thought the policeman was getting back to me. But it was Zee on the other end and I could tell she was trying to sound calm. It didn't work.

"Lucy Nan, I can't seem to find Idonia. Do you have any idea where she might have gone?"

Chapter Nineteen

"What time is it?" Ellis asked when I told her what Zee had said.

The clock on my dashboard said four o'clock, but then it always says four o'clock since it stopped running two years ago. I looked at my watch. It was a little after one.

"Has Zee gotten in touch with Idonia's niece Jennifer?" Ellis said when I told her the time.

"She didn't mention it, but surely Jennifer would know if Idonia has decided to take off to Savannah or something."

"She wouldn't go to Savannah. You know she wouldn't," Ellis said.

I did know it and so I didn't even bother to phone Jennifer at the high school but drove straight there. Luckily, Jennifer was on her lunch break when we arrived and when we explained the situation to the school secretary, she paged her right away.

"She assured me she was all right when I phoned her yesterday," Jennifer said when she met us in the office, "but frankly, I thought she sounded pretty stressed out. Are you sure she's not at the house?"

"Zee rang the bell and pounded on the door and she's tried to reach her by phone several times," I said.

Jennifer hesitated briefly then spoke with the secretary. "I have a key to Aunt Idonia's house. Just give me a minute to get my purse," she told us, hurrying back to her classroom. Fortunately, we learned, the secretary had been able to find someone to take her last class.

Ellis phoned Zee as we followed Jennifer to Idonia's and told her to meet us there. I wasn't surprised when Jo Nell and Nettie showed up as well.

"Did you check to see if her car's here?" I asked Zee when she skidded to a stop out front.

"Of course, but she always keeps it in the garage and I couldn't see inside," she reminded me.

"I told Idonia she was doing too much too soon," Jo Nell announced as we waited for Jennifer to unlock the door, and although my cousin is the world's greatest worrywart, this time I tended to agree with her. I tried not to think of our friend lying cold and still across her bed or crumpled on her kitchen floor, and I must've had Ellis's arm in a death grip because she cried out that I was cutting off her circulation.

A lopsided spray of drying evergreens tied with a red plastic bow rattled as Jennifer opened the door and stepped inside while the rest of us hovered briefly on the threshold as if our entering would bring the news we didn't want to hear. The house was quiet and dim except for the light from a table lamp Idonia always kept burning in her family room. A holiday edition of a popular women's magazine lay open in the seat of the worn green recliner where Idonia liked to sit. A pink poinsettia drooped in its pot on the coffee table and I stuck my finger in the soil. Idonia had overwatered it as usual.

"Aunt Idonia!" Jennifer called, softly at first and then more urgently until the rest of us began to take up the cry as we made our way through the house. There was no answer.

"She must have gone somewhere," Zee muttered, and nobody answered, probably because we were all thinking the same thing: *I hope she's gone somewhere.*

Idonia's bed had been neatly made and a still-damp towel was tossed over the shower curtain rail as if she had left it there in a hurry, which was most un-Idonia-like. The kitchen was clean and uncluttered except for a fat red candle surrounded by a wreath of pine cones that Claudia had given her for Christmas the year before on the kitchen table and a tin of cookies on the counter. Nettie lifted the lid and looked inside. "Charleston squares. Mattie Durham," she said. And we all nodded in agreement because Mattie always brought Charleston squares when anybody was sick.

Although I knew our friend had been there as recently as the day before, or even later, the house had an abandoned, neglected look, and it made me sad.

"Car's not here," Jennifer called out, looking into the connecting garage, and I felt weak with relief.

"Do you suppose she's just out running errands?" Zee said. "Lord help us if she is when she finds we've invaded her house!"

"No, here's something on the dining room table," Jo Nell called. "Looks like she's left a note."

Jennifer's name was on the outside of the envelope and she hurriedly ripped it open and read the contents, then silently held it for us to see. Idonia's usual neat handwriting could pass for an example in penmanship, but this note was written hastily on one of those greeting cards you receive unsolicited in the mail, and we sighed in unison when we read it: *Gone to meet Melrose. Don't worry. Be back soon.*

Jennifer sank onto a nearby chair. "Has she lost her senses? She doesn't even say where she went."

"Or why," I said.

Ellis and I exchanged looks before she spoke. "I don't want to alarm everybody, but Al Evans said Melrose has been acting kind of strange lately, and he didn't seem to know what to make of it. I don't like the idea of Idonia going off to meet him like this."

I agreed that Al had seemed worried about his cousin, and now I was worried, too, especially when I remembered that Idonia had seen Melrose hurrying from the church the night Opal was killed.

Jennifer's face was white. "Good Lord!" she said when I told them. "Why didn't she say something? Do you think he might have had something to do with what happened to Opal Henshaw?"

"He could've had other reasons for being there," Nettie reasoned. "Still, I think it's time we talked to the police about this."

Jennifer was already calling the number.

Guilt rode with me like a specter all the way to the police station. From what Al Evans had told us, Melrose might be unstable, and now Idonia had gone rushing off to meet him and we had no idea where she'd gone. I also wanted to wring her neck for making us worry like this.

Beside me, Ellis echoed my very thoughts. "I'm going to kill Idonia if that Melrose doesn't get to her first!" she said.

I shuddered. "Ellis Saxon! Hush your mouth!" It sounded awful when somebody spoke it aloud. I wished Augusta were with us, but just then it was more important to speak with the police.

"And I'd like to jerk a knot in that idiot Elmer Harris as well," Ellis added as we pulled into the parking lot behind the station. "That man doesn't have the sense God gave a billy goat!"

The chief had told Jennifer that because Idonia was a grown woman and had left of her own volition, he couldn't issue a missing person's bulletin. Besides, he added, he wasn't sure she'd been gone twenty-four hours yet. He did perk up when we told him she'd gone to meet Melrose, and asked us to let him know if we heard from her.

"Let's hope Kemper's here or Ed Tillman," I said as the six of us marched inside, an avenging army brandishing purses.

"There he is!" Jo Nell shouted, ignoring Paulette Morgan, the dispatcher who sat at the front desk, and I knew news of our arrival would be all over town in less than an hour.

Kemper seemed to cringe when he saw us, then immediately put up a bold front. "We need to talk," I said as we gathered around his desk. And supported by the others, I told him about seeing Melrose at the outlet mall in Commerce and how Idonia had glimpsed him hurrying from the church the night Opal Henshaw died.

"I'm beginning to think Idonia's gone off the deep end," Zee added. "She's completely bonkers about this man and she doesn't know a blessed thing about him."

Kemper sighed. Well, really it was more of a groan. He rubbed his face and then rubbed it again as if he could hide from us behind his hands. "Sit down, please," he said. I noticed someone had brought the required number of chairs, and so we did.

"It really would have been helpful if you had come to us with this earlier," he said, and he seemed to be staring straight at me.

I tried to explain that I *had* left a couple of messages for him earlier and that I didn't know Melrose had left town until I spoke on the phone with Idonia on my way to Georgia a few days before. That's when Kemper told us several choir members had seen a person of Melrose's description at the church the night Opal Henshaw was killed.

"Don't forget to tell him about the locket, Lucy Nan," Nettie urged me.

Kemper picked up a pencil and put it down. "I'm assuming you're talking about the locket that went missing the night your friend was drugged."

"Right," I said. "I don't suppose you've found it."

He shook his head. "What about the locket?"

"We think it's the same one the Tanseys' daughter, Dinah, is wearing in a photograph on their piano," I began.

Kemper leaned back in his chair and folded his hands over his stomach. He seemed to relax for the first time since we arrived. "Just because it looks like that doesn't mean they're the sa—"

"The Tanseys' daughter was married to Dexter Clark, the man who was killed out at Willowbrook," I said.

"Just how do you know this?" Kemper sat upright so fast I thought he might catapult over the desk.

I didn't answer. *Just let him stew awhile*, I thought.

Ellis spoke quietly. "And Dexter Clark was Opal Henshaw's nephew," she said, meeting his gaze.

"It's in Opal's obituary in today's *Messenger,*" Jo Nell said.

Kemper picked up the phone. "Paulette, see if you can round up Captain Hardy—and you'd better put on another pot of coffee, too."

"You have several messages on your answering device," Augusta told me when I finally got home later that afternoon.

"Do you know who they're from?" I asked. (Of course I knew she did. I don't want to say Augusta's nosy. Let's just say she's extremely curious.)

"Two are from your friend Ben. I think he wants you to call him, and your daughter-in-law, Jessica, phoned to ask how much fabric she would need for the curtains *you're* going to make for her." Augusta didn't even try to hide her smile as she poured some of her wonderful apricot tea into the fragile violet-flowered cups that had belonged to my grandmother. I turned on the tree lights in the living room and we sat on the sofa to drink it.

"I'm too tired to answer them now," I said, kicking off my shoes. "And you know very well I have no idea how much fabric she'll need."

Augusta patted her lap and Clementine came up and laid her big head there. "She gave her window measurements and I wrote down the yardage she'll need and left it by the phone," she said, stroking the dog's soft ears.

"Augusta Goodnight, you're an angel!" I said, raising my cup in salute. She flushed, but I know she likes it when I say that. "I just wish you could tell us where we could find Idonia," I added.

Augusta listened quietly as I told her about finding the note from Idonia and our subsequent meeting with several of Stone's Throw's finest. "Have they changed their minds about trying to locate Idonia?" she asked. I could tell she didn't want me to know she was worried, but the stones in her necklace turned cloudy when she touched them.

I told her I had heard Kemper tell Captain Hardy he was going to talk with Al Evans again and try to get some idea about where Melrose might have gone. The captain was heading out to Willowbrook to speak with the Tanseys.

"Melrose must have phoned Idonia sometime yesterday," I said, "and Kemper even suggested trying to trace the call, but Melrose had obviously used a cell phone.

"Jennifer has left a message for Idonia's son, Nathan, in case she turns up there but I seriously doubt if she went to Savannah. Poor Nathan! He must be a basket case by now. I wouldn't be surprised if he showed up on our doorstep tomorrow."

"You said yourself Idonia was looking forward to singing in Sunday's musical program at your church," Augusta reminded me. "I fully expect her to be back before then."

I wish I could've believed she meant it.

Ben and I had discussed going out that night and taking in a movie, but after all my running around in search of Melrose, then Idonia and our talk with Al Evans, I was more inclined toward a quiet night at home. Ben picked up a recent comedy on

DVD and we ordered a pizza and spent the evening in front of the television.

"I'm dying to find out what the police learned from the Tanseys but I know they won't tell me," I said, polishing off my second piece of pepperoni with extra cheese. "I'm sure it must have been one of the Tanseys who took Idonia's locket, but why do you suppose it's so important? I wish I knew where it really came from."

Ben poured another glass of wine. "There's one person who might be able to help you."

"I can't imagine who. We've questioned just about everybody we could think of."

He picked up my copy of *The Messenger* and turned to the article that included Opal's obituary. "Not everybody. What about Opal's brother, Terrance Banks?"

"The one who lives in Tennessee? I don't think they were especially close. How do you think he could help us?"

"Don't forget, this Dexter Clark was his nephew, too," Ben said. "He might know more about the relationship between Dexter Clark and the Tanseys' daughter than you give him credit for, including how she came by the locket she wore. After all, Opal's sister, Maisie, was Dexter's mother, and the boy's parents are both dead. This uncle seems to be the only one left to ask."

"Knoxville's a big city," I said. "How am I supposed to find him?"

Ben finished the last wedge of pizza before he spoke. "Opal's funeral's tomorrow, isn't it? Surely her only brother will be there."

Chapter Twenty

I was trying to decide what to wear to Opal Henshaw's visitation when Claudia phoned the next morning. "Sorry I didn't get back to you last night," she said, "but I was late getting home from the staff party. What's all this I hear about Idonia going off like that?"

I told her what Idonia's note had said and how we had gone to the police.

"Where in the world do you reckon she went? Have you heard anything more?"

"Not yet, but I'm hoping she'll get in touch with Jennifer or Nathan," I said. "Did you have a chance to talk with that girl who goes to the Tanseys' church?"

"Helen Harlan. She said Louella was at choir practice when Idonia's locket was stolen. They had an extra rehearsal that night to get ready for Christmas."

"So much for that theory," I said to Augusta, after assuring Claudia I'd let her know if I heard any more. "I was sure Louella Tansey was the one who took that locket."

Augusta clicked the remote and put her video exercise on pause. "Why Louella?"

"You saw the film from Ralph Snow's camera the same as I did," I said. "Remember how he focused on people in the entrance hall toward the end of the evening? The only men who even came near those stairs were our minister, Pete Whittaker, and Andy Collins, the man who plays the dulcimer, and I can't imagine why either of them would snatch Idonia's locket. The rest were women."

Augusta resumed her ritual, bending to touch one foot and then the other. "Perhaps, as Ben suggests, Opal Henshaw's brother will be able to explain the significance of the locket. I hope there will be an opportunity for you to speak with him at the service this afternoon."

"Or even earlier," I said. "Ellis and I will be on the lookout for him at the visitation this morning, and some of us will be staying to serve lunch to out-of-town friends and family who show up." I had taken one of Augusta's pound cakes out of the freezer and Jo Nell was bringing her "Joyed-It" jam cake to serve with the fruit and sandwich trays we'd ordered.

I saw Ellis's car pull up out back before I even put on my makeup and glanced at the clock to see if I was running late. "You're early," I said as she breezed in through the kitchen, stopping to drop the latest Sarah Strohmeyer mystery on the table.

"This is such a good read, I thought Augusta might like it," she said, helping herself to a slice of banana bread left from breakfast. "I know I'm early, but thought maybe you might've heard something from Idonia."

"Nothing yet but it's still early. I'd give anything to know what went on out at the Tanseys' yesterday."

Ellis plopped on the side of my bed and examined her leg. "Damn! I've got a run in these blasted pantyhose. Got an extra pair?"

I tossed her one of several I had invested in at the Budget Shop and she kicked off her shoes and shimmied into them. "I'll bet I know somebody who might tell us something," she said.

"If you mean Weigelia, there's not enough time in the day to drag it out of her."

She grinned. "Not if you have the right bait. She's been after me for ages for that old photograph my great-uncle Pruitt made of one of the first black schools in town way back when he had a studio here. I'll have a copy made for me and let her have the original. She ought to have it anyway since a couple of her grandparents went there."

I blotted my lipstick and found some simple gold earrings I thought suitable for the occasion. "Go for it," I said, hunting for my purse. "But don't take long. We want to have plenty of time to track down Opal's brother Terrance."

I brushed my hair and changed shoes three times before Ellis finally hung up the phone. "Well?" I said.

"I don't think she knew much more than we do, but Weigelia said Kemper seemed kind of upset about it. He went out there with Alonzo Hardy after they talked to Al Evans and it sounded like the Tanseys were pretty torn up over it. From what Kemper said, she—Louella—got all weepy, and Preacher Dave just turned kind of pale and clammed up."

"What about Jeremiah?"

Ellis shrugged. "I don't think Jeremiah was there at the time."

"Are they planning to arrest anybody?" I said.

"Doesn't sound like it. I doubt if they have enough evidence—yet, but Weigelia thinks something's brewing."

I hadn't been to Willowbrook since the morning Ben and I went there for my Christmas tree and were greeted by ghostly music. "I know they've boarded up the house, but I'm still curious about those hidden stairs. Wonder if the police ever checked that out again."

"If they didn't, I'll bet they will now," Ellis said.

Opal Henshaw and her late husband Virgil had belonged to Stone's Throw Presbyterian Church for as long as I could remember, and I was baptized there, so the line to pay condolences had already snaked out the door of the fellowship hall and people were clustered on the walkway by the time Ellis and I arrived. I passed my cake along to one of the circle members in charge of today's lunch and turned up the collar of my coat to wait along with the others, waving to Nettie and Jo Nell who were ahead of us in line.

As we shuffled slowly along I caught snatches of murmured conversation about the circumstances surrounding Opal's death, and since most people knew we were in the choir, Ellis and I received several sympathetic pats and words of condolence for having experienced the trauma of finding her.

Oohs and aahs of approval rose when Geraldine Overton passed us on her way in the fellowship hall with an arrangement of daisies and white chrysanthemums for the table, and Ellis poked me from behind. "Opal will be whirling in her grave when she finds out that's not artificial," she whispered.

Out of the corner of my eye I saw Myra Jennings and her daughter Alice working their way up to where we stood and wasn't surprised later when I felt a firm grip on my arm.

"I heard Idonia Mae had a frightful scare the other night out at Bellawood," Myra bellowed loud enough to wake those in the cemetery behind the church. "Is she going to be all right?"

I saw Ellis bite her lip and look quickly away. "Yes, thank you, Myra. She's doing fine."

Alice stuck her face so close to mine I could tell she'd had sausage for breakfast. "What was the matter with her? I heard she was *poisoned!*"

"It was something she ate, but Dr. Smiley says she's going to be okay," I said. Thank goodness the line surged forward just then and Ellis and I were able to inch inside the hall and leave them behind. If these two heard Idonia had disappeared, we'd never see the last of them.

"I think somebody's trying to get your attention on the other side of the room," someone ahead of us said, and I looked up to see Nathan Culpepper waving to us from the table by the kitchen where coffee was being served.

"Maybe he's heard from Idonia," Ellis said as we hurried over together, but as soon as I saw his face, I knew the news wasn't good.

"Any word?" I asked, trying to shield him from curious eyes.

"Nothing." Nathan sighed. "I don't know what else to do. I'm about ready to get in my car and start scouting the countryside." He poured coffee for Ellis and me and offered it silently. "The police told me you saw this Melrose fellow in Georgia. What was he doing there?"

"Beats me, unless he was doing the same thing we—uh—I was, which was trying to find out more about the Tanseys. I believe he was in Soso about the same time I was there. That's where the family lived before they came to Stone's Throw, and later he turned up at the mall in Commerce."

Nathan frowned. "And why, if I might ask, did you decide to go there?"

I took my time stirring sweetener into my coffee before answering, wondering all the while if Idonia had told Nathan there were doubts about the locket's origin, but as Nettie would say, the shit had already hit the fan. There was no holding back now.

"We think the locket Melrose gave your mother for Christmas might have originally belonged to one of the Tanseys," I began.

"You mean the man *stole* it?" Coffee sloshed as Nathan set down his cup.

"I don't know about that, but Dave Tansey was helping to park cars at Bellawood the night your mother was drugged and we believed there was a possibility a member of his family put that sleeping mixture in her drink," I said. "I thought if I talked with some of the people who knew them in Soso where he lived before, we might find out something about their background. After all, they're living out there at Willowbrook where a man died recently from a suspicious fall from a balcony." I didn't go into the fact that Dinah Tansey had been married to him.

"And Preacher Dave was seen at the church the night Opal died," Ellis added.

"Then, by God, why don't they arrest the man?" Nathan spoke so loudly several people turned to stare and Ellis and I hustled him into the kitchen where a couple of women from our circle arranged food on platters. I noticed that Anna Caldwell had brought her cream cheese salad with pineapple, apples, and pecans and hoped there might be at least a smidgen left for us.

We assured Nathan that the police probably didn't have enough evidence to arrest anyone yet but we had it on good authority (Weigelia's) that it would only be a matter of time.

"Meanwhile, my mother is who-knows-where with a man who might be not only a thief but a murderer as well!" he said.

Ellis was trying to convince Nathan to go back to Idonia's and wait in case his mother returned or tried to contact him there when the people who had been in line behind us signaled to tell us they had almost made their way to the front. As we hurried over I looked back to see him disappear through the door to the main part of the church and hoped he didn't intend to find Dave Tansey and confront him.

Ellis looked over my shoulder as we waited to speak to what was left of Opal Henshaw's family. "Which one do you think is her brother?" she whispered.

I shook my head. There were only a few people in the receiving line and none of them looked familiar to me.

I introduced myself to a matronly woman who looked as if all she wanted to do in this world was to sit down, and I didn't blame her. She turned out to be the sister of Opal's husband, Virgil, who died the summer before, and the younger man standing next to her, I learned, was her son. The son's wife, a teenaged boy, and two smaller girls comprised the family.

"Can you believe Opal's own brother didn't even come to her funeral?" Ellis said as we made our way back to the kitchen to help with lunch. "We'll have enough food left over to feed the multitudes."

And enough of Anna's salad left for us, I thought, eyeing the creamy squares on a platter of crisp green lettuce. But how were we going to get in touch with Opal's brother in Knoxville?

I kept an eye on the door the whole time we served the family, hoping that Terrance Banks would put in an appearance, but he didn't show. Ellis and I stayed after the meal to divide what was left of the food to take to some of the shut-ins in the community so the main sanctuary was full when we arrived for the service and we were directed to the balcony. Thank goodness we didn't have to sit on the first row because the only thing I could think of was poor Opal Henshaw tumbling over the railing.

Ellis nodded toward the area where Opal would have been standing, bending over the railing to reach the lopsided swag. "Can you imagine being shoved from behind like that?" she said under her breath. "Poor unsuspecting Opal!"

A shiver came over me as I looked involuntarily over my shoulder for some wicked unseen hand. Thank goodness Cissy, our organist, began playing softly, and since the hymn was "Nearer My God to Thee," I thought, *Maybe being in the balcony might have an advantage. Of course, I didn't want to be quite as near to God as Opal was, just yet.*

I was reading the memorial program when the family was ushered down the aisle to sit in the first pew so I didn't pay much attention to them until Ellis nudged me. "There's seven," she whispered.

I frowned. "Seven what?" All I could think of was that old tale, "Seven in One Blow," about a man killing flies, and I didn't see what that could possibly have to do with Opal's funeral.

"Seven *people*," she said. "There were only six for lunch."

I shifted to get a better look, and sure enough there was an extra man down there. *Oh, please, let him be Terrance*, I thought. He looked to be about the right age with graying hair and a slight balding spot in the back. A brief graveside service was scheduled for immediately after this one and in spite of the rising winds and falling temperature, I was determined to see Opal Henshaw all the way to the end.

"Let's sneak out the side door," Ellis suggested as the service ended, and I nodded in agreement. If we could get to the cemetery ahead of the others maybe we could station ourselves to head off Terrance when it was over before he could get away.

"Listen," I said as we stood for the family to recess. "Cissy's playing 'Oh, Come All Ye Faithful,'" and I felt tears welling in my eyes in spite of myself. Opal might have been aggravating at times, but nobody could ever say she wasn't faithful.

Chapter Twenty-One

Huddled together in the sparse protection of a large sycamore in the corner of the Henshaws' plot, Ellis and I waited for the family to be seated under the green canopy with Evans and Son in white lettering on the side. Al Evans, who didn't have a son, or at least any he was claiming, had been using the same awnings since his father died at least ten years ago and they were beginning to show the effects of the elements.

Al himself escorted the family of Virgil Henshaw's brother, carefully holding the arm of his wife as she made her way down the graveled path from the sleek black limousine, and I wondered if he had heard any more from his cousin, Melrose. As the town's decorous undertaker, Al Evans would hardly take to the idea of having criminal kin, and if Melrose *had* been responsible for what happened to Idonia or Opal, he might be inclined to cover it up, I thought. After all, isn't covering things up what undertakers do best? The more I pondered the idea, the more I suspected that Al might even have been the reason his cousin left town. But if so, why had they involved Idonia?

"What are you frowning so about, Lucy Nan?" Jo Nell said as she joined us. "I noticed your scowl two plots away."

"Tell you later," I said, keeping a watchful eye on Al, who seemed to be looking back at me, or I thought he was looking at me. It was hard to tell.

"We're going to try and have a word with Opal's brother when this is over," Ellis told her. "He's the one in the gray overcoat sitting on the end. It's important, so don't let him get away."

"Good grief, you talk like he's going to make a run for it or something." Jo Nell drew a fluffy white beret from her coat pocket and pulled it over her ears. "What's so important that you need to speak with him?"

We didn't have a chance to answer as everyone grew quiet when the minister began reading a passage from *Psalms*.

I looked at the people gathered around the grave site to see if Nathan Culpepper was among them but he wasn't there. I hoped he had taken our advice and gone home instead of tearing off on the warpath as he seemed inclined to do.

Beside me Jo Nell was standing first on one foot and then the other and I supposed she was either trying to keep warm or she had to go to the bathroom. Mercifully, the service was brief and those attending paid hurried respects to the family before rushing to the warmth of their nearby vehicles.

The cemetery emptied quickly but the three of us stayed behind while Opal's brother held a quiet conversation with Al Evans.

"I wish I knew where Al was going when he leaves here," I whispered. "He looks like he's hiding something, don't you think? Kind of like he has a guilty secret."

"I guess he'll be going home to get warm like everyone else. The poor man can't help it if he has a glass eye," Jo Nell reminded me.

Just then the two men turned and noticed us there, pausing as if they expected us to join them, so we did.

"I wonder if we might have a few minutes of your time," I said to Terrance Banks after the three of us introduced ourselves. I looked pointedly at Al but he stood there as if he had no immediate plans to leave until Terrance offered him his hand.

"I'll drop by before I leave," Terrance said. "And thank you again for taking care of things."

"It's freezing out here," I said after Al finally left us. "Why don't we go inside where we can be more comfortable?"

Terrance nodded, looking puzzled. "You knew my sister Opal, then?" he said, walking along beside us. The wind lifted his scarf as he glanced back at the open grave. His face looked lined and sad.

"Oh, my, yes!" Jo Nell said. "And Virgil, too. It's not going to seem the same without them."

"I'm a good five years older than Opal," Terrance said, "so we weren't very close growing up, and I regret that. My sister was probably around fourteen when I left home, and frankly, we didn't have a lot in common." He sighed. "I wish I had made more of an effort to stay in touch."

I thought about my own brother, Joel, whom I adored but hadn't seen in months and promised myself I would phone him in Oregon as soon as I got home.

We found the church parlor empty and quickly shed our coats in the warm confines of the room after coming in from the cold. Terrance settled on one end of the mauve-striped love seat and leaned forward, hands on his knees. "If any of you have any idea about the circumstances of my sister's death, I'd like to hear it," he said. "The police seem to think it might not have been an accident, but they haven't been able to pinpoint a motive or give me any kind of explanation." He drew in his breath. "I'd like to get to the bottom if this."

"And so would we," Ellis said. She told him how we had found Opal the night of our Christmas choir rehearsal and how Margaret had tried to revive her.

His voice was bleak. "But it was too late. She was already dead. What in God's name was she doing up in the balcony?"

"Straightening an evergreen swag," Jo Nell said. "It was crooked, you know."

"I see." A smile played on Terrance Banks's lips. "She would, of course. I realize my sister could be a bit—uh—overbearing at times, but I don't understand why someone would want to kill her."

"Neither do we," I said, "but there seems to be some kind of connection to a family here, the Tanseys, and a locket that belonged to their daughter."

Disbelief was obvious in his face. "What does a locket have to do with it?"

"That's why we wanted to talk with you," Ellis said. "Opal told the girl's mother that a locket identical to the one belonging to her daughter had been in her family for years. We thought you might remember it."

He frowned. "Do you know what it was like?"

"Gold with a raised design of a dogwood blossom—" I began.

Terrance nodded. "Set with six small pearls. It belonged to my grandmother, but Mother passed it along to the older of the two girls, my sister Maisie. I remember Maisie wearing it when she married, but I don't know what happened to it after that."

"I think I do," I told him. I hesitated to bring up the subject of Terrance's nephew, Dexter Clark, especially since I would have to be the bearer of bad news, but it couldn't be avoided.

Noticing my hesitancy, Ellis jumped in. "Your sister Maisie's son, Dexter, was married to the Tanseys' daughter, Dinah. Dexter must've given her the locket as a wedding gift."

Terrance nodded. "Or his mother did—probably as an engagement gift. That sounds like something our Maisie would do. She died several months before the two married." He frowned. "My sister spent the last years of her life worrying about Dexter, and I don't doubt for one minute that his behavior hastened her death." Terrance paused as if weighing his words before continuing. "It's a terrible thing to say about my own kin, but Dexter always was a sorry sort, reckless and rebellious—didn't give a damn about anybody but himself. What happened to his young wife was a senseless tragedy! I didn't even know it had happened until months later when I learned about it from a friend, and well . . . I just couldn't believe it."

"Believe it," I said. "He didn't even bother to tell her own parents until she was dead and buried."

"God only knows what Dexter's up to now," Terrance said. "I heard he got religion after that happened to his wife, and I hope it's true—we'll see. Called me not too long ago, left a message he wanted to get together, but I hadn't had a chance to get back to him. I reckon he just wants money. Far as I'm concerned, it's just as well Maisie's not around to worry about it."

Ellis and I exchanged glances, hoping Jo Nell would volunteer to deliver the grim news, but she was preoccupied with folding her scarf in neat accordion pleats and wouldn't even look up.

"I don't think you're going to have to deal with Dexter anymore," I said, and told him what had happened at Willowbrook.

Terrance Banks didn't speak but sat for a minute with his hand supporting his forehead. Despite his harsh words about his nephew, he seemed to be genuinely upset. Maybe he was thinking of happier times when Dexter was small. Had he read to him from *Winnie the Pooh*? Given him a tricycle for Christmas? Probably not, I thought. The man hardly seemed the cuddly uncle type.

"And you think this locket might have had something to do with my sister's death?" he said finally. "Why?"

"I'm sure you knew about Opal's bed-and-breakfast?" Ellis said, and Terrance nodded, wondering, I'm sure, what connection that might have with Opal's quick descent from the church balcony. "One of her guests," she continued, "a fellow named Melrose

DuBois, somehow came by that locket and gave it to a friend of ours for Christmas . . ."

"We can't be sure," I said, "but there's a possibility that he showed the locket to Opal before making a gift of it to—"

"And don't forget to tell him about Opal's fruitcake run," Jo Nell offered.

I frowned at her. "I was getting to that," I said. "A few days before Opal was killed, she and another member of our church circle took fruitcake and cookies to Dinah Tansey's family. You see, Dinah's father, Dave Tansey, is the sexton at our church. During the visit Opal noticed a studio photograph of Dinah on the piano, and she was wearing that locket in the picture."

"Did Opal ask the woman about it?" Terrance said.

"Yes, of course," I said, "but she was told that the locket in the photograph had been in the Tansey family for years and that it was probably one of several."

"Not so!" Terrance rose abruptly and walked to the window where he stood looking out at the playground where empty swings swayed eerily in the wind. "We were told our grandfather had that locket made especially for our grandmother for their wedding day with the date of their marriage inscribed on the inside." He turned and looked at us. "The woman was obviously lying, but why? Her daughter came by the locket honestly. It's not as if she stole it."

I didn't have an answer for that because it puzzled me as much as it did him.

"But that same night somebody did steal the locket from Idonia," Ellis said, and told him how our friend's punch had been doctored during the open house at Bellawood.

When Terrance spoke it came as a growl deep in his throat. "And a few days later my sister *accidentally fell* from the church balcony. And what, may I ask, are the police doing about this? I assume they've questioned these people—these Tanseys."

I replied that they had and I thought the police probably had a suspect in mind.

Apparently tiring of the view from the window, Terrance began to walk, making a circuit of the sofa, three chairs, and a table holding the ugly glass lamp Opal Henshaw herself had donated a few years before. I had to look away to keep from getting dizzy.

"It looks like an open-and-shut case to me," he said. "This family holds my nephew responsible for their daughter's death, and he ends up dying under suspicious circumstances on the property where the Tanseys live. When Opal identifies the locket as the one worn by our grandmother, they deny any connection to their daughter's marriage to Dexter. Seems to me they didn't want anybody else to know about it either—especially the police."

"But they know now," I said.

"And what about this Melrose you spoke of? Has anyone asked him how he came by the locket?"

Jo Nell spoke up. "Guess they would if they could find him," she said.

"Oh, Lordy! I thought we'd never get away from there!" Ellis wailed as we finally left the church. "First Nathan and now Terrance! Maybe between the two of them, they'll track down whoever's responsible for all this."

More power to them, I thought, circling the cemetery where Terrance had gone to inspect his sister's grave, now heaped with the fresh flowers she had considered a frivolous expense.

"Where are you going?" Ellis looked at her watch. "The day's almost gone and I need to run by the store."

"Thought maybe I might see Al Evans here but I guess he's gone on back to the funeral home," I said. "Ellis, I wonder if he knows where Melrose is."

"Why would he?"

"Well, think about it. If Al's cousin Melrose had anything to do with what happened to Opal, it wouldn't do a whole lot for his professional image."

Ellis dug in her handbag for a notebook and pen. "Maybe not, but I don't know how you could prove it. Could we stop by the market? I need to pick up oranges and coconut for the ambrosia."

So much for that notion, I thought. Idonia had been gone over twenty-four hours and all Ellis could think about was her Christmas menu. Yet I knew I needed to do the same. Julie would soon be home for the holidays and she would expect all her favorite goodies.

I was making out a grocery list in my mind when Ellis interrupted my thoughts. "Do you still have a key to the Green Cottage?" she asked.

"You mean the house where the Tanseys live? I think there's one in that box of things that belonged to Mimmer, but surely you're not suggesting—"

Ellis shrugged. "How else are we going to look for the locket?" she said.

I felt the same sensation in my stomach I remembered from the summer we were ten and she assured me it really wasn't that far to jump from the pear tree to the garage roof. I had to wear a cast on my ankle until September and missed out on swimming the rest of vacation.

"And how do you plan to make the Tanseys disappear?" I asked.

"Tomorrow's Sunday, isn't it? And I happen to know the congregation at Preacher Dave's church is having their Christmas program tomorrow night."

"What do we do about Jeremiah?" I asked. "He might not be the church-going type."

She shrugged. "I guess we'll have to cross that bridge when we come to it."

And maybe it was my imagination, but I could swear I felt a pain in my ankle.

"I'm not going unless Augusta comes, too," I told Ellis as we loaded groceries into my car.

She wedged the last bag in the trunk and slammed the lid. "She isn't going to like it—poking about in somebody's house when they're not there. You know how straitlaced Augusta can be."

"However, I sometimes make exceptions," Augusta said from the backseat. "Did you remember to get cranberries? I thought I'd make that salad Julie likes so much."

Chapter Twenty-Two

"Are you serious?" I asked Augusta as the three of us drove the few blocks to drop off Ellis and her groceries. Searching someone's home without permission is frowned upon in most earthly tribunals, so I could only imagine how it would go over in even *higher* courts.

"I can't think of any other way," Augusta said, speaking in a matter-of-fact manner. I glanced at Ellis, who chewed her bottom lip, a sure sign she was reasoning we might have jumped in over our heads. I thought of my two children and six-year-old grandson coming to visit me in the penitentiary and almost ran a red light at the corner. It surprised me that Ellis and I seemed more concerned about our planned illegal venture than our virtuous guardian angel.

"Of course, there's no need for the two of you to be involved at all," Augusta continued. "I could go there tonight—or even sooner. I see no reason to wait."

I pulled into Ellis's driveway and threw on the brakes. "Now, just hold your heavenly horses!" I said. "I'm the only one who's ever been in that house, and I know the layout. Besides, whose idea was this, anyway?"

"I do believe it was mine," Ellis reminded me. "And I agree with Augusta, the sooner we find out about that locket, the better. We haven't heard from Idonia since day before yesterday, and for all we know she could be locked up there somewhere, or even worse—"

I didn't want to hear the "even worse" part. "But how do we know the Tanseys aren't there? What if one of them walks in?"

"I've thought about that," Ellis said. "It would seem reasonable for you to have a key since your relatives own the property, and you could always give some excuse or other like . . ."

I waited. "Like what?"

"Like—uh—well . . . measuring for new countertops or something," she said. "Maybe the sink drips or the toilet runs. Can't you just make up something?"

"I'd rather not," I said.

"And you shouldn't have to," Augusta assured me. "Not when you have me to do your recon—reconnais—preliminary survey of the area."

I smiled. "I'd hate to be the one to lead you into a life of crime, Augusta."

This time the angel didn't smile back. Her words were solemn and her voice, sad. "You must be aware there is someone in this town who holds human life in little regard. This person has killed twice, and I don't believe they would hesitate to do it again. If I have to make this choice to prevent another such loss, then so be it."

"Hooray, Augusta!" Ellis applauded. "Just give me time to put away my groceries."

Although it was only six o'clock, it was dark when we started out a short time later, which wasn't surprising since the day before,

I remembered, had been the shortest day of the year. At Augusta's urging we stopped at a fast-food drive-in for milkshakes, although nobody seemed to be hungry but her.

"Your body needs fuel to go on," she reminded us.

The plan was for Augusta to find out if any of the Tanseys were at home. If not, using my grandmother's key, Ellis and I would enter and search for the locket we were almost certain was somewhere inside the house while the angel kept watch.

This time, Ellis drove and I sat in the passenger seat beside her holding an untouched milkshake in my lap. Augusta had ordered fries with her strawberry shake and sat in the backseat dipping each one in ketchup as she ate. Although I enjoy junk food as much as anybody, the greasy smell of the fries was causing a small uprising in my stomach.

"I don't see how you can sit back there and eat like we don't have a care in the world," I told her. "Aren't you even the least bit nervous?"

Augusta finished the last fry and dabbed her lips daintily with a paper napkin. "Think blue, Lucy Nan," she reminded me. "Take a deep breath, close your eyes, and think of a calm and beautiful place—a summer sky, a peaceful lake, a gentle stream."

Well, I tried, I really did, but all I felt was a tornado forming somewhere in my middle, and the closer we got to Willowbrook, the more I hoped we would find the Tanseys at home.

We didn't. The yellow-painted cottage sat bordered by huge oaks at the end of a lonely road, and the only thing that stirred on our approach was a gray squirrel scurrying across the grass in search of something to eat. The garage that housed the family's two vehicles was empty.

Ellis brought the car to a stop and parked boldly out front as if we had a right to be there. "Maybe you should go to the door and knock—just in case," she said, turning to me.

But holding up her hand, Augusta signaled for us to stay and silently slipped from the car. We watched as she walked up to the front door, hesitating for only a second before she disappeared inside—at least I assumed she was inside, although the front door never opened to admit her.

What would we do if any of the Tanseys drove up just then? What would we say? A hundred explanations came to mind but none was believable. I might be able to lie convincingly to Preacher Dave or Louella, I thought, but what could I say to Jeremiah?

The cottage, the yard, the car where we waited was shrouded in darkness now and I felt the bleakness of it creep into my head and inch its way down. I was afraid of Jeremiah Tansey.

"I guess they've all gone to church to rehearse for tomorrow's program," Ellis said, looking over her shoulder. "I hope it takes a long time." She shivered. "Why is Augusta taking so long in there?"

As if in answer, the angel suddenly slid into place in the backseat. "There's no one there now," she said, "but I wouldn't take too long if I were you. And it might be wise to move the car somewhere out of sight. Is there anywhere nearby where we could conceal it?"

"You mean so we could make a quick getaway?" I said. For some reason I wanted to giggle.

"What about that old shed just down the road? We could walk from there," Ellis suggested.

Or run, I thought, thinking more of the return trip. Mimmer had said the shed had once been used to weigh and store cotton, back when the fields were planted with cash crops, but now the sagging building contained only rusting pieces of outdated farm machinery and extra salt blocks for the cattle.

I watched for lights approaching the whole time Ellis turned back onto the road and drove the few yards to park behind the shed. In warmer weather weeds surrounding it would be so high it would be difficult to walk, but now dry grass only whispered under our feet. Ellis used a flashlight to find the narrow pathway through a thicket of trees and underbrush to the back of the Tanseys' cottage. Preacher Dave and others before him often used it as a shortcut to the shed and the cattle gate to the pasture across the road.

"I haven't the faintest idea where to start looking once we get inside," Ellis said as we made our way through the sparse woods Indian style. The moon was obscured by clouds, which was an advantage in a way because it gave us the cover of darkness, but it was difficult to see where we were going. I walked behind Augusta, keeping my eyes on the golden gleam of her hair.

"I suppose it depends on who took the locket as to where they might hide it," Augusta said. "Or, if they believe no one will come looking for it, they might not hide it at all."

I hoped we would be that lucky. A glance at my watch told me it was almost seven o'clock already and I didn't want to spend any more time in that house than necessary.

With Augusta stationed out front to alert us if anyone approached, Ellis and I let ourselves in the back door and stepped into a small laundry room that opened onto the kitchen. I felt like the guilty intruder I was and resisted the impulse to turn and run, but I knew Ellis would never let me forget it. "Okay, I'll take Jeremiah's room and you search his parents'," I said, feigning bravery.

"Be sure to leave everything the way you found it," she warned me, knowing some of my more careless habits. "We don't want them to even suspect we were here."

I had brought a container of Augusta's homemade candy—divinity, of course—and hurried to slip it among the packages under the family's small artificial tree just in case we were caught. If we were lucky, however, the Tanseys would never know who brought it.

The cottage was built in the Cape Cod manner with a half

story upstairs, which I assumed to be Jeremiah's, and as it turned out, I was right. The enclosed back stairway off the kitchen led to a long, narrow room with two dormer windows facing the front of the house. At least, I thought, from here I would be able to see the lights of an approaching car.

Jeremiah, it seemed, lived a rather Spartan lifestyle if it could be judged by the furnishings in his room, which contained a single bed, dresser, small table, and straight chair. On the wall across from his bed, shelves held a large television set with all the electronic attachments including a DVD, CD player, and speakers. But from the looks of my surroundings, I didn't think he spent much time there, and who could blame him? A computer sat on the table next to the bed and I was tempted to turn it on to learn if there was anything of interest there, but I'm just now getting accustomed to the one I use at Bellawood, and I didn't want to take a chance on messing with this one.

I didn't dare turn on a light so I used a flashlight to look through Jeremiah's dresser drawers which I found to be surprisingly neat. I don't even pretend to know a lot about current fashions for men, but I recognized some expensive brand-name clothing in Jeremiah Tansey's closet. For someone who worked as an unskilled laborer for a fencing company in nearby Rock Hill, he seemed to spend more on his wardrobe than my professor son, Roger. But being single and living at home, I reasoned, why shouldn't he?

Downstairs I could hear Ellis moving quietly about and when I was sure the locket couldn't possibly be in Jeremiah's room, I took one more look around, closed the door behind me, and went downstairs to help.

A glance out the living room window showed Augusta still keeping watch out front, wrapped to the teeth in her cape, and hugging herself for warmth, and I reminded myself to hurry as I knew she hated being cold.

"I found a box with a few earrings and a necklace or two in there but not much else," Ellis said, stepping from the couple's room. "I hope Santa Claus brings Louella a gift certificate for some decent clothes for Christmas. The contents of that woman's closet is just plain dismal."

"Sounds like she could take some pointers from Jeremiah," I said, and told her what I'd observed upstairs. Of course I knew I'd be the very last person appointed to snoop for the fashion police, I told myself as the annoying virtuous part of me waggled a finger, but I couldn't help what I saw.

It took the two of us several minutes to examine the contents of the curio cabinet in the dining room, being careful not to drop the souvenir cups, plates, and doodads from various vacation spots. I didn't dare to touch the lovely hand-painted cake plate that was displayed on the top shelf or the dainty china teapot beside it. Besides, it was obvious the locket wasn't here.

"What now?" I asked after a search of the buffet drawers proved disappointing. "Guess there's nothing left but the kitchen."

Ellis frowned. "Isn't there a small room on the other side of it?"

"You mean the pantry?"

"No, behind that," she said. "Looks like it's been added on."

"Oh, right! I forgot about that. One of the former tenants built it for his mother, but lately, I think it's just been used for storage."

"Sounds like a likely spot to hide a locket." Ellis pushed open the swinging door from the dining room and hurried through the kitchen, stopping abruptly at the closed door of the added room. "Damn! It's locked!" She tried the knob again, shaking it. "Well, this should tell us something. Now we'll never know if it's in here or not."

"Of course we will. We might not be able to get inside," I reminded her, "but I know somebody who can."

Augusta was so happy to be invited in out of the cold, she practically rushed inside in a blur and didn't even hesitate to debate the issue when Ellis told her we wanted her to let us into a locked room.

Ellis snatched up the jacket she had cast aside earlier. "I'll keep watch until it's open," she said, hurrying toward the front of the house. "Just try to hurry, please!"

But that last admonition proved unnecessary because Augusta had the locked door open before Ellis had crossed the room.

"Dear God!" I sighed, looking past her. And Augusta, who dislikes hearing anyone take the Lord's name in vain, barely made a face.

"What is it?" Ellis rushed to see and stood fixed in the doorway, her fingers fastened onto my shoulder. The small area in front of us contained the furnishings of a young girl's room, including a large rag doll in a rocking chair and an open book on the bed. In the narrow closet we found a limited array of clothing appropriate for a teenaged girl, and just about every space on the wall was covered with photographs of Dinah Tansey throughout most of the stages of her brief life.

Chapter Twenty-Three

"It seems to be some kind of shrine," I said, standing transfixed in the doorway. "How sad!"

"And creepy." Ellis walked over and looked closer at the book. "They've even left it open to mark the place as if she'll be back to finish reading it."

"What was she reading?" I asked, leaning over to see the title. I wasn't surprised to see Daphne du Maurier's *Rebecca*, which I had read a number of times during my teens.

"It's almost as if she never left," Ellis said, looking around.

"She didn't," I reminded her, "because she was never here. Dinah married Dexter Clark soon after high school before her parents even moved to Stone's Throw. She never saw this room."

So far Augusta had not spoken but I saw that she had stepped back from the doorway and now stood in the kitchen. The stones in her necklace, I noticed, were lusterless and dark. "I don't have a good feeling about this," she said. "I think we should leave right now."

"But we haven't even looked in here," I said, opening a drawer in the chest next to the bed. "If the locket is in this house, wouldn't this be the natural place to keep it?"

"Please, Augusta! We're so close. I'm sure we can find it." Ellis looked at the kitchen clock. "See, it's not even eight yet. Just give us a little more time."

The angel sighed. Her earlier confidence and enthusiasm seemed to have vanished into the night. "Very well, I'll be waiting out front, but do look quickly. However, I don't believe you'll be finding anything there."

"Well, Augusta was right . . . there's not much here," Ellis said, shutting a desk drawer a few minutes later. "I haven't seen anything but some old schoolwork, a couple of paperbacks, and a few letters."

I had found the dresser drawers to be almost empty as well except for a few pairs of stockings, underwear, and a modest bathing suit. "I guess this is what Dinah left behind when she ran off to marry that loser." I shoved the drawer back into place. "I can't understand what she saw in him. What a waste!"

While Ellis searched the closet, running her hands over shelves and crevices, I checked for a hiding place in the bedding, feeling under the mattress and pillow with no success. "Let's get out of here," I said finally. "This place is depressing."

Several pairs of shoes made a neat line across the closet floor and Ellis examined them one by one before carefully putting them back into place. "I'm with you," she said, and froze with her hand on the closet door. Someone was in the kitchen.

Heart thudding, I knelt behind the bed as close to the floor as I could get, but if one of the family was there, surely they would notice the door to the locked room was not only unlocked, but open.

Whoever was in there was now opening the refrigerator door and I heard the clanking of jars being shifted about. I dared to glance across the room at Ellis, who was attempting to flatten herself against the wall.

Something squeaked. An oven door? This was followed by a puzzling period of silence. I was working up the courage to make a dash for it when I heard another noise, one I couldn't identify, but it warned me the person was still there.

Ellis held a finger to her lips and began to move silently toward the door, hand out, as if she meant to close it quietly, when someone shouted, "Ah!"

I recognized that "ah" and it sounded even more heavenly than usual. Augusta! I jumped to my feet and joined her in the kitchen, where she stood at the counter holding something in a small plastic bag. "Ah!" she said again. "I thought I'd find it here!"

She had taken the top from the canister that held flour and the white powder lay scattered like snow on the countertop.

"What is it? Is it the locket?" Ellis reached for the bag. "It *is!* Won't Idonia be surprised when she sees it?"

But Augusta was already cleaning away the mess she had made and now she held out her hand for the locket. "We can't do that, Ellis. We have to put it back right away or they'll realize we've been here."

All this trouble for nothing! I thought. "So why look for it if we have to put it back?" I fumed. "At least let's open it and see what's inside. There must be a reason this is so important to somebody."

But the only thing we found inside was a yellowing photograph of a bridal couple and the engraved date of their marriage, just as we had been told. Augusta quickly buried the locket once more, replaced the top, and in an instant the countertop was gleaming. "Now that we know who took it, it will serve our purpose better to let the police discover it here," she said, quickly rinsing her hands at the sink.

Ellis frowned. "But we really don't, do we?"

"Don't what?" I asked.

"Know who took it," she said. "It could've been any of the Tanseys."

I watched as Augusta made sure the door to "Dinah's room" was locked, and one look told me she was wearing her "secret" face. "You know, don't you?" I asked. "You know who took the locket."

"Well, *who*? Don't keep us in suspense," Ellis said.

Augusta busied herself bundling up in her cape before stepping out into the night. "I'd rather not say until I'm sure," she said.

I hurried after her. "But how did you know where to look? What made you think to check the flour canister?"

"Why, I read it in a mystery," she said.

We had only walked a few steps from the house when Augusta stopped suddenly in front of us, her hand lifted in warning.

"What is it?" I asked, untangling my sleeve from a briar.

The angel spoke quietly. "I don't think we're alone out here."

I listened. "I don't hear anything," I said. It was hard to see in the darkness and I hadn't seen or heard a car approaching.

"Oh, come on, Augusta. It's freezing out here!" Ellis grumbled. "I think we're all on edge, and it's getting late. Let's just hurry and get home."

We couldn't very well spend the night standing out here in the woods, I thought, and was relieved when Augusta finally moved on.

The three of us walked as quickly as we could but it was impossible to be quiet, at least for Ellis and me, as we seemed to step on every brittle twig in our path, and dry leaves rattled in our wake.

Was there someone else in the woods? Augusta wasn't the type to be alarmed for no reason. Had one or more of the Tanseys returned and were now waiting to confront us here in this lonely place?

I was soon able to make out the dark outline of the shed just ahead of us, and Ellis and I started to run to the safety of the car parked behind it. But again Augusta signaled us to stop.

And that was when I saw them. In the clearing beside the shed two figures waited as if they intended to block our way to the car. It was too dark to see their faces but they didn't appear to be trying to hide. It was almost as if they *wanted* us to see them.

Should we run? Try to escape? Terrified, I looked to Augusta for advice.

"Uh-oh!" she said.

Uh-oh? What kind of angelic response was that? Of course she didn't have to worry, I remembered. Whoever waited for us wouldn't be able to see *her*, which would leave them free to concentrate on Ellis and me.

One of them spoke. "You might as well come on out. We know you're there."

As soon as I heard the voice, the fear that had formed a huge icicle in my middle began to thaw—a little.

"I hope you have a good reason for being out here," Kemper Mungo said.

Someone shone a flashlight in our faces. "Miss Lucy Nan? Miss Ellis? This isn't a very good place for you ladies right now." Speaking softly but sternly, Police Lieutenant Ed Tillman, my son's boyhood friend, came out of the darkness to meet us. "I'm going to have to ask you to explain why you're here," he said.

"Fine, as long as we can do it someplace where it's warm," Ellis said.

I agreed. The wind had picked up and the athletic shoes I wore to sneak around in weren't doing a very good job of keeping my feet warm. Augusta, I noticed, had vanished altogether.

We wound up sharing a Thermos of coffee in the police cruiser parked off the road not too far away. Augusta was somewhere close by. I sensed her presence and knew she'd never desert us even if she couldn't testify on our behalf in court. Ellis concentrated on relishing her steaming beverage and looked to me to take all the heat. And that was when I decided to tell the truth. Sort of.

"We went by to drop off some homemade candy but the door was locked," I said. "I hated to leave it outside—it's divinity, you know, and moisture just ruins it, so I just let myself in—"

Ed Tillman frowned. "How?"

"With a key, of course. My cousin owns the place and sometimes asks me to look in to see if everything's all right—with the tenant's permission, of course."

Well, that was an out-and-out lie. I could just imagine Augusta flinching.

"But the Tanseys weren't at home?" I could barely see Ed's face, but there was a question in his voice.

I let that hang in the air for a minute. "I thought I might find Idonia's locket," I said finally.

Kemper cleared his throat. "In other words, you searched the house."

Ellis, seeing my dilemma, finally jumped in—and about time! "Just looked around a little, that's all," she said.

"You must have known you were breaking the law," Ed said. "And what made you think the Tanseys had Mrs. Culpepper's locket?"

I couldn't believe these two were as thickheaded as all that, but this wasn't the time to say so. "Who else would have taken it?" I asked. "That locket was given to the Tanseys' daughter, Dinah, when she became engaged. There's a picture on their piano of her wearing it."

The two men exchanged looks which I took to mean they *thought* they knew something we didn't.

“I don’t suppose you found it,” Ed Tillman said.

I let that one hang, too, until the silence got too much for them.

“Are you trying to tell us you *did*?” This from Kemper.

“Well, you did ask,” Ellis reminded him. “What do you want us to say?”

Ed—or somebody—drew in his breath. “Then I’ll have to ask you to turn it over to us. That locket could be used as evi—”

“We don’t have it,” I told him.

“Then just where is it?” Ed was getting impatient.

Ellis finished her coffee and nudged me. “Should we tell them, Lucy Nan, or let them find it for themselves?”

I considered suggesting we make a game of it like I do with Teddy, letting them know when they’re getting hot or cold, but my better instincts took over. “Oh, for heaven’s sake, it’s in the flour canister,” I said.

“They never would’ve found it,” Ellis said on the drive home.

Augusta spoke from the backseat. “Probably not. You did the right thing, Lucy Nan. Now it’s their time to hit the ball.”

I smiled to myself in the darkness. The ball was in their court, all right, if they would just pursue it. After a serious lecture on the dangers and repercussions of what we had just done, we were warned to stay on our own side of the fence, so to speak, and leave the detective work to the professionals.

“What do you think they were doing out there?” Ellis asked as we turned into my driveway on Heritage Avenue.

“I think they were on a stakeout,” I said. “From what Weigelia tells me, Jeremiah seems to have cut and run. They must’ve been waiting for him to show up at home.”

“I’ve read all about that,” Augusta said. “It’s called ‘casing the joint.’ ”

Now that the police knew where to find the locket, I thought, the next step would be to obtain a search warrant, and it occurred to me we hadn't even told them about the locked room.

Ellis must have been thinking about it, too. "I was hoping we'd find at least some clue as to where Idonia might be," she said. "Tomorrow's the program of Lessons and Carols and she'd never miss that—not intentionally, anyway."

"Hey! It's not over till it's over," I said. "Maybe Nathan's heard from her by now." I didn't like the way this conversation was going.

"Isn't that a car parked over there by your hydrangea bush?" Augusta said as Ellis pulled up to the back steps.

I leaned forward to get a better look. Were the Stone's Throw police casing our joint, too? I had left the porch light burning and even with the headlights from Ellis's car, it was hard to distinguish one make from another. Julie wasn't due home for another couple of days and even in this poor light I would recognize her little red Honda.

"I think we'd better get out of here," Ellis said, and gunned the accelerator to back away, but Augusta leaned over to touch her on the shoulder. "Wait. It's all right," she said.

We watched as the driver's door of the strange car opened and a figure stepped into the light. "Where in the world have you been? I've been waiting out here for hours," Idonia said. "I thought you'd never get home!"

Chapter Twenty-Four

"And we'd like to know where *you've* been," I said, running to hug her. "Are you all right? We've been worried to death!"

Idonia practically shoved us up the steps. "First, I *have* to go to the bathroom, and then I'd really like something hot to drink. It's freezing out here."

"Does Nathan know where you are?" Ellis asked after Idonia's needs were taken care of. "He's been out of his mind wondering if you're okay."

Idonia waved that aside while she dunked an orange spice teabag in a cup of steaming water. "Oh, I left a message on his cell phone. He knows I'm all right."

"But does he know where you are?" I asked, and I was almost sure of the answer. If Idonia's son knew she was here he'd be in this kitchen with the rest of us.

"Well, you see . . . that's the thing . . ." We waited while she stirred sugar into her cup. "He'll have all these questions and it's late and I'm really tired." Idonia smiled coyly, which is *not*—I repeat, *not* her usual manner at all. "I'd rather not have to deal with Nathan until tomorrow."

Ellis was turning red in the face, which meant she was about two seconds away from giving Idonia Mae Culpepper a serious piece of her mind, but she'd have to get in line behind me. "Well, you're going to have to deal with us," I said. "Where on God's green earth have you been for the past two days?"

"Melrose felt uneasy about my staying here in town after what happened at Bellawood, so he arranged for me to meet him at this lovely little inn this side of Raleigh," she said.

Ellis frowned at her across the table. "You've been with Melrose all this time?"

Idonia sipped her tea before speaking. "Oh, it was all very proper, you understand—separate rooms and all."

"I don't give a rat's ass if you and Melrose made out on the courthouse lawn!" I said. "Would it have taken too much of an effort to give at least one of us a call?"

Alarmed at the tone of my voice, Clementine scurried into the sitting room where I knew Augusta waited to calm her. If only she could calm me!

Idonia spoke serenely as if she were addressing a small child, one who isn't very bright. "But that would defeat the purpose, wouldn't it? The object, after all, was for me to remain out of sight until all this has been cleared up." She tucked a stray lock of red hair into place and cleared her throat. "Of course I insisted on returning for tomorrow's Christmas service, although Melrose was dead set against it. But I just told him, 'Melrose,' I said, 'I haven't missed taking part in our Christmas music program for over thirty years, and I don't intend to start now.' "

Idonia drained the rest of her tea and stood. "And now, if you don't mind putting me up for the night, I'd like to get some sleep. I was going to ask Nettie for that spare room upstairs but she must've already gone to bed as I couldn't get her to come to the door. You know, I wouldn't dare mention this to Nettie, but I believe she's getting quite deaf."

Ellis, who also stood, held up a hand. "Whoa!" she said. "Do you realize, Idonia, that the police are looking for Melrose DuBois?"

The woman seemed genuinely puzzled. "Now why would they do that?"

"Let me count the ways," I said, listing them on my fingers. "First, he was seen at the church the night of Opal Henshaw's murder, and left town soon afterward—"

"*Murder?*" Idonia gasped.

"We're pretty sure it was deliberate," I said, continuing. "Also, he lied about that locket he gave you, which, if you'll remember, belonged to the Tanseys' daughter, Dinah, who was married to Opal's nephew Dexter Clark . . ."

"Remember him?" Ellis said. "Dexter was the fellow we found under the balcony at Willowbrook—deader than a doornail. The police are kind of curious to find out how Melrose came by that fascinating piece of jewelry."

Idonia sat again. "I've asked him about that, and there's a perfectly good explanation, if you'll—"

"Idonia, if you know where Melrose is, I think you'd better tell us," I said.

She looked down at her hands in her lap. "You'll know soon enough. He plans to be at church in the morning . . . and Melrose didn't know anything about that locket, I promise!"

"But why the disappearing act?" Ellis asked. "And why isn't he with you now?"

Idonia shook her head and smiled. "He has his reasons. You'll see. And now, if you don't mind, I really need some sleep."

"Only if you make a phone call first," I told her, and Ellis and I stood on either side of her while she spoke with Nathan, who happened to be staying at Idonia's. I could hear Nathan Culpepper's stormy ranting from a few feet away.

"He wants to speak with you," Idonia said, handing me the

phone, and I assured Nathan that his mother was safe with me and that I would deliver her to church in the morning. And then I laughed.

"What's so funny? What did he say?" Idonia asked.

"He wanted to know if I thought you were getting even with him for that time he played hooky in junior high," I said.

Idonia's eyes widened. "Nathan *played hooky* in junior high?"

Ellis left soon afterward and Idonia was settled in the guest room for the night when I remembered there was something I meant to do. I looked at my watch. What time was it in Oregon? It didn't matter. I picked up the phone and called my brother, Joel, whom I hadn't seen in almost a year. He plans to come for a long visit soon after the holidays.

It was late when, after a long chat with Joel, I finally crawled into bed and I should've dropped right off to sleep, but the events of the day kept playing in my mind. Idonia was safely back, thank goodness; the local police were aware of where the missing locket was hidden, and it looked as if they would make an arrest soon. Or as soon as they could locate Jeremiah Tansey. Had it been Jeremiah who buried the locket in the flour canister? Augusta seemed to think she knew who had put it there, but she wasn't sharing her secrets.

When at last I drifted off to sleep I dreamed of a young woman I took to be Dinah Tansey, only the Dinah in my dream was even younger than the girl in the photograph. She lay across a bed in a room with yellow walls and white curtains at the window and she was crying. It wasn't at all like the room we had seen at the Tanseys' cottage except for the locked door. But in my dream the door was bolted from the inside.

"There's something I want to run past you when we get a chance," I whispered to Ellis in the choir room the next morning. With Idonia there I hadn't been able to discuss with Augusta what was on my mind, and we had to rush to the church after a hurried breakfast.

Ellis adjusted her stole and mine. "We have an hour break between services. Maybe we can sneak away to the parlor. Can it wait till then?"

I nodded. I guessed it would have to.

"Will Augusta be in the congregation this morning?" Ellis asked, checking to see if her music was in order.

"You might not see her, but she'll be there both times. You know how she loves Christmas music," I said. "And Idonia says Melrose is coming, too."

Ellis sniffed. "He'd better!"

But try as I would, I couldn't find Melrose DuBois among the people attending the Lessons and Carols program although I scanned every row while our minister read the scriptures, and again during the offertory until I felt my eyes would cross.

Idonia's son, Nathan, sat in the second row flanked by his wife and daughter and I don't believe he took his eyes off his mother for one second. I didn't blame him. Idonia had a nervous, distracted look as if she wanted to bolt at any minute. A few days ago she had been pleased when she heard Nathan would be bringing his family, and now, after hours of rehearsals, all she could think of was the absence of one Melrose DuBois. God help him if he didn't show up for the eleven o'clock service, I thought, because if the police didn't track him down, I would!

Ellis closed the door to the parlor behind us and, kicking off her shoes, curled up on one end of the sofa. "What's going on?" she asked. "Has Idonia heard any more from Melrose? She seems in a bad way—did you notice? I'll swear, if that little jerk doesn't show up for church this morning I'm going to wring his neck."

"Let's hope he's there at eleven," I said. "He'd better not be leading her on! I felt bad about leaving her there in the choir room. I know she wondered where we were going."

"Maybe some of Cissy's turtle bars will cheer her up," Ellis said.

Our choir director always baked her fabulous cookies made with chocolate, brown sugar, and pecans to go with the other goodies choir members brought to eat between Christmas services. Most of us, I've learned, will grab any chance to have a party and I hated missing this one, but I needed somebody to tell me I wasn't crazy.

"Ellis," I began, "I had the strangest dream last night. Have you ever wondered if Dinah Tansey might still be alive?"

"Lucy Nan Pilgrim, you are totally, absolutely, and undeniably crazy!" my friend said. "What makes you think a thing like that?"

I told her about my dream and reminded her that Dinah's family wasn't told of the girl's death until after she was buried. "What if she never died?"

Ellis frowned. "Then who's buried in her grave?"

"Maybe there isn't any grave. Maybe Dinah Tansey is the ghostly woman who haunts Willowbrook."

"Now wait a minute, Lucy Nan, let's don't get carried away. You aren't thinking she actually lives in that room we found? Dinah would be in her twenties now and the clothes we found, everything was for somebody much younger."

Someone passed by the door and Ellis waited to continue until the footsteps went away. "And why in the world would she do it? She'd have to be—well, you know—"

"Crazy," I said. "I wish there were some way we could find out for sure."

"I believe there is."

I looked up to see Augusta standing before us. "The music this morning was lovely," she said. "But if you want any of those refreshments, you'd better hurry. I'm afraid the others have already taken care of most of it."

"How?" I said.

Augusta glanced at herself in the mirror that hung over the sofa. Today she wore a garment of what looked like golden filigree over a deep green satinlike dress that swirled when she walked and brought out the turquoise depths in her eyes. "How what?" she asked.

Today I had little patience with her vanity. "How can we find out if Dinah Tansey Clark is really dead?"

"If what I've read is correct, they have to issue a death certificate when someone dies. If you can find out where she was supposed to have died, they should have one on record," she said.

"Augusta Goodnight, you're a genius!" I threw my arms around her and sensed her serenity like a balm. "But how are we going to learn that?"

"Preacher Dave would be the most likely source," Ellis said, "but if she really isn't dead and the family is keeping her there in secret, he certainly isn't going to tell us the truth."

"Soso," I said, remembering my conversations with Aunt Eula and her kin in the small Georgia town. "Dinah was a friend of the Shackelfords' daughter Carolyn. Maybe she kept up with her after she married. I'll call Aunt Eula as soon as we get home."

But I immediately shoved that to the back of my mind when we processed into the sanctuary for the second time that day and that scumball Melrose DuBois was nowhere in sight.

"I'm worried about Idonia," Jo Nell had confided when we met briefly in the ladies' room earlier. "First she disappears and now she looks like she's about to jump out of her skin. It's that Melrose again, isn't it?"

"He's supposed to show up at one of the services this morning," I explained. "Idonia said she had his word on it."

"Ha!" Jo Nell snorted, letting the door slam behind her.

Ben smiled up at me from an aisle seat and I smiled back remembering he would be taking me to lunch after church at one of those new steak restaurants out on the highway. Roger sat near the front with Jessica and Teddy, and Julie would soon be home for Christmas. If only things would work out for Idonia! How rude and inconsiderate of that pipsqueak Melrose to put a damper on our holidays!

Nathan Culpepper stationed himself by the choir room door as soon as the service was over and I remembered that he expected his mother to go back to Savannah with him for Christmas. I wasn't surprised to find Idonia waiting for me as I hung up my robe. "Lucy Nan, you've got to help me," she said. "I can't leave with Nathan today—I just can't! Something's happened to Melrose, I know it."

I could see that this was not the time or the place to try and convince her that Melrose DuBois might not be the knight in shining armor she thought him to be. Instead I sent frantic eye signals to Zee and Jo Nell who stood behind her putting their music in appropriate stacks according to Cissy's directions, and Jo Nell, bless her heart, came over and put her arm around Idonia.

"We're so glad to have you back," she said. "Don't you dare scare us like that again!" And Idonia, ever the one with the stiff upper lip, began to cry.

"Honey, he's not worth it," Zee said with tears in her own eyes. "If the man's going to make you unhappy like this, you're well rid of him."

"You don't understand. He's in trouble—bad trouble, and if we don't find him, it might be too late." Idonia accepted a tissue and used it accordingly.

"What kind of trouble?" Ellis asked. "I thought you said you knew where he was."

"I did yesterday. It's today I'm worried about. I'm afraid he's gotten in over his head." Idonia sank onto the nearest chair. "Melrose has good intentions—I know he does, but he has no idea who he's dealing with, or, I'm afraid, how to go about it."

"How to go about what?" I asked.

Idonia took another tissue and shook her head. "Detective work. He's been taking a correspondence course in how to become a private investigator, and he says he's on the trail of the person who drugged my punch and stole the dogwood locket. Melrose thinks it's all tied up with the murder of that man you all found at Willowbrook and what happened to poor Opal Henshaw."

And Idonia Mae Culpepper began to cry anew.

Chapter Twenty-Five

"Please don't worry, Idonia," I found myself saying. "We'll work it out somehow. I think it's time to bring the police into this, and you're going to have to tell Nathan what's going on."

"Tell Nathan what?" Suddenly Nathan was standing beside us, and I saw Ben in the doorway behind him wondering, probably, what was taking me so long.

"Look, all of us have to eat lunch," I said. "Unless you have other plans, why not meet somewhere and discuss this calmly? Ben and I were thinking of Big Jake's out on the north end of town."

"I'm not hungry," Idonia said.

"Well, I am," Nathan told her, "and Big Jake's sounds just fine to me."

And so it was decided. Ellis had family coming for lunch, Claudia had already left for home, and Jo Nell was expecting some of her husband Paul's kin to drop by, but Zee and Nettie joined us at a table for eight, which included Sara and Millicent, Nathan's wife and daughter. Over two hours later when just about everyone else had left the restaurant and the busboy began pointedly sweeping under our feet, Nathan finally agreed to stay in Stone's Throw one more day to await news of the whimsical Melrose DuBois. Idonia, however, was to take her story to the local police.

"Lucy Nan, you will come with me, won't you?" she said when leaving the restaurant. "I mean, after all, you were at Bellawood when the locket was taken, and you said you saw Melrose at that mall in Georgia. Besides," she added, "those Tanseys, who seem to be mixed up in all this, work for your family, don't they?"

Well, what could I say? If there was ever a time a friend needed support, this was it, and besides, I was dying to find out what had happened after we left the Tanseys' place the night before.

Ben, who would be leaving that afternoon to spend Christmas with his son Greer in Atlanta, kissed me briefly before we left in separate cars. Because Greer is in his last year of residency at Emory University Hospital, he wasn't able to get away, and Ben didn't want him to be without family, even though they might not have a chance to spend much time together. "See you in a few days," he whispered, as I drove away, and I grew warm at the thought. We had agreed to exchange gifts at a ski resort in North Carolina in early January, and the fact that neither of us knew how to ski didn't bother us a bit.

Earlier I had phoned Eula Shackelford in Soso and left a message for Carolyn to call me at my cell phone number, but as yet she hadn't returned my call.

I found a familiar vehicle in the parking lot behind the Stone's Throw police station and a familiar figure in it. I wasn't surprised when Ellis got out of her car to join me in mine. "Zee called and told me you all would be here," she said, "but you might as well just stay where you are because they won't let you in the room while they talk to Idonia."

"Then how am I supposed to give her comfort and support from out here?" I wailed, settling down to wait.

"I hope they don't arrest her for being an accomplice—or,

what is it? An accessory after the fact," Augusta said from the backseat, startling both Ellis and me.

"Good grief, Augusta! You just about scared me to death," I said. "And that's not even funny."

"I didn't mean it to be," she said. "But I believe she'll be all right. Her son seems a solid sort, and I expect she'll be glad of his presence after all."

With eyes on the door where we hoped our friend would soon emerge, we settled in to make the best of the situation, and had been there only a few minutes when my cell phone rang.

Carolyn Shackelford Haney had a voice as rhythmic and full of humor as her mother's and I could hear a baby trying very hard to talk in the background. I told her I was looking for someone who had kept in touch with Dinah Tansey after her marriage to Dexter Clark, who might know where she died and was buried.

"It was somewhere in North Carolina," she said, "but I can't think of the name of the town. I kept several of her letters though, and if you'll wait just a minute, I'll go get them. I know Mama wouldn't throw them away."

I was going to tell her I would call her back, but she had already gone in search of the letters. A few minutes later I heard hurried footsteps approaching. "It was Asheboro," Carolyn said breathlessly. "I should've remembered because we drove through there looking at furniture once and I went to visit her grave."

"So you actually saw where she was buried?" I asked.

Carolyn didn't speak for a minute and when she did it was with emotion. "Dinah and I were friends since the fifth grade, but it was about a year after she died that I got a phone call from Dexter telling me what had happened. He cried, wanted to see me, to talk, I guess—seemed to be sorry . . . I don't know, but I did come. I came for Dinah. She was a gifted musician, you know. Played the piano and the flute. Dinah could've done something with her life. Instead she—" Her voice broke.

"That must have been a tragic experience losing a friend like that—and one so young," I said. "Carolyn, there's a reason I'm asking you this, but I need to know when Dinah died. Do you remember the date?"

"I sure do. It was April 17, 2002, the day my nephew was born. The little dickens was three weeks early."

I thought of the beautiful young girl dying too soon, and although it made me sad, it also made me furious. This could've happened to my own headstrong daughter, Julie. It might happen yet. "I'm so sorry," I said. "It seems like such a waste. What on earth do you suppose made her go off with somebody like Dexter Clark?"

Carolyn hesitated before she spoke. "I think she did it to get away from that house," she said.

But when I asked her what she meant, she wouldn't say any more.

"How do you know Dinah was really in that grave?" Ellis said when I repeated our conversation.

I hadn't thought to ask Carolyn if there had been a stone. "We'll have to wait until tomorrow and call about the death certificate," I said. "All the county offices will be closed on Sunday."

"No, we won't," Ellis reminded me. "Now that we know where and when Dinah was supposed to have died, we can access that on a computer."

Augusta sighed. "Glory be! I should've thought of that."

"I wish we had one with us," I said. Now that we were this close to learning the truth about Dinah's death, I couldn't bear to wait.

"What about your friend who works for the college?" Augusta asked. "Wouldn't she have one of those machines?"

"Claudia! Of course. I know she used to do a lot of freelance work from home," Ellis said. "Let's hope we can catch her before she goes off somewhere."

We were in luck. "Ohmygosh! Do you really think she might not have died? Wait a sec, let me turn off this food processor." Claudia, I learned, was in the middle of making clam dip for a family party. "I can look it up now if you can hold, or did you rather I call you back?"

I was going to tell her we'd wait when Ellis let out a shout, "Here she comes!" And I looked up to see Idonia coming out of the building with Nathan and his family.

At least they didn't arrest her, I thought. Not yet, anyway. "Idonia's just leaving the police station, and as far as I can tell, she's not in handcuffs," I told Claudia. "Just give me a call on my cell phone when you know something, okay?"

"Will do, if you'll fill me in on Idonia," she promised.

Nathan, I noticed, had a firm grip on his mother's arm and she signaled frantically for us to follow them as they left the station and turned in the direction of Idonia's house.

"I'll ride with you," Ellis said when I hesitated to follow. "We don't want to lose them."

Nathan's wife and daughter were leaving Idonia's as we drove up; they had things to do to get ready for Christmas, Nathan explained. He and his mother, he added, would be following them in the morning.

Augusta accompanied us inside, then disappeared, but I knew she was there listening. Like Ellis and me, she couldn't bear not to know what was going on.

Yawning, Nathan excused himself to take a short nap, as, he said pointedly, he didn't get much sleep the night before.

Good, I thought. Now Idonia can tell us what went on during her interrogation with the Stone's Throw police.

She didn't waste any time. "Bless his heart," she said as her son left the room. "I'm afraid he's a bit miffed with me."

"He'll get over it," I said. "What did the police have to say? They didn't tell you not to leave town, did they?"

Idonia sighed. "Oh, I wish! They really wanted me to tell them all about Melrose."

"And did you?" Ellis asked.

"I told them all I knew. Of course, I don't know where he is now. I wish I did!" Idonia went to the window and peered out at the empty street. "I'm afraid I was a little harsh on them, but Melrose is in trouble. I know he is, and they keep acting as if he's done something wrong!" She pulled herself up to her full stature and gave the curtains a jerk. "I told that simpleton Elmer Harris if he'd concentrate on finding the real killer instead of picking on innocent people, they would've cleared this up by now."

Idonia paced to the mantel and paused just long enough to adjust a candlestick. "And I'm not the only one who feels that way. Paulette Morgan—you know Paulette—dispatcher over at the police department—anyway, she told me Opal's brother was in there yesterday carryin' on something terrible about what happened to Opal. The man's no fool. He knows good and well it was murder."

I wasn't surprised. From what Terrance Banks had said when we spoke with him the day before, he was as determined to get to the bottom of this as we were.

"What else did they want to know?" I asked.

Idonia perched on the arm of a chair and spoke so softly I had to strain to hear her. "They asked where he got the locket."

I leaned forward. "Where did he get it?"

"From some booth at a flea market in Charlotte." Idonia flushed. "Oh, I know Melrose stretched the truth—okay, he told a whopper about it being a family heirloom and all, but he wanted it to be special, you see. He had no idea it had belonged to the Tanseys' daughter."

"And to Opal's family before that. I'm surprised Opal didn't mention it to him," Ellis said. "Didn't he show it to her?"

Idonia nodded. "Told him her grandmother or somebody like that—had had one just like it. She wanted to know where he got it, but of course he didn't want to admit it came from a flea market. Silly man! Didn't he know it wouldn't have mattered to me where it came from?"

Idonia turned away, I thought to hide her tears, but she stood and spoke with new resolve. "I want to speak with Al Evans. When Melrose disappeared after Opal died the police took a box of his belongings from the Spring Lamb. They turned it over to Al after they looked through it since he's his closest kin. I'd like to know what's in there."

Ellis grinned. "Lucy Nan thinks Al's been hiding Melrose. Thought they were in cahoots together."

"I did not!" I shot her a dirty look.

"Did, too! After Opal's funeral you wanted us to follow that poor man home. You know you did, Lucy Nan."

"Well . . . I thought he might know where Melrose was," I admitted.

"I wish he did," Idonia said, "but there might be something in the notes Melrose made that would give us an idea where to find him. I know he kept a notebook from that correspondence course he was taking. It's got to be in there."

I remembered what Idonia had said about Melrose taking a course in detective work and offered to bring her the box.

"I'll come with you," she said.

"Idonia, if Nathan wakes from his nap and finds you gone, I won't be responsible for what he might do," I told her. "If you'll call Al and tell him we're on the way, we'll be back before you can say, John Robinson."

"That's Jack Robinson," Ellis said as we left. "You've been around Augusta too long."

I heard her laughter before Augusta appeared on the backseat.

"I heard that," she said, "and who is this Robinson fellow anyway?"

My cell phone rang before I could answer but all I could hear was a football game in the background. "Brian, honey, turn that thing down!" Claudia hollered in my ear. "Sorry to be so late calling you back but my sister phoned right after I spoke with you, and I thought I'd never get away. You know how Gina is!"

I said I knew and what did she find out about Dinah Tansey?

"It was her all right. Died April 17, 2002. She was only nineteen, Lucy Nan. No wonder her mama looks so sad." And Claudia sounded close to tears herself.

"So Dinah's really dead," Ellis said when I told her. "Then who's been wearing those long dresses to try and frighten people at Willowbrook?"

And why? I wondered. And which of the family had created a shrine to Dinah's memory in a locked room?

Chapter Twenty-six

Idonia waited at the front door and Nathan was still asleep when we returned with the box of Melrose's belongings.

"The police must not have found anything of interest in here or else they wouldn't have given it to Al," I said as Idonia set it on the dining room table and hastily pulled off the lid. "If there's a clue in there to all that's been happening, you'd think they would've followed up on it."

Idonia frowned as she examined a small composition book. "You'd think," she said.

Or maybe they had, I thought. The local law enforcement officials now knew everything we did and probably more about the two suspicious deaths, the whereabouts of the locket, and the disappearance of Melrose DuBois. Well, almost all, unless they'd also found the locked room.

It was obvious that Idonia wanted to sift through the box alone so Ellis and I made a tactful exit. "You will call if you think you've found something?" I said. "Promise you won't go running off somewhere again."

"Lucy Nan's right, Idonia," Ellis added. If you find something that might lead to Melrose, for Pete's sake, let the police take care of it."

But Idonia was too busy reading to answer.

The call came about an hour later. I had dropped off Ellis at her place and Augusta had just plugged in the tree lights and was getting ready to light a fire in the living-room fireplace when Nathan Culpepper phoned.

"Is she there?" he demanded.

Although he didn't identify himself, I recognized his voice. "Idonia's not here, Nathan. What happened?"

"I woke up about ten minutes ago and she was gone. God only knows where she went this time! I'm calling the police."

"Wait, Nathan!" I called, but I was already too late. All I heard was a dial tone. When I tried to call him back the line was busy.

"Idonia's going to have a hissy," I told Augusta. "She's given Nathan the slip again and he's already put the police on her trail." Not that she didn't deserve it. I would seriously consider taking her name off my Christmas card list if I hadn't already forgotten to mail them.

Augusta silently closed the fire screen and unplugged the tree lights. "Did he have any idea where she went?"

"He didn't give me time to ask him," I said, calling Idonia's number again. This time I got no answer. "She must've found something in Melrose's notebook . . ."

We started for the door at the same time.

"How are we going to get in?" I asked as I parked in front of Idonia's. Of course, Augusta could've opened the door, I remembered, but as it turned out, she didn't have to. Nathan had left the house unlocked. His car was not in the driveway and on checking, I saw that Idonia's garage was empty.

"I don't see the box," I said, seeing upon entering that the dining room table was bare.

"She probably took it in her room so she'd have more privacy," Augusta suggested, and there it was on the floor between the bed and the rocking chair. A composition book, the speckled black and white kind, lay open in the seat of the chair. Although Melrose had used a computer for the course he was taking, he apparently kept his notes in longhand.

I passed the book to Augusta while I phoned Ellis, only to find no one there. "Idonia has disappeared again, and Nathan and the police are looking for her," I said, leaving a recorded message. "We've found the notes Melrose left and I'm afraid she's gone to find him. I'm hoping the notes will help us know where to look. You can reach me on my cell phone."

Augusta sat in the chair and read silently while I looked over her shoulder.

"Now we know what he was doing at the church the night Opal Henshaw died," she said. "It says here he went there to talk with Dave Tansey since it seemed the problems all centered around that family."

"And that's what he was doing in Soso," I said. "He was there for more or less the same reason we were, but I wonder why he didn't want us to see him."

She looked up briefly. "Probably because he knew you would inevitably ask about the locket he gave Idonia."

Melrose had continued his investigation, it seemed, by attempting to trace the origin of the locket.

"Look here," Augusta said. "He bought it from a place that sells estate jewelry . . . a man named G. Wayne Gravitt . . ."

Melrose's notes were precisely written in letters as neat and rounded as Melrose himself. From them we learned that he had gone back to the flea market where he bought the locket and found it had been included in a collection of items purchased from a dealer. From what Melrose wrote, G. Wayne was reluctant to tell him the name of the person who sold them, but Melrose

DuBois was not above bribery. He told the man he had seen a photograph of the locket with matching earrings and pretended interest in finding the earrings. It cost him a hundred dollars in the long run and he still didn't learn the name of the dealer. He was given instead a phone number. It only took seconds to find the listing under Tansey.

"I wonder why Melrose didn't take his notes with him," I said.

Augusta closed the notebook. "I suppose he had already found out what he needed to know."

I didn't have a clue how to get in touch with Nathan Culpepper, but I did know how to reach the Stone's Throw police. Ed Tillman, I was told, was off that day, and neither Kemper nor Captain Hardy was in, Paulette Morgan said. At that point I would've even agreed to speak with Chief Elmer Harris, but he had gone to Columbia to see his granddaughter in a Christmas pageant, I was told.

"I'm afraid Idonia has gone to the Tanseys thinking her friend Melrose is in some kind of danger," I told her, "and there's a good chance she might be in danger, too, so you need to get in touch with whoever's on duty *right now.* We—I'm going out there to see if I can find her, so please let them know where I am."

"You're going where?" Paulette asked.

"To the Tanseys out on Willowbrook Road—they know where it is, and if Nathan Culpepper calls, you can give him the same message."

"Will do," Paulette said. "Anything else?"

Isn't that enough? I thought as Augusta and I hurried to the car and headed for the Green Cottage on the outskirts of town. Paulette was dumb as a brick and the only reason she had that job was because her aunt was married to the chief's cousin, but surely she could remember a message as simple as that, I thought.

When we arrived the place seemed deserted and no one answered when I called their number on my cell phone. And then I remembered it was Sunday and the family would be at church for their Christmas program that night. I didn't know if the program was scheduled for late afternoon or evening, but I did know that the police had issued an APB for Jeremiah Tansey, so I would be surprised to find him here.

"It might be to our advantage if you turned the car toward the road in case anyone shows up," Augusta advised. "Meanwhile, I'll check the house to see if Idonia's there."

"Don't forget the locked room!" I called, but she had already disappeared inside. I let the engine idle and watched the road ahead until my eyes ached, feeling as if I were experiencing déjà vu from our adventures of the night before. The Tanseys had left a light burning in the living room, but except for that, darkness surrounded me and I was relieved when Augusta slipped in beside me. "No one's there," she said.

"Did you look in the locked room?" I asked.

"I looked everywhere," she said. "And, Lucy Nan, I've been thinking about that room since you told me what Dinah's friend Carolyn said." Augusta touched my arm. "I believe there was something very wrong in this family."

I had been thinking the same thing. Dinah married Dexter Clark . . . *to get away from that house*, Carolyn had said. I told Augusta about the dream I had about the young girl crying. "Only her door was locked from the *inside*," I said. "Dear God, do you think her brother, or even her *father*—"

"I think we'd better get to Willowbrook as fast as possible," Augusta said. "I just hope we're not too late."

The short drive to Willowbrook took only a few minutes but it seemed much longer and I had the door open as soon as we stopped. I saw Idonia's car parked out front about the same time I heard her scream.

"Wait!" Augusta said, and I felt her hand on my shoulder in an attempt to hold me back, but I was already running toward the house. A couple of the boards that were nailed over the entrance had been pried off and I heard some one crying inside. It sounded like Idonia.

"Let me go! I know he's here somewhere and you'd better not have hurt him!" she yelled. "Melrose, where are you?" This was followed by the sound of a scuffle taking place. I stood at the door listening to see if I could tell where it was coming from and wondering what to do when Idonia screamed again, and although the night was cold, I felt as if a fire burned inside me. I had to try and stop whatever was happening, but how? I stepped through the opening and into the entrance hall but it was so dark I couldn't see a thing, and almost jumped through the ceiling when someone touched my arm.

"You'll need this but don't turn it on yet," Augusta said, pressing a flashlight into my hand. Linking arms we made our way toward the noise, muffled now. It seemed to be coming from upstairs and I had started up when I heard someone pounding on the wall somewhere toward the rear of the house.

"Idonia! Idonia, I'm coming!" a man shouted. His voice sounded far away.

"Melrose?" I paused on the stairs. "It's Lucy Nan. Is that you?"

"Oh, Lucy Nan, thank God! They've locked me in this place down here and I can't get out. You've got to get the police!"

"They're on the way," I said, although I knew no such thing, and hoped they wouldn't hear me upstairs. I had been in such a hurry to find Idonia, I had left my cell phone in the car. Had Paulette Morgan relayed my message?

All was quiet upstairs until somebody cursed—a man. "You'll not get away with this!" Idonia said. At least she was still alive.

I froze when I heard the sound of a car pull up in front of the house. *Oh, please, let it be the police!*

"Lucy Nan, what on earth's going on in here?" Ellis said, shining a light in my face.

I hurried down to shush her and almost stumbled in the darkness on the bottom step. "For God's sake, be quiet!" I whispered. "Somebody's got Idonia upstairs and they've locked Melrose in the basement."

I felt Ellis stiffen beside me as Idonia cried out again. Below us, Melrose, or I thought it was Melrose, banged and clattered about as if he meant to send the old house crashing down on top of us.

Ellis grabbed a splintered board from the front door and stepped in front of me. "Come on!" she said, shining her light on the stairs. I was about to follow when the light came to rest on a pair of shoes. The shoes had feet in them.

"Run!" Idonia shouted, but it was too late.

"Jeremiah Tansey!" Ellis muttered under her breath.

"Looks like a party down here," Jeremiah said. "You didn't tell me you were going to invite your friends, but since you're here, let's all go into the living room—*now!*"

I switched on my light to see him shove Idonia in front of him with one hand while he held a gun in the other. Idonia's hands were tied in front of her and she had trouble maneuvering the stairs, although Jeremiah appeared to be accustomed to making his way around the house in the dark. He didn't seem to have noticed Ellis was holding the board. If she could just get close enough, I thought—

"Whatever that is you have in your hands, drop it right now!" he commanded as he herded us into what was once the drawing room, and Ellis did as she was told. "Now what in hell am I going to do with you?" Forcing us into a corner, he waved the gun about, mocking us. "First the old guy comes poking about, and now you!"

It occurred to me then that Augusta was no longer with us but I knew she would find a way to help if she could—and the sooner the better. If we all rushed him at once, I thought, he probably wouldn't be able to take aim. But if he did, I would surely be the one he hit. Still, I was contemplating such a move when a figure entered from the room behind him, the yellow gleam of her flashlight bouncing on each of us in turn. "Well, Jeremiah, what now?" Louella Tansey said.

"Thank heavens you're here!" I said. Surely he wouldn't shoot us in front of his mother. But why was she just standing there?

"What's all that racket about in the basement? Sounds like a wild man down there? And what are all these people here for?" Louella said.

"He has a gun, Louella," I shouted, "and he's locked—"

But Louella Tansey didn't seem the least bit concerned. I couldn't see her face in the darkness but her voice didn't sound at all like the mousy woman we knew. "Be quiet!" she said.

"As you can see, I have a little problem here," Jeremiah said. "I had the old man tied up down there but he must've gotten loose somehow." He gave Idonia a shove and she would've fallen if Ellis hadn't steadied her. "Then this one comes crashing in—pulled half the boards off the front door and came in here hollering for the old guy—and now these two! What am I supposed to do with them now?"

"Put them down there with that other one, I reckon," his mother said. "But we'll have to hurry, Jeremiah. The police have been here looking for you. We can't stay here any longer."

"And then what? Somebody's sure to find them, and you know they'll tell," he said.

His mother didn't answer, but her silence lay like a suffocating shroud around us.

If we could only delay them! "You were the one who killed Dexter Clark," I said to Jeremiah. "Why?"

"I'll tell you why," his mother answered. "Dexter was afraid to come to our house, afraid he might see Dave or me. My husband never forgave him because of what happened to Dinah. But Dexter got religion, it seems, and wanted to return the locket—"

"So we'd have something of hers to keep, he said," Jeremiah added. "When he called, I told him I'd meet him here. Hell, I didn't mean to kill him!"

"It was an accident," Louella added, with unmistakable impatience in her voice, "but nobody would've believed it."

"We had a slight disagreement," Jeremiah said.

Ellis spoke from behind me. "And you pushed him from the balcony?"

"We fought. He fell." Jeremiah's account sounded almost as if he were explaining away a broken lamp. "He was going to—"

"That's enough, son!" Louella spoke sharply.

I threaded my arm through Idonia's. If we had to run, I would try to pull her along. "Why are you doing this?" I asked. "What are you hiding here that you don't want anybody to see?" If I was going to be locked away—or worse—I wanted to know the reason why.

I didn't get one. "Come on, better get 'em on up there," Louella said, heading for the stairs.

Up there? I thought they were taking us to the basement. "I'm not going," I said, hanging back.

"I'm not either!" Ellis spoke beside me.

With a sudden jerk, Jeremiah wrenched Idonia away from me. "I don't think you'd like to see me shoot your friend here right in front of you."

"He means what he says," Louella said, stepping in front of us. "Get up the stairs, all of you."

"Where's Augusta?" Ellis whispered as we climbed the stairs ahead of them.

"She's here. Don't worry," I said.

"Shut up!" Jeremiah gave us a push from behind. "You know, with a little help, this old place would go up in a minute," he muttered aside to his mother.

If Augusta was going to help us, she'd better hurry, I thought. And that was when I heard footsteps above us—or was that just wishful thinking? But Ellis heard it, too. Her hand tightened on my arm, and behind us, Idonia gave an encouraging gasp.

Melrose DuBois stood at the top of the stairs with something that looked a whole lot like a gun and he pointed it at Jeremiah Tansey. "If you don't drop that gun right now, I'll shoot you where you stand," he said in a voice as solid and steady as the heart-of-pine stairs beneath us.

Chapter Twenty-Seven

"Melrose! Where did you come from?" Idonia would have run to him if we hadn't held her back.

"Idonia, honey! Are you all right?" he said, then added to Jeremiah, "I'd drop that gun *now* if I were you. I'm about mad enough right now to shoot you anyhow."

"Where did you get that gun?" Jeremiah asked, hesitating. But Ellis had had enough of Jeremiah Tansey. His gun clattered to the floor below as she gave him a push that sent him sprawling backward, his head banging on the treads.

"Oh no! You've killed him! Jeremiah, baby, are you all right?" His mother ran to gather him into her arms, and holding to the railing, I stepped quickly around them and made my way down the stairs to retrieve the gun he had dropped.

Ellis used her cell phone to call the police while the rest of us kept an eye on the two Tanseys. Jeremiah had managed to pull himself into a sitting position and now sat on the bottom step with his head in his hands while Louella hovered over him.

"Why didn't they send somebody out here the first time I called?" I asked.

"Because Paulette sent them out to Winternook," she said. "You know, that retirement community on the way to Columbia. "Told them Idonia was in big trouble out there."

And I'm not sure, but it sounded like a giggle came from Idonia Mae Culpepper.

"How did you manage to get upstairs all the way from the basement?" I asked Melrose.

"There's a narrow stairway that goes all the way up from there. I found the door to it down there while I was trying to feel my way out, but it was so dark, I couldn't see where it came out. That's where I was when I heard you, but I wasn't sure where I was."

"So how did you see the exit in the dark?" Idonia wanted to know.

"After I heard all that was going on, I was determined to try again," Melrose said. "I felt my way up on my hands and knees until I couldn't go any farther, but I knew there had to be an opening somewhere . . . and then the strangest thing happened. The door just started to open by itself. It was behind a bookcase in that big old room upstairs at the very back of the house. The bookcase just swung out, and let me tell you, I got out of there in a hurry!"

"You must've touched something," Idonia suggested. "A lever or a button or something."

"But I didn't!" Melrose insisted. "It just happened. And you know, this is a funny thing, too, but it smelled just like strawberries up there."

I couldn't see Ellis's face in the dim light, but I knew she was smiling, too. "But where did you get the gun?" I asked.

"There's a room down there you can't see from the other part of the basement and that's where he had me tied up until I managed to work loose. The door to it appears to be just another part of the wall, and it looks like it's been that way forever. That's where the stairs come out and that's where I found the gun along with enough stuff to stock a store," he said. "You wouldn't believe all the things down there: computers, televisions, jewelry, even a motorcycle. And guns—several guns. That one wasn't loaded, of course."

A motorcycle. According to Weigelia, Kemper had said that when Dexter Clark disappeared he had been riding a motorcycle.

Melrose put his coat around Idonia when she began to shiver and encouraged us all to go out to the car and turn on the heater, but Idonia didn't want to leave him with the Tanseys and neither did Ellis nor I. I could barely stand to look at Louella Tansey crouching beside her son. After all the terrible things he'd done, she still excused him, though she knew he was responsible for Dexter Clark's death and had probably sold the locket that had belonged to his sister. Of course it had to have been Louella who hid the locket in the flour canister, I thought. We should have known right away it wouldn't occur to a man to put it there.

Idonia sighed. "Surely that locket wasn't worth all this!" She directed her question to Louella who continued to fret over her son. "What was so important about that locket that one of you drugged my drink to get it back?"

"And it very nearly killed her!" Melrose added in a voice trembling with rage.

Jeremiah struggled to stand but a shouted warning from Melrose sent him back to his seat on the stairs. "Look," he said, "I only meant for it to make her sleepy. You've got to believe me! I didn't know it would—"

"Stop it, Jeremiah!" Louella said. "Can't you see my son is delirious? He has a head injury and doesn't know what he's saying. Why, he might even have a con—"

"Oh, shut up!" Jeremiah shoved his mother's hands aside. "It was your idea and you know it."

"And just whose idea was it to sell your sister's locket?" Louella snapped. "Of all the stupid notions, Jeremiah! Of course we had to get it back."

"The locket was your only connection to Dexter Clark—the only real link with your sister," Ellis said. "And when Opal Henshaw noticed that photograph of Dinah on your piano, she signed her death warrant."

"It wouldn't have been long," I said, "before Opal put two and two together and realized Dinah's husband was her nephew, Dexter Clark."

I assumed it was the police when I heard footsteps approaching outside a few minutes later, so I was surprised to see Preacher Dave Tansey standing in the doorway with a lantern in his hand. It was the kind you use for camping and gave out a warm yellow light.

"I saw all the cars over here and thought I'd better check it out," he began. And then he saw Jeremiah. "You!" he said. "I thought I told you to clear out of here. I suppose you know the police are looking for you. They say you killed the Clark fellow, and probably Opal Henshaw, too. And you might as well have killed your sister. Well, it's going to end, and it's going to end now."

Dave Tansey set his lantern on the floor and raised a rifle to his shoulder, pointing it at his son.

"No!" Louella threw herself on Jeremiah. "No! Don't hurt him! Please don't hurt him."

Jeremiah didn't speak but stared defiantly at his father as I was sure he had done many times before.

"Get out of the way, Louella. I don't want to kill you, too, although you deserve it for covering up for him all these years. If it hadn't been for the two of you, our Dinah would still be with us. I—I had no idea what was going on until I found her diary, and God help me, I read it. Did you know she left a diary?" His voice broke with a sob.

"But I didn't know. I didn't!" Louella reached out to him. "Not until it was too late. Our Dinah's gone . . . Jeremiah, he's all we have left!"

"Preacher Dave! Think what you're doing," I said. "This is against everything you believe in."

"Let the police take care of him," Ellis begged. "Don't ruin your life this way."

"It's already ruined," he said. "It's too late."

"No, it's not!" Idonia chimed in. "He's not worth it. Think of your congregation. They need you."

Still, he didn't lower the rifle but held it steady, ignoring our pleas and those of his sobbing wife. I looked at Melrose, who now held the gun Jeremiah had dropped, and waited for him to speak, to intercede, but Melrose only drew Idonia closer. Maybe he didn't care if Preacher Dave shot Jeremiah or not. Finally he stepped away from us. "Preacher, that's not a good idea. You're going to regret this. Now, listen—"

I jumped when I heard the clear, deadly click as Dave Tansey cocked his rifle. He meant to kill his son and there was nothing we could do about it. Melrose stood with the gun hanging loosely by his side. He was not going to fire on Dave Tansey and I didn't blame him, but what Dave was about to do was worse than being shot.

"I can't bear to think of what you did," Preacher Dave said to Jeremiah, and his voice was so full of heartbreak it made me cry. "Please, Daddy, no! I'm sorry, I'm sorry!" Jeremiah sobbed.

I felt as if we were part of a freeze-frame in a movie: the gaunt man with the rifle and the pleading son; the hysterical woman, the dark old house, the soft glow of the lantern, and the rest of us, stiff with dread. And then suddenly, Preacher Dave stepped back and lowered the rifle, and his face seemed to glow as brightly as the lantern at his feet. "Forgive me," he said, and turned and walked away.

"I can't believe she's really gone and done it," Nettie said. It was almost a week after Christmas and The Thursdays who gathered around my kitchen table didn't even pretend they were there to discuss a book.

"And she didn't even invite us to the wedding," Jo Nell said. "Looks like she'd want one of us to stand up with her."

"Nathan and his family were there," I said. "She said she didn't want a big wedding this time." Idonia and Melrose had been married in a tiny chapel the day before and were now honeymooning on a cruise ship in the Bahamas.

Ellis stroked Clementine's big head. "Sneaky thing didn't tell us she and Melrose got their license and blood tests when they were staying at that inn near Raleigh."

"And we were all frantic thinking she'd been snatched by the evil Melrose," Zee said, laughing.

Claudia smiled. "But he really did turn out to be her knight in shining armor, didn't he?"

"Sure did," Ellis said. "He had all of us believing that gun was loaded."

Since that frightening night at Willowbrook we had learned that Jeremiah Tansey, with his mother's knowledge, had been running a fencing operation dealing in stolen goods, which were stored in a hidden room in the basement at Willowbrook. When Dexter Clark met Jeremiah there to return Dinah's locket, he'd arrived when Jeremiah was unloading some of his plunder and threatened to tell his father. The two fought and Dexter fell or was pushed from the decaying balcony. He dropped the locket before he fell and Jeremiah, hoping to keep the meeting and the locket a secret from his parents, sold it, along with stolen estate valuables, to G. Wayne Gravitt, who asked no questions, and that's where Melrose came into the story.

Nettie folded a paper Christmas napkin in accordion pleats. "So it was Jeremiah who drugged Idonia's punch. But how did he manage to do it?" she asked.

"When the police finally arrived at Willowbrook that night they found a tape player hooked up to a microphone that could be controlled by a remote, along with a dress and wig in that hidden room in the basement, and the music he played was probably an old tape of Dinah's. Jeremiah was slender enough to easily fit into the dress. From a distance, no one could tell the difference," I told her.

"So he wore those to slip in and drug Idonia's punch," Jo Nell said. "But I don't understand how."

"Jeremiah's small," I explained, "and wearing the dress and wig he could walk right past that bunch at Bellawood, then go upstairs, and slip something in Idonia's punch. He and Louella didn't want that locket traced back to them as it would connect him to Dexter Clark's death. It must've been a shock when Melrose bought it and Idonia turned up wearing it."

"Remember when Idonia carried on so about being followed the night we went caroling?" Ellis said. "I wonder if that was Louella."

"Maybe. Those two were determined to get that locket back," I said. "It could just as easily have been Jeremiah."

"Was he the one who pushed Opal from the balcony?" Zee asked.

"The police seem to think Louella moved the swag and Jeremiah did the pushing, but I don't think they know for sure," I said.

"If only Opal hadn't noticed that locket in the photograph and told Louella about an identical one in her own family," Claudia said.

"That was before most people knew the body at Willowbrook had been identified as Dexter," Ellis added. "Unfortunately for

Opal, the police seemed to want that kept quiet. And, too, Opal had seen the locket Melrose bought for Idonia. She was bound to wonder how he came by it when she heard of Dexter's death."

"If Opal Henshaw hadn't been so hell-bent on delivering that fruitcake, she'd be alive today," Zee said. "I always knew that stuff was deadly!"

"She was only trying to do the right thing," I said, shaking my head. "And look where it got her."

Nettie sighed. "Poor Dexter! It's a shame he waited until Dinah's death to change for the better."

"Well, it won't help to dwell on that now," Jo Nell reminded her. "Are Cudin' Vance and his fiancée still planning to renovate the old home place?" she asked. "If I were those two I think I'd just find a nice little house in the suburbs."

I laughed. "The last I heard they were still interested, but Vance says they'll probably have to do it in stages, so if they start from the basement up we might not live to see it!"

Ellis got up and poured coffee all around. "I feel bad about Preacher Dave. It makes me sad to think of what he must have been through. His son and his wife are both in jail for murder, or accessory to murder. And can you believe that mealy-mouthed Louella? I wonder how long she knew that degenerate Jeremiah was abusing his own sister and still did nothing about it."

"That must be why Preacher kept Dinah's things in that locked room," Ellis said. "It really was a shrine of sorts. I expect he spent a lot of time in there just thinking of what could've been, and can you imagine how he felt when he found that diary? That's probably what drove him to what he almost did."

"I'm glad to hear his congregation has been supportive," Zee said. "They even helped move him into a small house next to the church out there. I guess your cousin will have to find another caretaker for Willowbrook."

"Pete Whittaker told me Dave Tansey had spoken to him

about forming a group with other churches in the area to reach out to abused children," I said. "I'm sure something good will come of that."

"I wonder what stopped him from shooting Jeremiah," Claudia said. "From what you all told me, he came close to killing his own son."

Nettie stirred sugar into her coffee. "Somebody told me Preacher Dave said he sensed somebody standing right behind him, and felt such goodness surrounding him he just couldn't pull the trigger. Kind of a wild tale if you ask me. I don't know whether to believe that or not."

I looked up to find Augusta standing in the doorway and smiled. "Believe it," I said.

Some of Stone's Throw Favorites

Ellis's Hot Clam Dip

One 8-ounce package cream cheese

½ pint sour cream

One 7½-ounce can minced clams, drained

Juice of 1 lemon

Dash red pepper, Texas Pete (or Tabasco), and Worcestershire sauce

Salt to taste

Cream the cheese and sour cream together and add the other ingredients. Heat in chafing dish until hot and bubbly, and serve with crackers or chips.

Serves about 6–8 (easily doubled).

Claudia's Marinated Mushrooms

1 pound fresh mushrooms, washed, or two or three 6-ounce cans whole mushrooms

1 onion, sliced

⅔ cup tarragon vinegar

½ cup olive oil

1 medium clove garlic, minced

1 tablespoon sugar

1½ teaspoons salt

Dash freshly ground black pepper

Dash pepper sauce

Put the mushrooms and onion in a jar or tightly covered container. Combine remaining ingredients and pour over them. Refrigerate until ready to serve.

—*In memory of* Meredith Camann—

Augusta's Spicy Meat Pies

Pastry:

2 cups all-purpose more plus more to cover surface

1 teaspoon baking powder

1 teaspoon salt

⅔ cup shortening

4 tablespoons ice water, more if needed

Sift dry ingredients together, blend in shortening with a fork or pastry blender, and add ice water a little at a time. Knead on a floured surface to form a ball.

Filling:

2 teaspoons vegetable oil

1 small onion, finely chopped

1 large clove garlic, minced

¼ teaspoon ground cinnamon

½ teaspoon ground red pepper (cayenne)

¼ pound ground lean beef

¼ teaspoon salt

3 tablespoons golden raisins, chopped

3 tablespoons pimiento-stuffed olives, chopped

1 cup canned diced tomatoes with juice

1 egg

Heat the oil in a skillet and add the onion and seasonings. Add the beef. Cook until the beef begins to brown and stir in the raisins, olives, and tomatoes. Cook about 10 minutes until almost all the liquid evaporates. Remove from the heat.

Preheat the oven to 425 degrees.

Roll out the pastry—thin for piecrusts. Cut as many rounds as possible using a glass or 3-inch cutter. Put about 1 or 2 teaspoons of the filling in each round, fold over, and crimp the edges. Brush the tops with 2 tablespoons water beaten with the egg. Bake about 12 minutes on an ungreased cookie sheet until golden brown. Serve warm. (These are kind of troublesome but very good.)

(Easily doubled.)

Martin Shackelford's Good-and-Easy Biscuits

1¾ cups self-rising flour plus more to cover surface

1 cup whipping cream

Preheat the oven to 425 degrees.

Mix the dough and roll out on a floured surface. Cut with a biscuit cutter and bake in the preheated oven about 10 to 12 minutes. Serve hot.

Anna's Cream Cheese and Apple Salad

One 3-ounce package lemon gelatin (Anna usually adds about ½ 3-ounce package more)

One 8-ounce package cream cheese, softened

One 20-ounce can crushed pineapple, drained (reserve juice)

⅓ cup sugar

2 cups tart apples, peeled and chopped

1 cup pecans, chopped

One 8-ounce container frozen whipped topping, thawed

Lettuce (optional)

Cream the dry gelatin and cream cheese together. Combine the reserved pineapple juice and sugar in a saucepan and bring to a boil. Add to the gelatin mix and stir until dissolved. Add the apples and pecans. Cool, then fold in the whipped topping and spoon into a 9×13-inch ungreased pan. Chill for 6 hours or overnight. Cut into squares and serve on lettuce, if desired.

Cousin Jo Nell's "Joyed-It" Jam Cake

1 cup butter

1½ cups sugar

3 eggs

1 teaspoon baking soda

1 cup buttermilk

3 cups flour

1 teaspoon each allspice, cloves, cinnamon, and nutmeg

1 cup seedless blackberry jam

1 pinch powdered ginger

Glaze (optional)

Preheat the oven to 300 degrees. Grease and flour a tube pan; put wax paper cut to fit in the bottom of the pan.

Cream the butter; add the sugar and eggs. Add the baking soda to the buttermilk and add to the egg mixture. Sift the flour and sift again with the spices. Add the flour mixture gradually to the butter mixture. Add the jam last. Bake for 1 hour and 20 minutes. This is good with a glaze made of the juice and grated rind of one orange, mixed with sifted confectioner's sugar. You don't want to get it too runny so measure a little at a time. It's also good just plain.

Mattie Durham's Charleston Squares

1 stick (½ cup) butter or margarine

1 cup sugar

2 eggs plus 1 egg yolk

2 cups all-purpose flour

1 teaspoon baking powder

½ teaspoon salt

1 teaspoon pure almond extract

1 teaspoon pure vanilla extract

1 egg white

½ cup firmly packed brown sugar

½ teaspoon vanilla extract

½ cup chopped nuts (pecans or almonds are good)

1 4-oz. bottle maraschino cherries, chopped and drained

Preheat the oven to 350 degrees.

Cream the butter and sugar. Add the eggs and egg yolk, one at a time, mixing well. Sift together the flour, baking powder, and salt and add to the creamed mixture. Add the almond and 1 teaspoon of the vanilla extracts. Spread the batter in the prepared pan. Beat the egg white and add the brown sugar and the remaining ½ teaspoon vanilla. Spread over the batter and sprinkle with the nuts and cherries. Bake for about 30 minutes. Cool and cut into squares. These are delicious and great for parties.

Aunt Eula's Lemonade Cake

One (3-ounce) package lemon Jell-O

¾ cup boiling water

1½ cups granulated sugar

¾ cup oil

4 eggs

2½ cups plain flour

2½ teaspoons baking powder

1 teaspoon salt

2 tablespoons freshly squeezed lemon juice

1 tablespoon grated lemon rind

1 tablespoon lemon extract

1 6-ounce can frozen lemonade

¾ cup powdered sugar, sifted

Preheat the oven to 350 degrees. Prepare a greased and floured 10-inch tube or Bundt pan.

Dissolve the Jell-O in the boiling water and set aside to cool. Mix the sugar and oil and add the eggs one at a time, beating well after each addition. In a separate bowl, mix the sifted flour, baking powder, and salt. Add to the egg mixture alternately with the gelatin mixture, beginning and ending with the flour. Beat thoroughly after each addition. Stir in the lemon juice, lemon rind, and lemon extract. Pour into the prepared pan and bake for 1 hour. While the cake is baking, thaw the lemonade and stir in the powdered sugar. Beat until smooth. Punch holes in top of cake while it's still warm in the pan and pour the lemonade mixture over it a little at a time. Let cool in the pan before removing. If you like lemon, you'll love this.

Cissy's Turtle Bars

Crust:

2 cups flour

1 cup firmly packed brown sugar

½ cup butter, softened

1 cup whole pecan halves

Caramel layer:

½ cup firmly packed brown sugar

⅔ cup butter

12 ounces milk chocolate chips

Preheat the oven to 350 degrees.

Combine the flour, brown sugar, and butter for the crust; mix well and pat firmly into an ungreased 9×13-inch pan. Sprinkle the pecans evenly over the unbaked crust. Prepare the caramel layer by combining the brown sugar and butter in a heavy saucepan. Cook over medium heat, stirring constantly, until the mixture begins to boil. Boil ½ to 1 minute, stirring the whole time. Pour over the pecans and crust. Bake for 18 to 22 minutes or until the crust is light golden brown. Remove from the oven and immediately sprinkle with chocolate chips. Allow to melt and then swirl. Cool and cut into bars.

Makes 3 to 4 dozen.